False **Friend**

False Friend

A Novel

Andrew Grant

Ballantine Books
New York

Published in the United States by Ballantine Books, an imprint of Random House, a division of Penguin Random House LLC, New York.

BALLANTINE and the HOUSE colophon are registered trademarks of Penguin Random House LLC.

Library of Congress Cataloging-in-Publication Data
Names: Grant, Andrew, author.
Title: False friend : a novel / Andrew Grant.
Description: First Edition. | New York : Ballantine Books, 2017.
Identifiers: LCCN 2016031067 (print) | LCCN 2016037966 (ebook) |
ISBN 9780399594304 (hardback) | ISBN 9780399594311 (ebook)
Subjects: LCSH: Police—Alabama—Birmingham—Fiction. |
BISAC: FICTION / Suspense. | FICTION / Thrillers. | FICTION / Mystery &
Detective / General. | GSAFD: Suspense fiction. | Mystery fiction.
Classification: LCC PR6107.R366 F35 2017 (print) | LCC PR6107.R366
(ebook) | DDC 823/.92—dc23 LC record available at https://lccn.loc.gov/2016031067

Printed in the United States of America on acid-free paper

randomhousebooks.com

1 2 3 4 5 6 7 8 9

First Edition

Book design by Diane Hobbing

For Tasha—*Tê kallistê.*

Nothing is so common-place as to wish to be remarkable.

Oliver Wendell Holmes,
The Autocrat of the Breakfast Table

False Friend

Chapter One

Saturday. Afternoon.

THE FLAMES WERE ALREADY TWENTY FEET TALL.

They were a fierce orange color, twisting and writhing above the gash they'd torn in the building's flat roof. Tyler Shaw thought they looked like the souls of sinners trying to escape the Hell that had somehow been unleashed inside. Clouds of dense, filthy smoke were spewing from a row of broken second-floor windows, staining the blue Alabama sky the kind of dirty black that hadn't been seen in Birmingham since the ironworks closed down. In his house across the street, lurking behind the faded bedroom drapes, Shaw could smell it. His eyes began to water. The fumes were bitter and sharp, not sweet and welcoming like the smoke from the barbeque pits and campfires he'd missed so much while he was away. And he could hear the sirens. The place would soon be swarming with fire trucks.

And with police.

Why? The word bounced frantically around inside Shaw's head. Why was this happening? And why now? Had he made a giant mistake, coming back? Was it all over for him? Was he finally finished?

Chapter Two

Saturday. Afternoon.

COOPER DEVEREAUX SCANNED THE PACKED ROWS OF SEATS ALL AROUND him for the hundredth time, and what he saw only confirmed his conclusion: Despite the name of the play—and the alarming number of people who'd come armed with family-size boxes of Kleenex—*he* was the only one in the place who was truly *misérable*.

Devereaux had wanted to spend his Saturday afternoon at his cabin, working on its damaged roof. But Alexandra, his—what? girlfriend?—had other plans. She'd been desperate to see the show together, and was so delighted when another lawyer she'd done a favor for had bagged her tickets for the matinée that Devereaux hadn't had it in him to disappoint her. And on balance, he figured that sacrificing one afternoon's satisfying labor was a small price to pay to make her happy. He'd been separated from Alexandra for eight years, and Devereaux was ready to do—almost—anything to strengthen his newly-repaired relationship with her. And with Nicole, their seven-year-old daughter. He'd only recently discovered that she existed, and was still just getting to know the little girl. Devereaux glanced down at her, stretched out in the seat between him and Alexandra. She looked up and smiled, then went back to watching the play. Or pretending to. Devereaux could see that she was paying more attention to the banged-up doll she'd insisted on bringing than to the action on the stage. *Smart kid,* he thought.

Devereaux had mentioned his lack of enthusiasm for Alexandra's play-going scheme to a couple of the other detectives in his squad the day before, but they'd told him not to worry. A trip to the Alabama Theatre was worth it just to see the inside of the building, they'd said. Devereaux didn't agree. The contractors who'd handled the refurbishment certainly hadn't skimped on the gold leaf or the extravagant palette of colors, but the result made Devereaux feel giddy. The red and green octagons decorating the underneath of the long sweeping arches reminded him of the suckers on an octopus's tentacles, reaching around to grab him. And the broad illuminated dome set into the gilded ceiling made him feel like a flying saucer was hovering overhead, waiting to spirit him away. Or perhaps that was just wishful thinking . . .

Devereaux was aware that his attention was wandering. His head kept filling with images of the flawless monochrome interior of his apartment in the City Federal Building. It was only a couple of blocks away. Could he sneak out, head over there, grab a beer, listen to some real music, and be back before the final curtain? There was time. But no. He couldn't take the chance. Alexandra would notice. She'd be upset, and that was the last thing he wanted. So he fixed a smile on his face, dragged his attention back to the stage, and realized he'd lost track of what was happening. This Valjean guy and his cronies wanted to go beyond some barricades? OK. But weren't they the ones who'd built the barricades? Why pick that spot if they wanted to go past? Why not build the barricades farther away? And why stand around singing about their own lack of planning skills? What was the point in that?

Before he could torment himself any longer Devereaux felt his phone begin to vibrate. He discreetly checked the number and saw it was his boss, Lieutenant Hale. An opportunity to escape? Devereaux felt a flood of relief wash over him. He turned to mime 911 to Alexandra and felt a tiny part of that relief turn to guilt as she shot him daggers in return. Then he pushed the feelings away, slipped into the aisle, and hurried to the foyer to answer the call.

"Cooper? Apologies. I didn't want to pull you out of the show." Hale's voice sounded distant and hollow, so Devereaux guessed she had him on speakerphone.

"Don't worry about it." Devereaux crossed to the ornate, circular, four-person French-style lounge chair below the chandelier in the center of the rectangular space. No one else was sitting on it, but Devereaux decided he'd prefer to stand, anyway.

"You're not enjoying it?" Hale sounded surprised. "Actually, that can wait. We've got a situation. At a school, out on 31st Street, Southwest. Near Jefferson Avenue."

"Jones Valley?"

"Right. You know it?"

"I went to it. For a while, anyway. It was my first high school."

"You must be mixing it up with somewhere else. This one's a middle school."

"It's the same place. They changed it after I left. What happened there?"

"A fire. A big one. Lots of damage, by the sound of it."

"Anyone hurt?"

"No reports of any casualties. Shouldn't have been any kids around as it's not a weekday, and there's no on-site janitor or maintenance guys anymore."

"Good. Want me to head over there?"

"No. No point. The uniforms are already canvassing the area, and no one will be able to get into the school itself for another couple of days, because it's not safe. But listen. A battalion chief from Fire and Rescue just called. This isn't confirmed yet—his science guys need more time to collect samples and run tests—but his gut feel is that the blaze was started deliberately."

"Lightning striking twice."

"What do you mean?" Papers rustled on Hale's desk. "There's no mention of previous fires in the report."

"It was a long time ago." Devereaux glared at an usher who'd appeared from an anteroom at the far end of the lobby, apparently ready to shush him. "November eleventh, 1961. The date was in the school crest. Some crazy student torched the place. Burned it to the ground. Maybe history's repeating itself."

"Maybe it is. But we'll get to that later. For now, step one is to interview the witnesses. The battalion chief needs some very specific information, until the lab work comes back. He laid it out in an email, which I'll forward to you. The uniforms have got the local residents covered, but we also have a passerby who called 911. I want you and Tommy to go talk to him. Right away, while his memory's still fresh. And before he reads anything about it in the press. I'll include his deets in the email."

Devereaux crossed the shiny black-and-white-tiled floor, stepped outside, and paused beneath the illuminated canopy on Third Avenue as he felt the warm air engulf him. He imagined his old school in flames, and couldn't help but smile. Not because he'd particularly disliked the place. But because he was struck by the irony. Today he was being sent to investigate the fire. Back when he was a student, he'd have been the first one the police would have blamed for it.

Labor Omnia Vincit, the school motto said. *Labor overcomes all difficulties.* Despite the creepy Nazi overtones, Devereaux had always found it to be true. Especially as it didn't stipulate what kind of labor . . .

Chapter Three

Saturday. Afternoon.

Squeezed onto a triangle of land to the west of the city, between Third Avenue North and Valley Creek, the *Birmingham Tribune* building had been dividing local opinion for nearly forty years. Some saw it as an iconic brutalist masterpiece, and lauded its intelligent, innovative design. They pointed to the way the front of the building was shaped like the prow of a ship, so that its protruding second floor could shelter the entrance and allow both the set-back higher floors to have their own outdoor balcony spaces. But the majority thought of it as a hideous monstrosity. They loathed its rough, textured concrete. Its sharp angles. Its parallel strips of featureless black windows. The bad feeling ran so high that its harshest critics likened it to a child's drawing of an ocean liner, and said they wished they could push it into the nearby water and let it sink.

Diane McKinzie didn't have an opinion on the building's appearance, one way or the other. She was too used to the place. It had been around her whole life—opening the year she was born—and her father had started taking her there before she could walk. She'd visited constantly throughout her childhood, and when she got a job there right out of college it felt like she was coming home.

Please let it be a quiet day! Diane thought as she reversed her Mini into the last shaded spot in the parking lot. She had good news, from a personal point of view, and couldn't wait to get home and share it with her son, Daniel. She'd just heard from an old friend. An editor in

New York. His company was publishing a new biography of J. Robert Oppenheimer, the legendary physicist who'd led the Manhattan Project in World War II. *The destroyer of worlds,* as he'd described himself. The book sounded fabulous, casting new light on the difficulties the young Robert experienced in getting along with other students, and the trouble he landed himself in politically, later in life. There was no doubt about it, Oppenheimer was a fascinating guy. He was one of Daniel's heroes. And Diane's friend was going to send him an advance copy of the book—the kind normally reserved for reviewers to use. That meant Daniel would get it months before it hit the shelves. He could potentially be the first person in the world, outside the publishing industry, to read it. He'd be delighted! And Diane loved to see him happy. He was so smart, and he worked so hard, despite not being in the best situation at school. He deserved a little special treatment from time to time.

At first Diane had thought about telling Daniel about the book the next day, when they were planning to visit the McWane Science Center in downtown Birmingham together. But she soon rejected that idea. She knew herself too well. She'd never be able to keep it a secret that long. No. She'd tell him that night, over his favorite dinner . . .

Diane was still looking forward to the evening when she got back to her desk. She had to write up some notes from the interview she'd just done, to account for her time. She couldn't be too careful these days. The era when journalists could be out of the office for hours—days!—at a time without anyone turning a hair was long gone. She also had to confirm some technical details with the one remaining staff photographer for a job she was planning for the following week. But mostly she had to make sure that all the important people saw she was there, working hard. And then, if she was lucky, she could get on the road early for a change.

THE MAESTRO OF FLAME, HERE IN THE MAGIC CITY!

"Extraordinary. Magnificent. Out of this world. Whoever did this, they obviously work with fire the way Michelangelo worked with paint or marble!"

This was the view expressed by Mr. Jonathan Ford when he made a call from his cellphone at 3:11 pm this afternoon to report seeing flames beginning to erupt from the Jones Valley Middle School at 2000 31st Street SW. Mr. Ford, a thirty-six-year-old insurance company executive from Vestavia Hills, was on his way to collect his son, Jonathan Ford Jr., from a community service litter clearance exercise organized by their church when he spotted the outbreak of the inferno.

"I knew right away I was witnessing something special," Mr. Ford told this reporter after making his call to 911. "The majesty with which the fire spread told me that this was no accidental blaze. It had to be intentional. The work of an expert. No. An artist. Someone with a level of skill and vision, combined with an exceptional degree of technical brilliance, the like of which has never been seen in the United States before. In fact, if you think about it, to have such a genius living and working right here in Birmingham is a pretty amazing privilege!"

Chapter Four

Saturday. Afternoon.

THE ADDRESS LIEUTENANT HALE HAD GIVEN DEVEREAUX WAS IN HOME-wood, coincidentally not too far from Alexandra's house. On their way to the theater Devereaux had noticed the traffic backing up, as usual, on the Red Mountain Expressway so he started out using 20th Street and Highland Avenue to bypass the worst of it. He thought he'd made good time but when he reached the house on Yorkshire Drive he saw that Tommy Garretty's car was already parked outside. That was the way it went with Garretty. He was taller than Devereaux. Younger. Slimmer. He came from a large, wealthy family over the mountain that had always supported him, no matter what he chose to do with his life. And he had the instinctive ability to always back the right horse—the quickest route, the shortest line, who'd come out on top in the Iron Bowl before the season had even started, you name it. Devereaux had hated him the first time they'd met. He'd cursed Lieutenant Hale for making them ride together. But try as he might, he couldn't stay mad at Garretty for long. And as if to underline what he missed without him, Devereaux had recently ended up being partnered with someone else—Jan Loflin, a detective on loan from Vice—after a round of de-partmental musical chairs. That had turned out to be a temporary arrangement, fortunately for all concerned, and Devereaux was very glad to have things back to the way they were before.

Devereaux pulled up behind Garretty's car and took a moment to survey the property. The street sloped so steeply that what started as the first floor on the right-hand side of the house had become the second floor by the time it reached the left, with a two-car garage beneath. Aside from that, Devereaux guessed the overall style would be described as faux English. The rest of the structure was symmetrical, with triangular gables at each side, a dormer window in the center of the neatly-tiled roof, and walls that were rendered in cream and punctuated by dark wooden beams. The place was huge. It loomed over its neighbors, and Devereaux noticed that the more traditional single-story homes on both adjoining plots were up for sale. He couldn't help wondering if that was just a coincidence . . .

"What kept you, Cooper?" Garretty climbed out of his car and slapped Devereaux on the back. "Couldn't tear yourself away from the show?"

"You got me." Devereaux tried to smile at his partner, but his heart wasn't in it. The play hadn't been his cup of tea, but it was at least an opportunity to spend time with Alexandra. The disappointed look on her face as he'd left his seat was beginning to haunt him, as was something else. An observation an old girlfriend who'd worked in Dispatch had once shared with him. *When a citizen calls in to volunteer information, it's even money you're answering the phone to an asshole.* "Come on. Let's see what this yahoo has to say for himself."

Devereaux rang the bell and the door was answered after a couple of minutes by a man in his late forties. He was a shade over six feet tall, and his deep tan was accentuated by the white linen pants and crisp sky blue shirt he was wearing.

"Jeff Nelson?" Devereaux showed the guy his badge. "Mind if we come inside a minute? We have a few follow-up questions regarding the fire you witnessed."

Nelson nodded, glanced over his shoulder, then gestured for the detectives to step quickly into the hallway.

"Honey?" Nelson ushered Devereaux and Garretty into the first room on the left, over the garage. "A couple of guys are here. I need to talk a little business with them for a minute, so give us some space, OK?"

The room felt like a cross between an office and some overpaid designer's idea of an old-fashioned London club, though the air was scented with sweet potpourri rather than the stench of cigar smoke. The walls were paneled in dark, richly polished wood. Oil paintings of fox hunts hung on either side of the window, beneath shiny brass accent lights that snaked out from the top of their gilded frames. A pair of Chesterfield sofas met at right angles in the far corner, and a twin pedestal mahogany desk with a green leather inlaid top sat opposite the door. Behind it was a green leather chair with a double row of antiqued brass tacks around its edges, and the floor was covered by a tightly woven oriental rug. The furniture was all lightly distressed, which made a nice contrast with the flawlessly smooth walls, though Devereaux would have placed good money that the majority of the action it had seen had taken place in a factory.

"Will this take long?" The guy closed the door and turned to face the detectives.

"It shouldn't." Devereaux nodded toward the Chesterfields. "Mind if we sit?"

"Sure, I guess." Nelson waited for the detectives to settle themselves, one on each couch, then retreated to the far side of the desk and lowered himself into the chair.

"OK." Devereaux took his notebook out of his jacket pocket. "Just a few quick questions, and we'll be out of your hair."

"I don't know what else I can give you." Nelson shrugged. "I told the 911 guy everything I could think of."

"I'm sure you did." Devereaux opened his notebook. "But run us through it again, just in case. Let's start at the beginning. You were driving on, what, Thirty-first?"

"Right." Nelson nodded.

"Where were you heading?"

"Home."

"Where had you been?"

"Why does that matter?" Nelson glanced at the door.

"We don't know what matters at this point." Devereaux kept his voice neutral. "So we need to build a full picture of what happened. The more you can tell us, the more it'll help."

"I'd been to a gallery." Nelson's voice was noticeably quieter. "I have someone who helps me with antiques, that sort of thing. I'm looking to invest in a few new pieces."

"There's a high-end antique gallery near Jones Valley school?" Devereaux raised his eyebrows. "The neighborhood must have changed some since I was a kid."

"It's not that near the school." Nelson glanced at the door again. "It's a home gallery. In Wenonah. And the owner doesn't advertise."

"Interesting." Devereaux nodded slowly as if he was weighing what he'd heard. "I'm a bit of a collector myself. Maybe I'll get the address from you sometime. Meanwhile, let's get back to the fire. Tell me what you saw, in as much detail as you can."

"There's not much to tell." Nelson placed his hands flat on the desk. "I was driving by the school—"

"What time?"

"I'm not sure." Nelson looked at his watch. "About three-twenty, probably?"

"OK. And?"

"I saw it was on fire, so I called 911."

"Did you stop?"

"No. I didn't see the point. You don't need to stop to say *There's a fire* and give an address. It takes, like, two seconds. But it's OK—I have hands-free. I didn't break any traffic laws, if that's what you're thinking."

"It wasn't." Devereaux took out his phone and pulled up Lieutenant Hale's email. "Now, with these next questions, Jeff, I need you to think real carefully before you answer. The information's going to one of the top guys at Fire and Rescue. It's important. Got it?"

Nelson nodded and put his hands back on his lap.

"Good. So, the flames. Were they concentrated in one place, or spread out across the building?"

"They were in one place, I think. It's hard to be sure. The school's kind of side-on to Thirty-first, and the main building's quite deep. All the smoke looked like it was coming from somewhere around the center, maybe. You'd have got a better look from the next street on the right, whatever it's called. Dowell? That's where the main entrance is."

"OK. Now, still thinking about the flames. From what you could see, were they spreading fast? Or staying pretty much in the same place?"

"I'm not sure. It was more the smoke that I could see."

"OK. The smoke. What color was it?"

"Black. Kind of oily looking."

"That's good. And what was it like? Dense? Or wispy?"

"Oh, dense. That's for sure. I couldn't see through it at all."

"And what about the smell? Did the smoke have any kind of odor to it?"

"You bet. It was foul. Gross. Like a garbage dump was burning, rather than a school. It made me want to puke. That was another reason for not hanging around there."

"What about artificial smells? Chemicals? Gasoline? That kind of thing?"

"Oh. No. Nothing like that."

"OK. Now, think about the building itself. The doors and windows. Were any of them left open? Or broken?"

"Well, there aren't any windows on that side. Just brick walls. I think there's a door, though. Like an emergency exit. It was closed. I'm pretty sure. Look, Detective, are we nearly done here?"

"Nearly. I just have one more question. People. Did you see anyone there, at the scene?"

"No." Nelson glanced at the door again, this time for a little longer. "I don't think so."

"Was there any cover nearby? Like trees, or bushes? Could anyone have been hiding, watching the fire?"

"I don't remember any bushes. There are a few trees, but they're too small. They look freshly planted. No one could hide behind them."

"Any walls? Or ditches?"

"No. Just scrubby grass."

"What about vehicles? Does the school have a parking lot?"

"It does, but it was empty."

"Did you see anyone driving away? Don't just think about cars. Think trucks and bikes, too. Or any vehicles being driven erratically, anywhere in the area?"

"No. Nothing. It seems like a quiet neighborhood, when the school's out." Nelson pushed his chair back and got to his feet, again glancing toward the door. "Look, Detectives, how about this? Leave me your numbers. Or your email, or whatever. If anything comes back to me, I'll let you know. Right away. I guarantee."

Neither detective showed any sign of moving.

"I have a question." Garretty waited for Nelson to stop fidgeting and look at him. "Your wife. Does she know about the fire? About you calling 911?"

"Yes, of course she does." Nelson looked down and stared intently at the gold embossed border on the desktop.

"That's good." Garretty leaned forward. "Because I want to tell you something. About an old case of mine. It was years ago, not long after I got my shield. A young woman had disappeared. She'd been on a night out, downtown, and she never made it home. A guy contacted us and told us he'd seen her, walking alone down Fourteenth Street. What he didn't add until two weeks later was that he'd also seen her coming out of a converted loft building on the corner with Fifth Avenue. He kept that part quiet because the loft was opposite the entrance to a skeevy strip club called Geraldine's Stairway to Heaven, and he didn't want anyone to know where he was when he spotted her. Anyway, the owner of the loft had come after the woman and killed her, but we were looking for a random guy off the street. And in the next two weeks, three other women lost their lives. Three women we could have saved, if the witness had told us everything up front when he'd first had the chance."

"That's tragic." Nelson glanced at the door again. "But why are you telling me about it? Do you think *I'm* holding something back?"

"I don't know." Garretty crossed his arms. "Are you?"

"This is unbelievable!" Nelson came out from behind the desk. "I volunteer to help, and you come into my house and start making accusations? Do you want me to bring my lawyer into this?"

"OK, let's all just settle down." Devereaux levered himself up from the couch and blocked Nelson's path. "I'm sure Mr. Nelson's nothing like that guy, Tommy. And I'm sure that if he has anything else he needs to tell us, he'll find a discreet way to do it. Right?"

Nelson didn't respond.

"You know what else?" Devereaux closed his notebook. "It's getting late. I skipped lunch, and now I'm starving. I don't want to go all the way back downtown to eat. So I was wondering, Mr. Nelson. Is there anyplace around here worth trying?"

"Maybe." Nelson's focus was switching rapidly from one detective to the other. "Depends what kind of thing you want to eat."

"I'm flexible about the food." Devereaux slipped the notebook back into his pocket. "The location's the important thing, right now. It needs to be close. The kind of place you could get to from here without it being a big production. And it would have to be quiet. With some privacy. Where you could talk without being overheard all the time. Do you know anywhere like that?"

Nelson thought for a moment. "Sure. I know a place. It's ten minutes from here. Hold up. I'll give you directions."

Chapter Five

Saturday. Late afternoon.

ALEXANDRA WAS THINKING ABOUT OPENING A BOTTLE OF ZINFANDEL.

It felt like a night for red wine, sitting alone in her kitchen after returning home from the show. A night for a heavy red wine. Because it struck her that she'd gotten used to feeling Devereaux's presence around the house in the weeks they'd been back together. And that she liked it. But at that moment, after taking just a single glass out of the cupboard, she was feeling something else. Something unwelcome. Devereaux's absence.

Spending time in that house without Devereaux wasn't a novelty. Alexandra had only bought the place after they'd split up—after she'd kicked Devereaux out—eight years earlier. She'd moved there from Vestavia Hills because she wanted to homeschool their as-yet unborn daughter, and after cutting her hours and switching to consulting for other law firms rather than practicing in her own right she'd needed to trim her budget. She'd never resented the changes she'd had to make. But somehow, in the glow of having attention paid to her as more than just a lawyer or someone's mom, and the fascination of seeing Nicole responding to a second parent, she'd forgotten the reality of being in a relationship with a cop. Of never being able to depend on having time together. Never knowing when the phone would ring and call him away. Never knowing when he'd get home. What state he'd be in. Emotionally, as well as physically. Whether he'd get home at all . . .

Was it worth it? That was a tough question. What would she do if a friend came to her with a similar situation? That was much easier. She'd tell her to put it down on paper. Make two columns. Put the pros on the left. The cons on the right. See how they stacked up. And see if you found yourself wanting one side to be longer than the other . . .

Alexandra left the wine to breathe for a minute, took a legal pad from the drawer she used to store her homeschooling supplies, and sat down at the kitchen table to write. Superficial as it was, the fact that she was taking action made her feel better. At first she felt a strange shyness about listing such personal details, but point by point she began to build some momentum. She was feeling so good about the process that when Nicole appeared in the doorway after fifteen minutes and asked if they could do some drawing together instead, she was reluctant to stop.

Much to her surprise, Nicole took the rebuttal without complaint. Another point in the plus column for Devereaux, Alexandra thought. Nicole's behavior was markedly better since he'd been around. In the past there'd have been a half-hour tantrum to deal with. Now the little girl trotted back upstairs without a word.

Back in her room, Nicole crossed to her toy shelves and took down two of her dolls. A little girl, and a mom.

Soon after that, she reached for a third doll.

A paramedic.

Chapter Six

Saturday. Late afternoon.

DEVEREAUX PARKED IN THE SHADOW OF THE TALL SIGN ADVERTISING THE famous Meat 'n' Three lunchtime special in the Homewood Diner's triangular lot and made his way inside. A waitress he didn't recognize asked him where he'd like to sit, and he picked his usual booth to the side of the entrance to the kitchen. He didn't find the slatted benches particularly comfortable, and he thought the pink gingham-patterned Formica tabletop was pretty much of an atrocity, but it was the spot Nicole had chosen on the couple of occasions in the last month he'd brought her for a secret ice-cream treat when Alexandra had gone to bed early, so he felt an affinity for it. The waitress fetched Devereaux an iced tea without waiting to be asked, then left him alone to study the menu. Three minutes later his phone buzzed. It was a text from Garretty:

Incoming . . . !

Devereaux smiled and ordered a black coffee and a slice of peach pie, figuring those should keep him occupied for the little time he'd be there on his own. He also asked the waitress to bring over another couple of menus.

Nelson arrived nine minutes later, with Garretty hard on his heels. They weaved their way through the uneven rows of square wooden tables to reach Devereaux's booth then slid onto the opposite bench, waited for their iced teas to arrive, and sat in silence for another thirty seconds.

"Good call on the diner, Jeff." Devereaux set down his fork. "Great pie."

"The chicken fried steak smells good, too." Garretty made a show of sniffing the air. "I might have had to get me some of that, if I didn't have a date tonight. How about you, Jeff? Are you hungry?"

Nelson picked up his menu, then threw it straight down again and turned to face Garretty. "Look. Three menus. You knew I was coming. So why did you have to follow me? Where were you? Waiting outside my house? What if someone had seen you? Those stupid-looking cars you drive stand out a mile. What are you trying to do to me?"

"We didn't know you'd come *here*. We hoped you would. But if you're pissed, blame him." Garretty nodded toward Devereaux. "This was all his idea."

"Where else did you think I'd go?" Nelson pushed the menu away.

"Who knows?" Devereaux shrugged. "Maybe here. Maybe to an antiques store in Wenonah . . ."

Nelson didn't respond.

"Your wife didn't know anything about the fire, did she?" Garretty leaned in closer.

Nelson shook his head.

"OK." Devereaux pushed his empty plate away. "Here's the deal. You need to come clean. We may have a serious crime on our hands, and we can't afford to waste any time. So if you stop dicking us around and tell us what you know, we'll do our best to keep your personal business out of the paperwork. But make us run around and dig it up another way, we'll let the chips land wherever they fall."

Nelson took a long sip of tea then sagged against the back of the bench, his head leaning on the whitewashed wall behind it and his eyes focused on the tiled ceiling above. "Well, like you've obviously guessed, the woman who sells the antiques isn't just my advisor. My wife doesn't know anything about it. She thought I was running errands this morning. Innocent stuff. But you know how it goes. Time got away from me. I realized I was running late, didn't want to look suspicious, and was hurrying back when I saw the fire at the school. What could I do? I didn't have time to stop, but I couldn't not report it. What if someone had been trapped inside? So I kept going, and called 911 from the car."

Neither detective said a word.

"OK, OK." Nelson squirmed in his seat. "I admit it. I don't have hands-free. I was holding the phone while I drove. I'm sorry!"

"It's good that you told us these things." Devereaux waited for Nelson to look at him. "We're not here to judge your personal life. And we don't care about the phone. But there's something else you're holding back. Don't deny it. I could feel it at your house. I can feel it now."

Nelson bent forward until his forehead was touching the table, then straightened up halfway. "All right. Yes. There's one more thing. I think there might have been someone else there, near the school, when the fire started."

"Who?"

"I don't know." Nelson took out his phone, opened a photograph, and slid it across the table. "But, here. Look."

Devereaux looked at the blurry image on the screen, then passed the phone to Garretty. The building in the picture was completely unfamiliar to him—the school he'd attended on the site had been demolished and replaced in 2011—but the new structure wasn't what caught his eye. Nor was the smoke pouring out of it. It was the figure standing on the steps of the modern brick and concrete church on the opposite side of the street to the school.

"I can't see his face." Garretty had latched onto the same thing, and was using his fingers on the phone's screen to enlarge the image. "Or his hair. His hood's in the way. But it's probably a male. Probably an adult. We need to look into this. Jeff, I need you to email a copy of this picture to me and Detective Devereaux right away."

"No problem." Nelson took the phone and sent the email. "Am I in trouble now?"

"Why didn't you tell us about the photo right away?" Devereaux checked his phone to make sure the complete message had come through.

Nelson covered his face with his hands for a moment. "I was going to. That's why I took it in the first place. I thought it would help. Then I thought, if I give this to anyone there'll be a record of where I was, and when. What if my wife heard about it? How would I explain it? So I was wavering, and then I saw how bad the picture had come out. I figured someone might ask why, and I'd have to admit I'd taken it while I was driving. Then they might have asked why I hadn't stopped to take a better one, and I'd have had to get into the whole thing of where I'd been and why I was hurrying, which I didn't want to do. I didn't realize the other guy was there till I saw him in the picture when I got home. And then I convinced myself it wouldn't matter, because he must have gotten a much better view than me and had probably come forward as a witness. He did come forward, right?"

Devereaux shrugged his shoulders. "That's one of the things we're going to check. Now go home. And stop running around behind your wife's back. We'll be in touch if we need you."

The detectives walked out of the diner together and paused at the side of Devereaux's car, blinking in the bright sunshine.

"Want me to call the lieutenant?" Garretty checked his watch. "Bring her up to speed?"

"No." Devereaux took out his keys. "I'll do it. You've got a date tonight, right?"

"Right. At the Red Pearl. With Joanne."

"How's that going?"

"Good, knock on wood. Hey, I have an idea. Why don't I call the restaurant? Make it a table for four. You and Alexandra could join us. Make it a double date. What do you say? Might help get you out of the doghouse for ditching her at the theater."

"Who says I'm in the doghouse?"

"Cooper. Come on. Alexandra was planning this trip for how long? And you walked out halfway through. Who do you think you're kidding?"

"It wasn't my fault I had to leave. It was work."

"And you think that matters? Seriously, Cooper. You should come."

"Thanks, Tommy. It's a nice thought. And I'd like to. But we'd need a sitter for Nicole. There's only one girl Alex trusts, and she always seems to be booked up these days. So, no. I'll head home. I'll make it up to her some other way. You enjoy your date. Try the crispy shrimp, if you haven't had it before. It's sublime."

"I will. But listen to me, Cooper. You've got to face the music. Get it over with. Girlfriends' tempers aren't like wine. They don't improve with time. Trust me on this."

Chapter Seven

Saturday. Evening.

HOME AT LAST! HOME AT LAST! THE WORDS ECHOED INSIDE DIANE McKinzie's head as if she were being tormented by a shrieking sideshow clown with a lung full of helium.

At last? Sure. If she was a shift worker, and didn't start until lunchtime. But as it was? The sun had been down for over an hour. So much for getting home early . . .

Diane gently slid her key into the lock. She held her breath then pushed the door, making sure to stop before it reached the point where the hinges squeaked. She cursed herself for the millionth time for not having oiled them. Slipped through the narrow gap into her hallway. Eased the door closed, welcoming the dark as it enveloped her. Started toward the foot of the staircase, ears straining for the slightest sound. And tripped on something.

It was one of her son Daniel's giant, gross sneakers. She made a mental note to speak to him about not putting them away properly—again—in the morning. Maybe. But for now she just had to concentrate on getting upstairs, to her room. Silence was critical. She took another step toward the staircase, knowing which floorboards were likely to creak and avoiding them by muscle memory. She slid her feet smoothly across the polished wood. Figured she'd made it a third of the way. Took another step. And—

"Um, hello!" The voice boomed out in the darkness. "Where do you think you're going?"

"Daniel?" Diane's heart rate skyrocketed. "Sweetheart? Where are you?"

There was no reply.

"Sweetheart?" Diane was working hard to keep her breathing under control. "I'm sorry I'm so late. I thought you'd be in bed already. I was trying not to wake you. I got held up at work. There was a fire at a school, you see, maybe an arson attack, and I had to write an article about it. It'll be in the paper, tomorrow. You'll be able to read it."

There was no response.

"Daniel, my angel, did you hear me?"

The house remained silent.

"Danny-love, where are you?"

Her son still didn't answer so Diane reached out and switched on the hall light. There was no sign of him in the long corridor that stretched to the kitchen at the back of the house, though he had dropped one of his old hoodies on the floor halfway down. It was lying beneath the gap in the series of her father's most famous articles that lined the wall. Diane hated seeing the forlorn little picture hook, sticking out, bent and empty. She cursed herself for still not having had the frame's glass repaired, then took another step forward. She looked through the archway into the living room, and finally saw him. He was sitting on the couch, bolt upright, eyes focused on the drapes that covered the window in the opposite wall. His arms were crossed rigidly over his chest, rumpling the wording on his T-shirt and ruining the pun it made by misplacing *pi* and *pie*. As usual, his hair looked like it could use a wash and it had obviously been a while since his plump, grubby bare feet had seen water.

"Danny?" Diane moved toward her son. "What are you doing? How long have you been sitting here in the dark?"

"Maybe you'd know if you'd been here." Daniel's voice was deep for a fifteen-year-old, and it was loud. "If you weren't always at *work*. It's Saturday, and you couldn't be bothered to spend any time with me. Again."

"Now, come on." Diane crossed her arms. "That's not fair. You know I have to work. I don't get to pick my hours. I'd much rather spend my weekends with you, my sweet. You know that! How did the community service go, by the way, with the church. Was it fun?"

"I didn't go." Daniel turned to glare at his mother. "Don't change the subject. And you're lying, anyway. Nothing you say is true. You don't *have to* work. Dad gives us plenty of money. You should stay home and take care of *me*. You could if you wanted to. If you were a good parent. Or you could get a different job, like my friends' moms have. One with better hours. If you cared. If you were fit to be my mother."

"Daniel!" Diane took a step toward him. "That's a horrible thing to say."

"You're a horrible person." Daniel stood and glared down at his mother. Even at fifteen he already towered over her. "How often do you leave me all alone? How many nights are you late home? And what are you even doing? You can't possibly be at the office all that time."

"Of course I'm at the office. Where else do you think I could be?"

"Then why are you never there when I call?"

"I am there!" Diane's voice was shrill. "Unless I'm in an editorial meeting. Or out researching a story."

"Right." Daniel nodded sarcastically. "*Researching* one of your little stories. Instead of helping me with my homework. Or cooking me real food. Or hanging out with me. I should go live with Dad. I never should have stayed with you. Or let you change my last name. *McKinzie* sounds so stupid. My life's a nightmare because of you. You're the worst mother in the world."

"Well, I'm sorry, Daniel, but I'm doing the best I can."

"That's not good enough. You're a mess. And even when you are here, you're like a zombie half the time. You stumble around. You can't hold a conversation. You can't string a sentence together some days."

"That's because I'm tired! And tiredness isn't a crime. I'm a single parent, and I have a very demanding job. It's not easy to juggle both things. But listen. Enough of that. I have exciting news. I got an email from a friend today, and—"

"I'm going to bed." Daniel walked out of the room and switched off the hall light, leaving Diane in the dark. "I have to study tomorrow, before we go out. Wake me at eight."

Diane was trembling so much she had to carry her glass of water in both hands as she climbed the stairs. She reached her bedroom, made sure the door was properly closed, then took the little bottle of pills from its hiding place in the hollowed-out bible on her night-stand. She had no recollection of the rest of that evening. Just like she had no memory of so many other evenings. And weekends. And holidays . . .

Chapter **Eight**

Saturday. Evening.

HOME AT LAST. THE WORDS SOUNDED FOREIGN AND OUT OF PLACE TO Devereaux, even as they were running through his head.

Home? Would he ever get used to thinking of Alexandra's house in that way? He'd spent more time at her previous one, over in Vestavia Hills. The one she'd sold after they broke up. That place certainly didn't hold many happy memories for him. He associated it with getting dumped, unsurprisingly. And the reason he'd been there so much was that he'd been serving one of his longest suspensions during the final weeks of their relationship. He'd shot someone in order to save his partner's life. But that someone was fourteen years old, and all hell had broken loose. Devereaux was benched, and he never did well when he had too much time on his hands. And what made it worse was that he couldn't understand what all the fuss was about. You don't have to be a certain age to pull a trigger, and no one had forced the kid to point his gun at a police officer's head. Would the public have preferred to end up with a dead cop? And if they would, why was he wasting his time *Protecting* and *Serving* them? He'd known other ways to make a living, as his Porsche and his penthouse bore witness to.

Maybe things would work out differently this time? Although Devereaux wasn't honestly a big fan of the house itself. He preferred his apartment at the City Federal. He liked its light, and its space. Its elegant, balanced proportions. Its close connection to the heartbeat of the city. The building's crazy neon sign that blazed extravagantly at night. But for all its advantages, there were three things that the apartment did not have. Alexandra. Nicole. And a shot at having a real family of his own.

Devereaux slid his key into the lock and gently opened the door. The hallway light was on, but there was no sound of music or TV. He was hoping that Alexandra was still awake, but crept silently inside so as not to disturb her if he was too late. He reached the kitchen and found a note on the table, handwritten on yellow legal paper and held in place by a half-full bottle of wine:

Sorry! Zonked. Had to hit the hay. Hope you're OK!
There's pot pie in the fridge . . .
See you in the morning!
A xx

Devereaux smiled. He hadn't realized he was hungry until he read Alexandra's note. He took the pale blue Le Creuset pot from the fridge, set it down on the table, and ate the pie without waiting to heat it. When he was done he stacked the dirty utensils in the dishwasher, started down the hallway, then paused at the bottom of the stairs. He was tired, but didn't feel like he'd be able to sleep just yet. His mind was still chewing on something. It was searching for a name. Of a guy he'd known in the lost years between school and the Police Academy. A torch artist. And an absolute asshole. Kevin something, was he called? A vile cowardly snake of a guy who set fires just for the thrill of lurking in the shadows and seeing other people's stuff get destroyed. He didn't need to do it. He didn't gain from it in any way, other than witnessing the pain he caused. Devereaux had done his best to ignore the guy until a fire he'd set had spread to a friend's mother's house. Then he'd offered Kevin some helpful advice about relocating to another city. Immediately. And permanently. Devereaux had never seen the guy again, and had hardly given him a second thought since he disappeared. But now something had brought him to mind.

The picture that Jeff Nelson, the 911 caller, had taken.

Devereaux sat at the bottom of the stairs and pulled up Nelson's email on his phone. He enlarged the photo as far as it would go and stared at the grainy image of the man standing outside the church.

Who are you? he thought. Lieutenant Hale had confirmed that the guy's description didn't match any of the other witnesses who'd been interviewed that afternoon. Could he be a sick asshole like that Kevin guy, causing damage just for the hell of it? Could he be—

"Daddy?" Devereaux hadn't heard Nicole's light feet sneaking down the stairs behind him. "Who's that man?"

"No one, princess." Devereaux slammed the phone facedown on his lap and braced himself for one of the spectacular tantrums he'd seen Nicole throw when Alexandra didn't give her something she wanted. "No one I can tell you about, anyway. He's from my work."

"That's OK!" Nicole flashed a wide smile and turned to dance back up the stairs. "I understand, Daddy."

Chapter Nine

Saturday. Late evening.

THE LAST FIRE TRUCK HAD BEEN GONE FOR A GOOD FEW HOURS BY THE time Tyler Shaw risked sneaking back to his window. He'd been lying low, desperate to avoid the attention of the police who'd been swarming all over the neighborhood, hammering on doors and no doubt asking all kinds of questions about what had happened at the school.

Shaw reached out and cracked the window an inch, praying that the coast really was clear. He took a deep breath and almost choked on the traces of smoke that were still lingering in the air. It was truly foul. But how foul? He continued to sniff, trying to discern what sort of particles might be present. Rotten, obnoxious ones, obviously. But the kind that are someone else's problem? Or the kind that should remain his secret?

Shaw cast his mind back to the time he'd spent at the school. He thought of the thick, solid floor, and imagined the layers of varnish that would have built up to protect it by now. He tried to remember what his distant science lessons had taught him about flames. About how they rise. And finally he turned and gazed at his icons. Each one carefully displayed. Each one inspiring him. Telling him that he was safe. That it was time to move on to the next phase of his growth, now that fate had brought him back to Birmingham and given him the perfect platform.

Fate, and the timely demise of an old lover . . .

Chapter Ten

Sunday. Early morning.

DEVEREAUX HAD LAIN AWAKE RAKING OVER OLD MEMORIES UNTIL AFTER two am, but he still managed to shut off the alarm the next morning before it woke Alexandra. He knew she liked to sleep late on Sundays so he slipped on a robe and tiptoed downstairs, fired up her fancy coffee machine, and made a triple espresso to take with him into the shower. He kept the sharp jets of water as icy as he could bear and didn't set foot back out of the stall until he felt the caffeine begin to infuse some life into his sleep-deprived brain. Then he shaved, grabbed a shirt and some pants from the freestanding rack he'd brought from his apartment, and made the nine minute drive to police headquarters.

The fourth-floor conference room was Devereaux's least favorite place in the building, other than Captain Emrich's office. The procedural briefings that were frequently held there tried his patience—he hadn't joined the department to be treated like a performing seal by a bunch of politically-correct paper-pushers who hadn't walked a beat or made an arrest since the previous century—and on top of that the room simply had a depressing vibe. It looked like it hadn't been decorated since Reagan was President. It smelled vaguely like a locker room. Its cheap, outdated furniture was on the verge of falling apart. Plus the last time Devereaux had been there the room was being used as the nerve center for a case involving a missing boy. Ethan Crane. An orphan. Devereaux had also grown up without parents, so the investigation had touched on areas that cut uncomfortably close to the bone for him. And it had also revealed some truths about his own family background that he was in no hurry to revisit.

Devereaux took a deep breath before opening the door, and wasn't surprised to find that Garretty had already arrived. He was sitting on the far side of the battered, rectangular conference table, with a giant carry-out coffee cup in one hand and a half-eaten croissant in the other.

"Where is she?" Devereaux gestured toward the three empty mugs lined up near Lieutenant Hale's customary place at the head of the table. "Getting more coffee?"

Garretty shook his head. "Collecting a couple of visitors from reception. One of them's from the Bureau. She told me to give you a heads-up if you arrived before she got back."

Devereaux shook his head and made his way around the table to take a seat near to Garretty. He found it strange that Hale was still so convinced he had an issue with the Bureau. He'd been seriously annoyed a couple of years previously when he'd been all set to join them, only for their acceptance to be withdrawn at the last minute without a word of explanation. But now, thanks to what he'd learned during the Ethan Crane investigation, he knew the reason for their change of heart. He couldn't argue with it. And he'd made another discovery since his original application. The existence of Nicole. Transferring to the Bureau would have involved leaving Birmingham, at least temporarily, making it much harder to get to know his daughter. Or to patch things up with Alexandra. Plus he had certain financial interests in the area dating back to his pre–police department days that were better handled in person.

Devereaux heard voices from the corridor and a moment later Lieutenant Hale appeared in the doorway. She was wearing pale gray pants and a plain white blouse. She had on flat shoes, as usual—at five feet eleven in bare feet she generally tried to avoid anything that accentuated her height—but her shiny black hair was braided and intricately coiled on top of her head in a way that added at least four inches. And it did more than that. It hinted at a late night in swanky surroundings. Devereaux was intrigued, but he knew better than to ask where she'd been. Hale kept her work and private lives relentlessly separate, and wearing her hair that way to the office was the closest Devereaux had known her to come to bridging the two worlds.

Another woman entered the room after the lieutenant. She had the kind of piercing blue eyes and high, chiseled cheekbones that Devereaux certainly would have remembered if he'd met her before. But with her short neat blond hair, unremarkable black business suit, and boringly practical briefcase, he would have pegged her as a Bureau employee even without Garretty's warning. Following behind her was a man in his early forties. He matched Hale for height, even with her fancy 'do, and seemed as broad as the two women combined. He was wearing a black baseball cap, steel-rimmed glasses, a short-sleeved white shirt with a gold shield above the breast pocket, and black utility pants. From the way the guy slammed his messenger bag down on the table, Devereaux guessed the newcomer was as unimpressed with the surroundings as he was.

"Cooper, Tommy, let me introduce our guests." Hale took her seat and gestured for the others to make themselves comfortable. "We have Special Agent Linda Irvin, who's the new profile coordinator from the Bureau's Birmingham Field Office. And Donald Young, Battalion Chief, Birmingham Fire and Rescue." Hale waited for the murmur of acknowledgments to die down before continuing. "Thanks for coming in on a Sunday morning, guys. It's not an ideal time, I get that, but I don't want any grass to grow under our feet. We're going to be seeing a lot of media attention on this one. And feeling a lot of heat from upstairs, too. A lot of taxpayers' dollars went up in smoke yesterday, and folks get very angsty when that kind of thing happens. So, let's get down to business. The first question is, are we actually dealing with a crime here? Chief? What do we know for sure?"

"That's a good question, Lieutenant." Young pulled a marker pen from his bag and pointed to a long sheet of lining paper that was taped to the wall next to the door. It was the last of the pieces that had been used to keep track of the Ethan Crane investigation—the others had all been filled up and then archived when the case was closed, leaving only rough triangles at each top corner where they'd been torn down by one of the civilian aides. "May I?"

"Please." Hale swept a little pile of pastry crumbs onto the floor and rested her forearms on the table. "Go ahead."

"You guys know as well as I do, arson's the easiest crime in the world to commit." Young got to his feet. "But it's also the hardest to prove. Anyone can do it, and the fire itself destroys its own evidence. So does the water we use to put it out. But the good news is, we've got a lot of experience, and we know what to look for." He drew a shape like a giant capital *E* on the sheet of paper. "Here's the rough outline of the main Jones Valley school building." He added an oval line, taking in the central bar of the *E* and half the depth of its trunk. "This is the perimeter of the damaged area. What we do is start here, collecting ash and other charred debris, and work back in till we can identify the exact point of origin of the fire. Sometimes with arson we're looking at multiple points, but in this case there's only the one." He drew a large dot in the center of the oval. "Here. Then we look to see if there could have been an accidental cause—a gas leak, an electrical fault, even a dropped cigarette. We figure out how high up the fire started—cigarette fires usually start at ground level, gas leaks near the ceiling, and so on. This one started low down. Then we trace how the fire spread." He hatched in a rectangle on either side of the dot he'd drawn. "This one burned hot and moved fast—hotter and faster than a naturally occurring fire would, probably due to an accelerant being used. The accelerant's the key. If we can find evidence showing which type's been used, then *bingo*. So we take all the ash and debris back to the lab, along with some control samples from elsewhere in the building, and run everything through the chromatographs. That's when we can put it in writing."

"How long till that's done, Chief?" Hale rested her hands on the table.

"Another twenty-four hours." Young sat back down. "Maybe forty-eight."

"Any way you could put a rush on that?" Devereaux drummed his fingers on the tabletop. "It would be good to be sure what we're dealing with."

"No." Young shook his head. "Can't be done. We've got to wait for the last of the water to dissipate. Make sure the structure's safe, physically, and that there's no buildup of harmful gas. Check for hazardous materials, like asbestos. And in case it is arson, we have to make sure there aren't any other devices in there. Either timed deliberately to go off later, or ones that failed to work before. My guys' safety's at stake here, and I can't compromise on that."

"We understand, Chief." Hale brushed back a strand of hair that had come loose. "We know you can't sign off on anything right now. But on the QT?"

"Between you and me?" Young shoved his pen back in his bag and zipped it closed. "Lieutenant, I've seen a lot of fires in my time, in everything from henhouses to high-rises. If this one got started on its own, I'll show my butt on the town hall steps."

"That's good enough for me." Hale nodded. "So, question two, where do we go from here? Next steps? Linda—any thoughts?"

Irvin laid her hands on the table, palms down, fingers spread, and leaned forward slightly for a moment before standing up and moving to the sheet of paper that Young had drawn on. She took out a pen of her own and started to write:

Insurance fraud
Vandalism
Revenge
Secondary crime

"Statistically speaking, these are the top four motives for arson in the United States." Irvin struck through the first word she'd written. "We can discount fraud. Usually it's top of the list, but it doesn't apply here, as the school's public property." She moved her pen down to the last item on the list. "So, I've been trying to think—could anyone else benefit financially from the fire? Could it have been a cover for a theft of some sort? Was there anything of value in the building? Computers? Sports equipment?"

"Not in the area that was burned." Young shook his head.

"I'll put out some feelers, just in case." Devereaux scribbled a note in his book. "See if anyone's trying to fence anything educational. But I've got to say, it's a long shot. There are much better places to steal computers from than a school, where grubby kids will have had their sticky hands all over them."

"What about a contractor, looking to clean up on the rebuilding job?" Garretty scratched the side of his nose.

"I don't see it." Hale frowned. "How would anyone guarantee they'd win the contract? Or that there even would be a contract? Schools are getting consolidated right and left in Birmingham. The Board of Education will probably just move the kids to other schools, bulldoze the site, and sell the land. Too much risk for too little chance of reward, I'd say."

"Agreed." Irvin drew a line through *secondary crime* and moved the tip of her pen up to *vandalism*. "We have a problem here, too. Vandals usually start small and build up, but I've done some checking. There are no reports of smaller fires or similar kinds of damage in the neighborhood in the last three months. Therefore," Irvin moved the pen down and circled *revenge,* "my money's on someone with a grudge. And a box of matches."

"A pissed-off student." Devereaux nodded. "Just like in '61. History's repeating itself."

"It could be." Irvin moved back to her seat. "Or it could be a parent this time, feeling like the school had failed his or her kid. Or a staff member, who'd been fired or passed over for promotion."

"Revenge. That's an interesting angle." Young eased back his cap to scratch the side of his closely cropped head. "Because here's something else you guys might want to factor in. All schools have sprinkler systems, right? Well, Jones Valley's was totally outdated. It was due to be replaced this summer, but the program's running behind. If you wanted to do the maximum amount of damage, you couldn't have left it much later. In another couple of weeks, the new system'll be in place. After that, a fire like this one wouldn't have half the impact."

"How many other schools have old systems?" Irvin got back to her feet and drew a second ring around *revenge*.

"Only two." Young pulled his cap back into place. "The others have all been switched out already."

"Interesting." Irvin twiddled the pen between her fingers. "Seems like the sort of thing a staff member's more likely to know about than a student."

"That's what I was thinking." Young nodded.

"What about the Board of Education?" Hale steepled her fingers. "Someone there must know about the upgrade program, if it's city-wide?"

"I would guess so." Young shrugged.

"OK." Hale put both hands on the table. "Good work, everyone. I can see the outline of a plan here. We're going to pursue the revenge angle. Hard. We'll need to take a good look at a lot of people. School staff. Board of Ed employees. Students, including recent graduates. And parents. Linda, can you pull a list together? And prioritize it? Let's make this process as efficient as possible."

"Happy to." Irvin sat down and took a notebook from her briefcase.

"Tommy, I want you to arrange the interviews. Use anyone from the squad you need."

"I'm on it, Lieutenant."

"Good. I'm sure that's our best move right now. But I want us to follow a second angle, as well. As insurance. Just in case we're wrong. At least until the lab results are back. So, let's play the percentages. Cooper, I want you to arrange a canvass of all the gas stations in the city. And all the home improvement stores. Anywhere that sells gasoline, or any other flammable liquid that could be used as an accelerant. I want to know about anyone making suspicious purchases. Or even asking questions about that kind of stuff. And I want someone talking to the hospitals. Checking for burn victims. Who knows, if we're lucky, our guy might have hurt himself when he set the fire."

"Got it." Devereaux scribbled a quick note. "I'll liaise with uniform, borrow some guys, and get them on it right away."

"Excellent. Any other ideas before we wrap this up?"

"Nothing from me." Young reached for his bag.

"Nor me." Garretty drained the last drop from his coffee cup.

"I have one other suggestion." Irvin put her pen down on the table. "Whoever did this, their behavior pre and post offense will be quite distinctive. Beforehand, I'd expect a buildup of tension to an intolerable degree. Afterward, they'll be noticeably different. Erratic. Any alcohol or drug use is likely to increase. Anxiety will build up tremendously, as they worry about being caught. It could lead to a complete meltdown. So, my thought is this: We release an appeal to the public. Ask people to report any of their friends or relatives whose behavior shows the kind of changes I've described. Stress that it's for their own good. A *help us to help them* type of thing."

"Interesting." Hale picked up one of her mugs, swirled the dregs of her coffee around for ten seconds, then put it back down. "I see where you're coming from. But I'm wary of the volume of calls that might involve. We could end up drowning in absolute dross."

"Sure." Irvin clasped her hands together. "There could be a lot of calls, and they'd have to be managed effectively. But I'm wary of the prospect of more fires. There could be more damage. Maybe casualties as well in the future. And if extra call-screening facilities are needed, I'm sure the Bureau could help."

"OK." Hale lined her mugs up so that the handles were all pointing the same way. "Go ahead and draft something. But let's not put it out just yet. Let's wait and see what we can dig up on our own, first. Now, is there anything else? Anyone?"

"I was thinking about Jeff Nelson's photograph." Devereaux looked up from his notebook. He'd actually been thinking about Kevin, the arsonist he'd known years ago, and drawing doodles of snakes. "Remember the mystery guy he caught on his camera phone? He didn't come forward. None of the other witnesses mentioned him, and no one knows who he is. So what if we're on the wrong track with this thing? Fraud, revenge, these are all rational motives. But what if this is something else? What if someone set the fire because he just likes setting fires? The guy in the picture, maybe? Hanging around, enjoying the destruction he'd caused."

"I've heard of cases like that." Hale frowned. "Chief? Any thoughts?"

"Not really." Young shook his head. "Psychology's not my field. I do the *what* and the *how*. The *why*'s up to someone else to figure out."

"OK." Hale picked her mug up again, as if she was hoping that some fresh coffee would have magically appeared. "Linda?"

"It's certainly possible." Irvin paused for a moment. "And if it's not inappropriate to say so, it would be excellent from my point of view. Much more interesting than someone trying to screw a few dollars out of State Farm or get back at their eighth-grade math teacher. But I'm sorry. I have to put my practical hat on here. The odds are way, way against it. You know, Ockham's Law. Hear hoofbeats, think horses. Not zebras. Not unless you've got a very good reason to."

"You're probably right." Hale stood up and hooked her index finger through the handles of all three of her mugs. "But I hate loose ends. Let's make sure we find the guy, even if he's just another witness."

Chapter Eleven

Sunday. Morning.

IN HER HEART, ALEXANDRA KNEW THAT DEVEREAUX WASN'T GOING TO come. But she stood outside the Trinity Presbyterian Church for another five minutes anyway, tuned out the roar of a leaf blower in a nearby yard and the drone of the cars passing by on the street, and poured all her mental energy into the vain hope that he'd miraculously appear in time.

Part of her was worried about Devereaux in case he was bleeding to death on a filthy floor somewhere. That's what he'd told her had happened to his father, who'd also been a cop. But mostly she was embarrassed. The one thing about living as a single mother that she hadn't enjoyed was enduring the looks she received from the other worshippers at the church she'd attended since she was a baby. No one said anything unpleasant about her. Not openly, anyway. But she could read the disapproval on their faces. She'd hoped that would go away once she was reunited with her child's father, as unlikely a companion on the road to redemption as Devereaux may be. And yet here she was, alone with Nicole again. And she wasn't just back to square one. It was worse than that. It wasn't just the judgment she was dealing with. Now she could sense pity, too.

Alexandra delayed until she heard the first chord being played on the organ inside the simple, single-story building, then left the shade of her favorite oak tree and called for Nicole to follow her inside. But when she reached the door there was no sign of her daughter. She looked around, momentarily panicked, and saw Nicole racing around between the spherical bushes at the side of the driveway, a frenetic blur against the green of the leaves and the reds, blues, and silvers of the shiny cars in the church's small lot. Suddenly furious, Alexandra called again, louder, and as soon as Nicole was within reach she grabbed her daughter's wrist and dragged her inside.

Alexandra made for the rearmost pew, anxious to avoid drawing attention to herself, and the moment she settled in the seat she felt her flash of anger turn to guilt. Nicole hadn't done anything wrong. All kids like to run around in the fresh air, making up games. Alexandra certainly had, when she was Nicole's age. And who can blame a child for exercising her imagination? Nicole wasn't to blame for the change in their circumstances. Alexandra reached across and stroked Nicole's hair. She was blessed to have a daughter with such a divine temperament, she told herself, as she watched the little girl sitting demurely with her two little dolls next to her, arranged so they were holding hands.

Nicole waited for her mother's attention to be drawn to the hypnotic rhythm of the pastor's soothing words, then moved her dolls onto her lap. She took hold of the little girl doll's hand, pulled, and smiled as the slender wire that ran up the mother doll's sleeve tightened around its neck . . .

Chapter Twelve

Sunday. Morning.

SCREW OCKHAM, DEVEREAUX THOUGHT, *WHOEVER HE WAS*. HERE WAS a much better rule: *Think snake, grab stick. Start beating the undergrowth.* Leave the horses and zebras for someone else to worry about.

Devereaux stopped at his desk on the third floor for just long enough to get the ball rolling on the canvassing that Lieutenant Hale had asked for, then he hurried outside to his car. He felt a touch of regret as he fired up the engine and headed west on First Avenue instead of east, thinking about Alexandra walking into the church without him. But the closer he came to the Jones Valley campus, the more his curiosity took over. He pictured his old school being consumed by flames, and all the misery of his childhood being burned away along with the buildings he'd been so bored in. Then his imagination kicked up a gear, and visions of smoldering, desolated European cities filled his mind, flooding back to him from the WWII movies he and his father had loved to watch together when he was a kid. Even from a mile away he could feel his adrenaline level rising as he anticipated the untamed, elemental violence of a fire in its full fury. But the images in his head still left him completely unprepared for what he saw when he turned onto Dowell Avenue from 31st Street and approached the school's main entrance. It was as if the blaze had sucked all life out of the structure, leaving just a hulking, extinct carcass. It was dull. Inert. And above all, dirty.

The redbrick walls above the row of jagged, broken windows in the school's central block were stained black from the smoke. Sections of chain-link fence had been knocked down, and sagging swathes of police tape had been strung across the gaps. The grass banks and verges had been torn up by the fire trucks' enormous tires. A handful of the saplings that had recently been planted around the edge of the parking lot had been uprooted. The parking lot itself was caked in dried mud caused by the torrents of water used to defeat the flames. And the whole place stank as if that water had been taken directly from a sewage plant.

There were cars parked on both sides of Dowell Avenue and 30th Street. The vacant lot opposite the side of Powderly Baptist Church was also full of vehicles, and that gave Devereaux an idea. An extra few minutes couldn't make things much worse with Alexandra at this point, so he pulled his Charger onto the sidewalk at the bottom of the church steps—hoping it was as big a giveaway as Nelson had suggested—grabbed a BPD windbreaker from the trunk, and waited for the congregation to come out.

"Pardon me, miss?" Devereaux tried to hand a business card to the first worshipper to make her way down the steps, five minutes later. "Is there anything you can tell me about the fire that happened across the street yesterday?"

The woman shook her head and hurried away.

"Sir, do you live in the neighborhood?" Devereaux offered a card to an old man who walked with a cane. "Did you see anything suspicious going on at the school?"

Soon too many people were swarming past Devereaux for him to address them all individually, but still no one stopped to speak to him. Devereaux wasn't disheartened by that. He wasn't expecting to be given any information. He just wanted the chance to take a good look at the stream of parishioners. To see how they reacted when they spotted him. To pick up on anyone who seemed too keen to avoid him. Or who paid him too much attention, like one guy he soon had his eye on. A man who'd managed to recirculate through the crowd three times, and was now standing in the exact same spot at the top of the steps, between the right-hand pair of rectangular pillars, as the guy Nelson had photographed.

"Come on." Devereaux gestured to the guy. "Come down here. Let's talk. Maybe we can help each other out."

The guy didn't reply. He stood stock still for a moment and a pink rash began to spread up from his neck and across his face. Then he started down the steps, trying to dodge to Devereaux's right and break away down Dowell Avenue.

"You looking to get shot?" Devereaux had anticipated the guy's move and caught up to him in three strides, grabbing him by the collar. "Knock it off. I only want to talk to you. Let's start with your name."

"Cooper?" The guy twisted around to face Devereaux, and looked like he was ready to burst into tears. "Cooper Devereaux? You don't remember me?"

Devereaux bundled the guy into the Charger's passenger seat and drove down Dowell Avenue until he reached a spot where he could park well clear of any other cars.

"Of course I remember you, now." Devereaux killed the engine and turned his head. "You're Swedish Dave. But give me a break. I haven't seen you since tenth grade. That's a lot of years. Your face has changed a little bit. I expect mine has, too."

"No." The guy shook his head. "I'm not *Swedish* Dave. I'm just Dave. Dave Bateman. I made the Swedish part up to try and sound more interesting when I was a kid. No one calls me that anymore."

"Dave Bateman, that's right." Devereaux tried to keep the annoyance out of his voice. He'd come in search of a snake, but all he'd found was a bunny rabbit. He should have spent his time waiting for Alexandra outside her church, instead. "That's what I meant. So what are you doing with yourself these days, Dave?"

"Not much." Bateman seemed to shrink into his seat. "I'm working retail right now."

"But you were planning to be an actor, right? Or a singer?"

"I was going to be the next David Bowie. Only it didn't quite work out. I've been selling Hi-Fi, mostly, since I quit school. When I've been in work."

"There's nothing wrong with that. It keeps the wolf from the door, right?"

Bateman shrugged.

"Do you live around here, Dave?"

"No."

"So what are you doing here?"

"Going to church."

"Do you come every week?"

Bateman nodded.

"Did you go yesterday?"

"Yesterday was Saturday."

"I know. But did you go to the church yesterday? Say around 2:20 pm?"

"Why would I do that? Services are on Sundays."

"Dave, I have a picture of you. Standing at the top of the steps, where you were just now. Wearing a hoodie. A passing motorist took it. Don't make me pull out my phone and show you. Just confirm you were here, tell me what you saw, and we can both go home."

"OK."

"So you were here?"

"All right. Yes. I was."

"You were watching the fire."

"I guess."

"What can you tell me about it?"

"Nothing much."

"But you did see it?"

Bateman nodded.

"You could see the smoke?"

Bateman nodded again.

"What color was it?"

"Black."

"Was it thick? Or thin?"

"Thick. Real thick."

"And the flames? I heard they were a hundred feet tall."

"No way. More like twenty. Thirty at the most."

"OK. Good. But I want you to think carefully now, Dave. Did you see anyone else? Watching the fire? Running away? Driving away?"

"Not really. I mean, a few cars went by. People probably saw the fire from their houses. I guess someone called 911, because the fire trucks came pretty soon. That's when I left."

"Why didn't you call 911, Dave?"

Bateman shrugged.

"Seriously, Dave, why didn't you call? Most people see a fire in a school, they call 911. Why didn't you do that?"

"I didn't want the fire trucks to come so fast, I guess."

"Why not?"

"I don't know. Give me a minute."

"Come on, Dave. It's a simple question. Give me a sensible answer and we can both get out of here."

"Just give me a minute!" Bateman's voice had dropped a couple of octaves, turning into a kind of bass growl, and he started to rock jerkily back and forward in his seat. "I told you. I need to think."

"OK, Dave." Devereaux eased to the side, making sure there was nothing between his elbow and the side of Bateman's head, just in case. "Take your time. No one's rushing you."

Bateman's movements gradually became less frenzied, and after another minute he turned his head and stared out of the side window.

"All right." Bateman turned to Devereaux a few seconds later, his voice back to its usual pitch and a look of childish excitement on his face. "I'm ready. You might want to write this down. Because I'm confessing. The reason I didn't call 911? That's easy. It's obvious. It was me who set the school on fire. I did it. At last."

Chapter Thirteen

Sunday. Late morning.

DIANE MCKINZIE READ THE TEXT MESSAGE FOR A SECOND TIME, THEN pushed her bedroom door closed and leaned against it.

This is good news, she told herself. *This is good news!*

Except that somehow she was going to have to break the consequences of it to Daniel.

This is not good news . . .

Daniel slammed his bedroom door so hard that the nameplate—Professor Daniel McKinzie, Department of Theoretical Physics—broke free from its mounting and slammed into the wooden floor, adding another deep dent to the scored and scratched surface.

"Daniel!" Diane bent down to retrieve the enameled metal square. "Your grandfather had that made specially for you! Now you've bent the corner again. If you do that one more time, I'm taking it away. I'm serious!"

There was no response from inside the room.

"Daniel, come on." Diane tried in vain to keep the wheedling tone she hated so much from entering her voice. "Come out. Please. Let me explain. You know I don't like talking to you through the door."

Diane heard a familiar *ting* sound from behind her so she hurried back to her room to check her phone. Part of her hoped it would be her contact at the police department again, saying the previous tip-off was wrong. That there hadn't been an arrest in the school arson case, after all. But that was crazy! Think of the scoop she could get. That's what journalists live for! Or *should* live for. But she wasn't just a journalist anymore. She had other responsibilities now. Had done for a long while. Not that anyone noticed. Or cared. She had too many balls to keep in the air to stay sane, unless—maybe no other reporters would find out about the arrest until tomorrow? Then she could ignore the last message. Or pretend she hadn't seen it. Her editor would never know. Or would she? Because turning her back on an opportunity like this—it would be career suicide. And in the current environment? No. She couldn't risk it. She'd just have to find a way to smooth things over with Daniel. Get him to agree to reschedule their plans for the next weekend . . .

By the time Diane retrieved her phone she was back to hoping that the new message wasn't from her police contact, after all. But when she checked the screen, she was momentarily confused. It was Daniel's name that was displayed. Diane figured an old message must have been resent due to some network glitch, but she clicked on it, anyway, to be sure. And she found that she was wrong. The text was marked as unread:

I will speak to you in ten minutes. Wait for me in the living room.

Chapter Fourteen

Sunday. Late morning.

TYLER SHAW TOOK ONE OF THE LENGTHS OF TWO-BY-FOURS OFF THE cart and replaced it in the vertical rack at the hardware store. In other circumstances he'd have taken it. As a rule he preferred to be safe rather than sorry. And he could always find a use for a good length of wood. But as things were, he couldn't risk getting too much. He had a long way to carry it, and no one he could trust to help.

Next up was the paint section. Shaw parked the cart at the end of the aisle and walked slowly up and down each side, carefully contemplating all the available colors. Blue would be best, he decided, eventually settling on a deep shade of cobalt. It was the most powerful. Perfect for what he had in mind. And he could pair it with blue lightbulbs, for an even greater effect. He'd need to pick up a couple of packs. Unless he just painted some regular ones? No. What was he thinking? This was not a project to skimp on. He'd buy some colored ones. But not any batteries. Those, he could steal from his work. Paying for them would just be a waste. And all the other stuff, he already had.

In fact, once he was through the register, he'd have everything he needed. Everything apart from time. If he was going to get the real work under way on schedule, he'd need to get the preparations nailed down double-quick . . .

Chapter Fifteen

Sunday. Late morning.

DIANE MCKINZIE'S TONGUE RECOILED FROM THE METALLIC TANG OF the blood but she continued to suck the tip of her finger, anyway, anxious to stem the flow before it dripped onto the pale yellow fabric of the couch.

She hadn't realized she'd been picking at the scab again until she felt the familiar, warm stickiness reach her palm. She'd been too busy trying to figure how much later she could afford to leave and still get to the coffee shop in time to meet her source and get the scoop on the school fire arrest. She really should have left already, but if the traffic on I-65 was kind—it was Sunday, after all—and if she found somewhere to park right away, and if there wasn't a line, and . . . and if Daniel didn't keep her waiting much longer! He'd said ten minutes. That was fifteen minutes ago. She'd changed her clothes and grabbed her purse the moment she got his text. He was usually so punctual. But of course, not today! He must still be pissed about having to change their plan. And she still hadn't figured out what to say to him about that. Maybe if she offered to—

"What have you done to the floor?" Daniel had appeared in the arch between the living room and the hallway. He leant his shoulder against the wall, thrust his hands into the pockets of his jeans, and stared at her. He was barefoot, his hair was washed and brushed, and he had on a T-shirt so new the fold lines from the packaging were still visible. It was black with a picture of three rappers wearing their signature hats and heavy gold chains, only each of their faces had been replaced with Einstein's, and a caption at the bottom of the image read RUN EMC². "You're always telling me not to wear shoes in the house. You're such a hypocrite."

Diane looked down and saw that her heels had cut a series of zigzag-shaped scratches in the polished wooden boards as she'd fidgeted. *One more thing she'd have to fix. If she could ever get the time . . .*

"Maybe if you wore normal shoes, this kind of thing wouldn't happen." Daniel sneered. "Why do you have to dress like that, anyway? Maybe things would work out better if you put more effort into your writing, instead of worrying about how you look. I read your 'article,' by the way. The one you stayed out late for, yesterday. Was that really the best you could do? It was terrible. Making out like you know what happened at that school. How could you possibly know?"

"It's what journalists do, Daniel." Diane clamped her eyes shut for a moment, desperate to stop any tears from escaping. "We investigate. Talk to people who do know. Build—"

"Investigate. Right. Talk to people. Uh-huh. Come on. What were you really doing last night? Where were you?"

"I've explained that to you, and I'm not going over it again." Diane moved her purse onto her lap and started to rummage through its contents, looking for a Band-Aid for her finger. "Now, I have to get going. I have work to do, and I'm already late. So let's talk about the museum. I'm—"

"It's not a museum!" Daniel levered himself off the wall, pulling his hands from his pockets and clenching his fists.

"OK." Diane held up her hands. "The science center. Whatever. The point is, I will still take you. Just not today. I'm sorry."

"You're sorry." Daniel rolled his eyes. "What good is that? Was Albie's mother *sorry* when his Greek teacher disparaged him? Was Oppie's mother *sorry* when he had problems taking the bus to school? No. Because they were real parents. They did what was needed to help their sons. How can I fulfill my destiny and become the greatest physicist of the twenty-first century when I'm lumbered with *you*?"

"Daniel, that's not fair." Diane gripped her purse tight, distorting the fine Italian leather. "I'm doing everything I can to help, you know that. You're on track to become an outstanding scientist. But you're only fifteen! You're in high school! Postponing one trip by a few days isn't going to hurt your future career."

"No. Your betrayals and your broken promises are what's going to hurt it." Daniel glowered at his mother, then turned and walked away down the hallway. "My high school's a joke. It's a waste of time. An asylum for losers. Lobotomy candidates. The corporate slaves of tomorrow. I shouldn't even be there. I should just teach myself. And you know what? I will. You go. Investigate your little story. I've got stuff to do. I need to design a new syllabus. As of this moment, I'm officially withdrawing from the public educational system."

Diane sat for a moment, staring blankly at the spot where Daniel had been standing. Then she shook her head as if snapping out of a daydream and got to her feet. She hurried down the hallway. Let herself into the garage through the door from the utility room. Pulled out her key and unlocked her dad's old car. And paused. That car had been her father's pride and joy. It was a 1967 Volvo P1800 in white, with limited-edition Empi-style wheels. Volvo wasn't most people's idea of an exotic brand, but this car was an exception. With its two-door coupe body; sweeping, sexy curves; and low, sporty stance, it was frequently mistaken for an early Ferrari. Diane remembered the looks they'd get from pedestrians and other motorists when her dad took her out for drives on the rare Saturday or Sunday he wasn't working when she was a little girl. She still liked to drive it herself on weekends, and sometimes late at night when she couldn't sleep. But there was a snag. The reason her father had ordered that particular make, model, color, and specification was because he wanted to have the same car as Simon Templar. Simon Templar, aka The Saint. Hero of the Leslie Charteris novels. Played in the cult TV show by Roger Moore. For complete authenticity her father had imported it specially from England. That meant it was right-hand drive, and had stick shift. Not the greatest combination for cutting through city traffic. Maybe having to parallel park. Probably with an audience. No. Diane figured that even though it was the weekend, she'd be better off using her trusty—and already dented—Mini Cooper.

What would her dad have made of her Mini? He'd have hated it, Diane thought. He'd have wanted an original, not a prettified faux imitation. He'd liked things done right. Which begged the obvious question, what would he have made of her life? Diane was pretty sure she knew the answer to that one.

Diane locked the Volvo's door, blinked away another impending flood of tears, turned, and bumped into a tall stack of three-foot-cubed cardboard boxes that had been pushed against the wall. The top one wobbled, then fell, hitting the hood of the car before tumbling onto the hard concrete floor in front of her. She lashed out with her foot, caving in the side of the box and bursting open its top flaps. Styrofoam packing chips flooded out like giant hailstones, blocking her path. She kicked out again, sending a slow-motion plume of chips floating high into the air. Then she jumped into the middle of the heap, kicking and stomping and spinning around in the narrow space, bouncing dizzily between the wall and the side of the car. Struggling for breath, she eventually slowed down, picked up handfuls of chips instead, and flung them around her, not stopping completely until the garage looked like the inside of a giant urban snow globe.

A couple of errant chips were clinging to her hair when she climbed into her Mini, still breathless, five minutes later. *Useful little things,* she thought, pulling them free of the static. *Not what they're designed for, of course. And not why I bought them. But if I can also use them to keep me from doing more destructive things, that's got to be good, right?*

Chapter Sixteen

Sunday. Afternoon.

"THIS IS THE GUY?" CAPTAIN EMRICH TURNED AWAY FROM THE OBSERVA-
tion window and glared in turn at Devereaux and Hale. "Are you sure?"

"What's the problem?" Devereaux glared back. "You wanted someone more photogenic?"

"No. Although, really?" Emrich gestured through the window at
Bateman, who was cowering behind the scratched metal table in the
interview room rather than sitting at it. Aside from his gaunt face and
thinning hair he could have been mistaken for a scared little boy who'd
borrowed his father's clothes. "I hear you've pulled in an old buddy of
yours, and I see *him,* and I'm supposed to take it seriously? What are
you trying to pull here, Devereaux?"

"What do you mean, you *see* him?" Devereaux raised his eyebrows.
"You can tell if someone's guilty just by looking at them? That's some
mighty fine police work right there, Captain. I'm truly impressed."

"That's enough of your bullshit, Detective." Emrich scowled. "And
given that you know this man, you shouldn't be questioning him, anyway."

"I agree." Devereaux nodded. "Best if someone else takes it from
here."

"I'm sorry, Captain." Lieutenant Hale resisted the temptation to
smile. She'd never thought she'd hear Devereaux admit to being on the
same page as the captain. The two of them being in the same room

was usually a recipe for disaster. They were a year apart in age. Both had been born in Birmingham. But they were poles apart in every other respect. Devereaux did little to hide the fact that he'd happily take Emrich into a blind alley and come out alone. And the word in the department was that Emrich was only delaying his inevitable move into politics in the hope of finally making one of Devereaux's many suspensions stick. "I thought the same thing. But there's a problem. The suspect has refused to talk to anyone else. There's no point antagonizing him, if we want to get this thing cleared up as quick as possible."

Bateman sat up straighter when he heard the door to the interview room squeak open, and by the time Devereaux had taken the seat opposite him and laid his slim beige folder on the table, a look of childish enthusiasm had returned to his face.

"Cooper, good. I didn't know where you'd gone. Let's—"

"Hold on, Dave." Devereaux held up one hand. "Don't say anything. Not before you get yourself a lawyer." He suppressed a smile of his own, thinking of the consternation he'd just caused in the observation room.

"Do I need one?" Wrinkles appeared along the length of Bateman's forehead.

"I think you should get one, yes." Devereaux nodded. "If you're worried about the cost, remember what I told you earlier, in the car. The city will provide one for you. It won't cost you a cent."

"Do I have to get one?"

"No." Devereaux folded his arms. "You don't have to. But my advice is, you should. This is a serious situation, and you need to protect yourself."

"You think I don't know how serious this is?" Bateman slammed his hand on the table. "You think I'm an idiot? This isn't school. I can protect myself now!"

Devereaux didn't respond.

Bateman took a few moments then pressed his palms together as if he was praying. "OK. Let's get this straight. There will be no lawyer.

Just you and me. And I want to get it done right now. Can we just cut the crap and get the show on the road? Please?"

Devereaux took a pen from his jacket pocket—one of the cheap disposable ballpoints he regularly pinched from restaurants and hotels because he didn't want murderers and rapists touching his personal property—and slid it across the table along with a piece of paper from his folder. "Here. Sign this. It says you've declined your right to a lawyer. Anything you tell me is worthless otherwise."

Bateman scrawled his name across the bottom of the page without even reading it. "There. Can we get started now?"

"I guess." Devereaux pulled out his notebook. "OK. The ball's in your court. Tell me what happened."

"Easy. I set fire to the school. Jones Valley. Yesterday afternoon. I'm officially confessing. Do I have to sign to that, too?"

"We'll come to that. First, tell me how you did it."

"How?" Bateman scratched his left wrist. "Oh. Well, I got a bunch of gas, took it—"

"What did you take it in?"

"One of those special red containers. Four gallons."

"Where did you get it? This container?"

"At a DIY store. Out on Flintridge Drive. In Fairfield."

"Got a receipt?"

"No. Not anymore."

"Dave, we talked to the manager of that store. They have no record of any of those containers being sold."

"Do their records go back ten years? Because that's how long ago I bought it. I've been planning this a long time."

"OK. What about the gas?"

"I got it at the Shell station on Arkadelphia Road, just off 20/59."

"Really? Because we checked. No one's filled a container with gas there in the last three months."

"I didn't fill the container. I filled my car. Then I syphoned the gas into the container back at my house. Last Tuesday. And the gas, I do have a receipt for."

"What did you do next?"

"Nothing, till yesterday. Then I drove to the school. Parked in my usual spot that I use for church. Broke into the school. Splashed the gas around all over the place. Threw down a match. Then watched it burn, till the fire trucks came."

"Why didn't an alarm go off, when you broke into the school?"

Bateman shrugged.

"And how come no one saw you?"

"Someone did! They took my picture. Outside the church. That's what you said."

"True point." Devereaux closed his notebook. "OK. I'm going to check out everything you've told me, Dave. Don't worry. It's standard procedure. But before I do, there's one more thing I need to know."

"OK. What?"

"Why, Dave? Why did you do it? Torch the place?"

"You're going to make me spell it out?"

"Absolutely. Motive's a key thing. This is a high-profile case. Lots of tax dollars are up in smoke. People are pissed. So I've got to go by the book. I need you to tell me."

"Cooper, please! You of all people."

"What's that supposed to mean?"

Bateman held his hands an inch above the table for a moment, moving his fingers as if he was playing scales on an invisible piano. "OK. You remember Principal Oliver? You must. You were in his office enough times."

Devereaux cast his mind back and recalled a thin, gray figure in a baggy suit lurking behind a giant, ornate wooden desk. He regularly hauled Devereaux over the coals about his grades, and threw out veiled threats about curtailing his extra-curricular activities, though without having the balls to ever act on them. In the hierarchy of assholes who Devereaux held grudges against, Principal Oliver didn't even make the top twenty. "Right. I do. He was a weasely little guy. I never liked him. He was always harassing me about something or other."

"And when you were in his room, he never . . . oh God. This was a mistake."

"What was? Setting the fire?"

"No. Telling you. I figured you knew. But maybe you don't. I don't want to talk about it anymore. Can I go?"

Watching Bateman squirm in his seat brought another memory to Devereaux's mind. Of seeing a younger version of the guy sitting out-side Oliver's office. Small. Red-eyed. Fidgety. And Devereaux remem-bered feeling no sympathy for him whatsoever. He'd been too busy keeping his own activities out of the school's spotlight. Plus his atti-tude had always been, *If you can't do the time . . .* But now he was beginning to worry. Maybe he'd missed something. Maybe Bateman hadn't been the one at fault . . .

"It's all right, Dave." Devereaux tried to make his voice sound warm and unthreatening. "Whatever it is, you can tell me. And if I can help you, I will. You have my word."

"Like that's worth anything."

"Come on, Dave. I'm not the bad guy here. Tell me what happened. What did Oliver do?"

"Nothing." Bateman shook his head. "It doesn't matter. I want to go."

"You can't go, Dave! You're under arrest. That's why you've got to tell me. If there's something that explains what you did, that shifts the blame onto someone else, I need to know. That's the only way I can help you now."

"I don't care." Bateman turned his head and lowered his gaze to the floor. "I'm not saying another word."

"Would it be better to write it down? Would that be easier than say-ing it?"

Bateman shook his head.

"Do you want to talk to someone else, instead? Another detective? A counselor?"

"No." Bateman's voice was barely above a whisper. "It's OK. Let me write it."

Devereaux read every tiny, spidery word on the three pages that Bate-man had covered, then laid the legal pad down on the table. He felt a wave of calmness and clarity wash over him, the way it always did when a violent outcome became inevitable. Or preferable. But this time the feeling was tinged with regret. He'd been there at the school when the things Bateman described had happened. He could have stopped them. If only he'd seen the signs.

"I'm sorry you had to go through this, Dave." Devereaux could barely meet Bateman's gaze. "Truly. And I'm sorry I have to ask, but it's important. Was anyone else involved?"

"A few times." Bateman shivered, as if an icy blast of wind had cut through the room. "Sometimes Oliver let people watch. I don't know their names. And I didn't look at their faces. I was too ashamed."

"Other adults?"

Bateman nodded.

"How about other students?"

"Never in the room with me." Bateman shrugged. "But there probably were others."

"Got any names?"

Bateman shook his head.

"Where's Oliver now?" Devereaux opened his notebook.

"I've got no idea." Bateman started to play his imaginary piano again. "I haven't seen him or heard of him for years. Not since he retired. I think he moved away. Maybe left the country."

"Are you sure?" Devereaux turned the legal pad facedown. "Because in a situation like this, let's say you'd been to see him one time. A while ago. Just to talk things through. Hoping to reconcile, perhaps. And he had some kind of accident? Like, a terminal one? No one would take a very close look at that. I certainly wouldn't, and this is my case."

"You think I killed him?" Bateman stopped moving his fingers and looked up. "Honestly, I wish I had. I wanted to. Many times. But I didn't have the nerve. I'm a coward. That's why I had to burn the school down, instead."

"All right, Dave." Devereaux nodded. "I'll make you a promise. I'll find Oliver, if he's still alive. And I'll make him pay for every single thing he did to you. But there's just one thing I don't understand. The school. It's the wrong one. The one we went to, where the bad things happened? It was demolished years ago. This new one's not even a high school. So why burn it? What was the point?"

Bateman covered his eyes for a moment, then dropped his hands to the table. "Look, I get it. I should have done something before. I know that. I tried to. Over and over. Every time I wussed out. And every time I hated myself a little bit more. But is it my fault they demolished our old school before I could set it on fire? No. And what else could I do? Travel back in time? No. So it might have been too little, and it might have been too late. But at least I finally did *something*."

WHO IS TO BLAME?

Does the guilt lie at Jonathan Ford's door? Or at the Birmingham Police Department's? This reporter examines the rival candidates:

First under the microscope is Jonathan Ford, who had the simple task of driving from one place to another at the correct time to act as a witness. He failed. He's clearly a moron. But can the fault of derailing one part of the plan be placed entirely on his shoulders?

Even without Mr. Ford's unreliable contribution, experienced police officers should have been capable of detecting a burning school on their own. They should have done this quickly enough to have the flames doused in time to retrieve the clues the genius had left for them like toys for a roomful of imbecile children. They, too, failed. Their failure was immense. But was it the critical factor?

With all the failure in the air, perhaps a measure of blame should also be borne by the genius? After all, a person of such colossal intellect should know better than to formulate a plan that depends on the competence of regular mortals.

And in conclusion? The actors in this particular scene may have fluffed their lines, but the public should be assured: The play is not over! In fact, the drama has only just begun. The only question is: Where will the genius stage the next act? No doubt the answer will soon be revealed . . .

Chapter Seventeen

Sunday. Late afternoon.

OF COURSE THE DAMN PORSCHE WAS IN THE WAY!

Alexandra had forgotten it was there until she hit the button to open her garage door. And of course it wasn't actually a Porsche anymore. It was a Ferrari now. A red monstrosity. At least she only had to put up with it temporarily. Just until Devereaux's Porsche was fixed. Although she still couldn't understand how it took twelve weeks and counting to replace one lousy rear speaker. Or how Devereaux came to choose such impractical cars in the first place. Or how he was able to pay for them. The cost of his old one hadn't really struck her when she originally met him, when she was a full-time lawyer. She was used to being around people with expensive toys back then. But now that money was tighter, it stood out to her a little bit more. And then there were the whispers at her church. *A detective's salary. A sports car . . .*

The Range Rover was the only luxury item Alexandra had held on to from her days in the law firm, and she wasn't happy about having to keep leaving it in the driveway. Still, she told herself as she scooped the grocery bags out of the trunk and waited for Nicole to climb down from the back seat, that's a small price to pay for no longer being alone in life. Isn't it?

In the kitchen, a big hunk of bacon was the first thing to come out of the tall paper sack. Then the olive oil. The stewing beef. A carrot. And an onion. Which rolled onto the floor the moment she let go of it. *What on earth was she doing?* Alexandra stopped lining the ingredients up along her countertop and slammed her nearly-new cookbook closed. *Screw you, Julia Child!* Boeuf Bourguignon was a ridiculous choice for Birmingham in September. The weather was far too hot. And the dish was far too much work. She'd be crazy to go to all that effort for someone who probably wouldn't appreciate it. Who probably wouldn't even come home to eat it. However much she hoped he would . . .

"Nicole! Come here!" Alexandra dumped the meat on the lowest shelf in the refrigerator. "Change of plan. We're going out for dinner. Want to pick a place?"

"No, Mommy." Nicole scurried along the hallway. "We can't go."

"Why not, Pumpkin?" Alexandra spun around, surprised that her daughter had responded so quickly. "Aren't you hungry?"

"You said you'd make that beef thingy." Nicole plonked her hands on her hips. "You said you would. So you should."

"I didn't know you liked it so much." Alexandra wondered if she should back off on the wine content next time.

"I don't. But Daddy does. It's his favorite. You said you'd make it. What'll happen when he comes home and you haven't and we're not here? He'll be sad."

"Pumpkin, that's very sweet of you. But remember what I told you about Daddy's job? About how sometimes he has to stay out all night to catch the bad guys? Well, I think tonight might be one of those nights."

"No." Nicole shook her head. "He's coming home."

"I wish I could agree with you, sweetheart." Alexandra leaned down to straighten a rogue strand of her daughter's hair. "But I'm not sure you're right this time."

"I am." Nicole batted Alexandra's hand away. "Daddy's coming home. You'll see."

How did I get myself into this? Alexandra asked herself as she looked down at her daughter's defiant scowl. *What has being back with Devereaux done to me? I argue for a living. And here I am, up against a seven-year-old, hoping I'm going to lose . . .*

Chapter Eighteen

Sunday. Evening.

DIANE MCKINZIE THOUGHT SHE'D MADE IT ALL THE WAY TO HER BEDroom door without giving herself away. She hadn't tripped on any footwear. She hadn't trodden on any creaky boards. She hadn't even breathed until her fingers gripped the handle, started to turn, and—

"Mom!" Daniel's voice echoed along the corridor. "It's no good sneaking around. I can hear you. And I want to talk to you."

Daniel was lying in bed with his head on the pillow and his periodic table comforter pulled right up to his chin. The room was warm—the air conditioner was on the blink again—and for a moment Diane was worried that he was sick. But she quickly dismissed that idea. She'd already have heard about it if there was something wrong with him. He wasn't the kind to suffer in silence. Then her attention was drawn to his feet. How far down the bed they were—she remembered how lost he'd looked when she first put him in that bed as a toddler—and how large they'd grown, sticking straight up like the poles in a circus tent. She was tempted to say something, just to break the silence, but thought better of it. Daniel didn't respond well to personal observations.

"Your room's looking nice." Diane noticed that most of the floor was visible, and the portraits lined up on two of the walls—Copernicus, Galileo, Kepler, Newton, Tesla, Einstein, and Oppenheimer—were unusually straight and level. "You've done a great job of picking up."

"Why are you so late home?" Daniel raised his head a little. "What have you been doing?"

"I've been working, Danny." Diane moved closer to the bed and made to sit on the edge. "You know that."

"Don't!" Daniel glared at his mother. "And don't lie to me. Where have you been, really?"

"Meeting a source, like I told you." Diane backed away again. "Then I was at the office. Mostly. I did have to go out and interview a couple of other people. And to quickly grab something to eat."

"You had dinner? Where?"

Diane hesitated. "Gianmarco's."

"Without me? Why didn't you come get me? This is outrageous! I had to heat up leftovers. You're so selfish."

"I'm not selfish, Daniel. I had to go there with someone. We had things to discuss."

"What kind of things?"

"None of your business."

"Oh, right, because you're embarrassed to be seen with me. You think you can't have an adult conversation with me around. Even though I'm smarter and know more than every single person who works at your stupid newspaper. Including you."

"Daniel, you're very smart, yes. But that's not a very nice attitude. You're not being very gracious right now."

"Who cares? I'm right. Aren't I?"

"It's getting late." Diane took another step back toward the door. "We both have to be up early in the morning. Let's call it a night."

"Wait!" Daniel raised his head a little higher. "What aren't you telling me? Who exactly were you with? Was it someone from your work?"

"It doesn't matter who it was. Now, goodnight."

"Were you on a date? You were, weren't you? How could you? You're disgusting! You leave me home alone. You don't bother to feed me. And why? So you can go out and cavort around with some asshole? You're a disgrace."

"Daniel! That's enough. I was not on a date. I do not go on dates. I was meeting with a person I've known for a while. We were discussing something important. And confidential. Which is all I'm going to say about it."

"If it's so innocent, why did you try to hide it? Why did you lie to me?"

"I'm not hiding anything! And I didn't lie."

"You did. Just not very well. If you're going to lie, you should at least try to do it properly. You can't even do that right. You're pathetic. I hate you. Now leave me alone. And close my door on the way out. It's time for me to sleep."

Diane double-checked that her own door was properly closed, then sank onto her bed. She pressed the heels of her hands against her eyes, breathed deeply, and willed the encounter with Daniel to show itself in a better light. She had to be ready, in case the guy she'd gone to dinner with asked about the rest of her evening, the next time they spoke. If there was a next time. So: She got home. Happily, her son was still awake, despite all the extra work he'd been doing on his science projects. They chatted for a while—he was very interested to hear about her day, as usual—then he settled down to sleep in preparation for his very demanding school schedule. Yes. That should do. It sounded reasonable. As long as she could summon the willpower to keep things lined up the way she needed them to be. But it was all just so very, very tiring. She was worried she didn't have enough left in the tank. And she wondered if it was wrong of her to sometimes wish Daniel had gone to live with his father . . .

She was pretty sure it wasn't wrong of her to fall back on the vodka and pills, given the circumstances. They were medicinal. And taking them was far better than lots of other things she could be doing.

Far better than lots of things she'd already done.

Chapter Nineteen

Sunday. Evening.

THE GARAGE DOOR WAS OPEN.

All the way open. Not just a crack. Wide enough that anyone passing by would be able to see the stupid Ferrari. Devereaux wasn't a fan
of that car. He preferred his tasteful, sapphire blue Porsche, and
couldn't wait for it to come back. He wasn't a fan of the dealer scoring
points off a rival by using their latest model as a loaner. It seemed like
a cheap shot. And he certainly wasn't a fan of inviting strangers to
invade his privacy. His lifestyle raised enough unwanted questions as it
was.

Devereaux had been orphaned when he was six, and the rest of his
childhood had been spent passing through a succession of gruesome
foster homes. And he didn't fare much better at school. But not because he was stupid. Or lazy. His problem was his attitude. He balked
at following the path his teachers laid out when he could see a quicker
way. Or a better one. And what he learned in the classroom stayed
with him when, after graduating with no money for college and little
hope of regular employment, he was left to spiral unwillingly down
through the unwanted leftover dregs of society. He soon found himself
surrounded with criminals and drug addicts, but he was never tempted
to follow their examples. He ignored the dopers, but kept his eye on
the burglars and thieves and extortionists while they did their work.
Then he stepped in. He took their proceeds for himself, and knocked

the low-lifes out of the game by whatever means were necessary. Or desirable.

Devereaux had finally come unstuck when he went after a gang that accidently killed a clerk during a botched gas station stickup. He was swept up by the police in the chaotic aftermath, and because a man had died in the commission of a crime he was linked to, Devereaux was looking at a murder charge. It was almost the end of the road for him. It would have been, if an old cop named Tomcik—one of the officers who'd worked his father's case—hadn't stepped in and brokered a deal: Devereaux's testimony against the shooter for a walk.

Tomcik was pleased with the way Devereaux stood up at the trial, and was delighted when the younger man cut himself free from his dubious associates and asked for help to get into the Police Academy. It wouldn't be possible today, but things were different when Devereaux was in his early twenties. Tomcik was well enough connected to get the problematic areas in Devereaux's record tidied up a little, and back then the department didn't mind too much what lines their recruits had previously crossed as long as the experience made them better cops. And as long as they didn't ever cross those lines again.

Devereaux had a much healthier bank balance than the other recruits in his class, thanks to the giant heap of cash he'd accumulated in his past life. Some of it he gave away in the form of anonymous donations, when he could identify the original victims of the other people's crimes. But the bulk he kept and invested in a variety of creative ways, which generated a return that was far greater than his salary. He felt no guilt. He'd taken the money from lawbreakers. And he felt he deserved compensation for the misery he'd been forced to endure in foster care, without two cents to rub together.

If someone had told Devereaux during those dark days that the time would come when he'd be pissed because someone had left a garage door open, he'd have laughed in their face. He acknowledged the thought and reached down for the bottle of wine he'd bought earlier in the day. It was a 2012 Louis Latour Bourgogne Pinot Noir, which the clerk had assured him would work well with Boeuf Bourguignon. It had something to do with tannins, the guy had explained. Devereaux hadn't really followed, and he didn't really care as long as the wine tasted good. And Alexandra liked it. He just hoped he wasn't too late.

It was nice of her to leave him food in the fridge when he missed dinner. But not as nice as sitting across from her as they ate. And chatted. And held hands. And watched Nicole play. And . . . whatever else might happen after the little girl was tucked up in bed. He smiled, looking forward to the evening. Then cursed when he felt his phone vibrate in his pocket.

"Cooper?" It was Lieutenant Hale. "We have a problem. Another fire. At another school. Inglenook. It's a K–8 this time."

Chapter Twenty

Monday. Early morning.

THE GRATING SCREECH OF THE ALARM SHATTERED HER DREAM AND FOR
a moment Alexandra lay inert in the bed, too shocked to silence it.
Then she thought about Devereaux and shot out an arm, her fingers
scrabbling urgently for the Off button.

She needn't have worried. Devereaux wasn't there. He'd come to
bed after she was asleep, and left before she was awake. She only knew
he'd been there at all by counting the shirts on the weird rack he'd insisted on putting in the corner of the room. Why couldn't he just use
the closet she'd cleared out for him, like a normal person? And this
disappearing act of his had been happening a lot recently. He'd only
been living there—semi-officially—since the middle of August, and
already a pattern was forming. It wasn't a pattern she liked. She
knew—or at least hoped—that he was doing good work. And she understood that following in his father's footsteps was important to him.
So was it selfish of her to want more of him for herself? Surely a relationship should be about sharing more than a house?

The lawyer in Alexandra was still debating the issue as she pulled
on clothes and hurried downstairs, running through dozens of argu-
ments both for and against. Then, growing tired of listening to the
voice in her head, she switched on the radio. NPR was running a seg-
ment on the two school fires. People were calling in. They were angry.
Some were scared. Most were demanding action. One even threatened
revenge if any children were hurt before the arsonist was caught. Alex-

andra felt bad for Devereaux, having to deal with that kind of hysteria. She felt guilty about the critical thoughts she'd been having. But not bad or guilty enough to stop herself from taking a cheap shot at him. She shoved his Honey Smacks back in the kitchen cabinet and took out the ingredients for cranberry oatmeal. That had been her go-to breakfast back when it was just her and Nicole in the house. Nicole loved it. She scarfed it down by the bowlful because it was so delicious. And it was healthy. Not like Devereaux's stupid sugary cereals.

Alexandra waited for the oatmeal to reach just the right consistency, then ladled it into two big bowls. She carried them to the kitchen table and set them down just as Nicole walked in and took her seat.

"What did you make *that* for?" Nicole crossed her arms. "I don't like it anymore. I want froggy cereal. That's what Daddy always gets me."

Chapter Twenty-one

Monday. Morning.

THE STAFF AT HAWKINS & LEACH ELECTRICAL, INC. HADN'T KNOWN Tyler Shaw long enough to realize how out of character his behavior was. It was a Monday morning. He was on time. He was cheerful. And he wasn't drunk.

Anyone watching him carefully might have picked up on a few things that reflected his true nature more accurately. Like the way he parked his van in a handicapped space because it was the nearest to the stockroom. The way he whistled the tune to the Crimson Tide fight song when he came in through the main front entrance; not because he supported Alabama, but because he'd noticed that the receptionist always used an Auburn mug. Or the way he picked up a number of components that couldn't possibly be needed on the jobs he'd been assigned for the day.

There were at least two facts that none of his co-workers could have divined, however. The kind of labor he'd been engaged in that had put him in such a good mood. Or that there was plenty more of that labor left to come . . .

THE SUN ALSO RISES, BUT WILL THE LIGHT EVER DAWN?

As the sun once again blazes its incandescent trail across the Birmingham sky, the city's sleepy inhabitants are on the verge of learning some momentous news: The genius has made the next move!

As the celestial rays mingle with the plumes of smoke still issuing forth from the devastated remains of another school, one question remains: Will the asinine authorities comprehend the significance? Will the pattern be clear to them yet? Will it ever be? Or will the dunces keep on chasing their tails until the genius chooses to reveal the method behind the masterfulness?

For what it's worth, this reporter's money's on the latter option.

Chapter Twenty-two

Monday. Morning.

"COOPER! A WORD." LIEUTENANT HALE WAS EMERGING FROM THE fourth-floor conference room just as Devereaux arrived, and she took his elbow and steered him back toward the elevator. "Let's make this quick. Irvin and Young are waiting in reception. But I have a question first. Your voicemail. On your cellphone. Is it broken?"

"Not that I'm aware." Devereaux shrugged his arm free.

"Then why do I have some guy calling me every five minutes, complaining about you not responding to your messages?" Hale shot a fierce glare over her shoulder and continued walking. "He says he left you a bunch. At least one every day for the last week?"

"Oh." Devereaux hurried to catch up. "This is Chris Lambert we're talking about?"

"You know him?"

"Unfortunately." Devereaux scowled. "He was an instructor at the Academy when I was there."

"So why don't you call him back?"

"Because he's an asshole."

"Can't you just call him and see what he wants?" Hale reached out and hit the call button for the elevator.

"I already know what he wants. My *input* on some project he's working on. He said so on the tenth message he left. Or was it the eleventh. Anyway, what he means is he wants help. Or money. And I'm telling you, he's not getting either of them from me. He's a useless parasite and I don't want anything to do with him."

"Cooper, I understand you don't like the guy." The doors parted and Hale stepped into the elevator car. "No one likes him, from what I hear. But that's not the point." She held out a hand to stop the doors from closing. "The point is, if you don't respond, he'll keep on bugging me. And I don't want that. I have enough on my plate already. So you're going to call him. Today. Whether you want to or not. OK?"

Lieutenant Hale led the visitors into the room, got them situated, then asked Chief Young to get the ball rolling.

"Happy to." Young was wearing the same outfit as the previous day, but his expression had changed to one of pure sunshine. "All right, then, ladies and gentlemen. Do you want the good news? Or the weird news?"

"The weird." Agent Irvin had switched to a dark navy suit, and looked as if she'd startled herself by jumping on the question so fast.

"Let me start with the good." Young smiled. "Inglenook School, where the incident occurred last night? It had the new kind of sprinkler system. Remember I was telling you about those? So the damage was fairly minor. The blaze was controlled, and we were able to extinguish it pretty easily once we got on-site. Which we did very fast. It also meant there was more evidence left for us to collect. And we were able to take it to the lab right away for analysis."

"That is good news." Hale shifted her chair slightly to avoid the sunlight that was streaming in through the broken blind on the end window.

"Now for the weird." Young winked at Irvin. "Pop quiz time. What do you get if you mix Styrofoam, gasoline, and benzene? Or soap?"

"A very clean kind of bomb?" Garretty's attempt at humor fell flat.

"Not even close." Young's smile faded away. "The right answer? Napalm."

"Seriously?" Hale put down her cup. "Napalm? That's . . . insane."

"Insane." Young nodded. "But true. It makes a version of napalm, anyway. The military's kind is more sophisticated, of course. But the home-brew variety will still do a number on anything it comes in contact with. Or anyone. Believe me."

"And someone's attacking our schools with it?" Hale sighed. "Wait till the press gets hold of this."

"School." Young held up his hand. "Inglenook. That's the only one we can be sure about right now. Jones Valley, we're still waiting on one more test. Should be done by this afternoon."

"But the odds of it being different?" Hale raised her eyebrows.

"Not for me to say." Young crossed his arms.

"Assuming there is only one torch artist in play here, I guess your old school buddy's off the hook." Garretty nudged Devereaux's arm. "Confession or no confession."

"Right." Devereaux peeled a loose strand of laminate that had been bugging him off the tabletop and dropped it on the floor. "We're going to have words about that, him and me. But if he's out of the picture, the real question has to be, why napalm? What's wrong with a bottle of gas, a rag, and a match?"

"Good point." Irvin leaned forward. "The choice of napalm is very important here. It tells us something critical about the perp. What he's doing is demonstrating a degree of technical proficiency that far outweighs the demands of the crime. It's an assertion of intellect. Of competence. A gesture, if you like, driven by the feeling of being undervalued in everyday life. By someone who feels they're being continually disrespected. Or that they're not getting the credit they believe they deserve for the work they do. Or did."

"So you think it plays into the revenge angle?" Devereaux removed another annoying laminate strip from the tabletop.

"Right." Irvin nodded. "It has to be someone reasonably intelligent, to figure out how to make the napalm. Someone organized, to source the ingredients. And with sufficient self-control to wait until they can strike at a time of minimum risk. It could be a teacher. Current. Or retired. I'll see if any of them worked at both schools. It could be someone at the Board of Ed. Or a former student. I'll get updated, prioritized lists to you by lunchtime."

"Interesting insight." Hale steepled her fingers. "I like it. But tell me one other thing. This sense of being undervalued, or disrespected. Does that have to come from a personal perspective? Or could the perp be feeling it on behalf of someone else? Even multiple someone elses?"

"A kind of vicarious version?" Irvin pulled a deep frown. "Yes. There have been documented cases. But they're much less common. Why?"

"Come on." Hale pulled a laptop out of her briefcase, sending a slew of papers cascading onto the floor. "Gather round. There's something I want to show you all." She set the computer on the table in front of her, waited for the others to take up places where they could see, then clicked on the track pad. "Tell me what you think of this."

A video clip began to play on the screen. The picture was grainy and dark, and showed a group of men at a meeting. It was shot from the second row of the audience, apparently covertly, and focused on a heavyset man in jeans and a denim shirt who was addressing the crowd from the front of the room. The audio was muffled, but it was still possible to make out what he was saying:

"And I tell you brothers—no more!" The guy was striding from one side of the room to the other, and jabbing the air with his index finger to drive home his points. "We've been pushed to the limit. To the limit? Beyond the limit! We will accept no more! *I* will accept no more. Not one more job lost. Not one more of us kicked to the curb. Not one more year of loyal service forgotten. Not one more family ignored. Not one more future destroyed. And why? So that some rich asshole can buy a bigger Mercedes? Or go on a second skiing vacation? Or a third? Hell no. I'll burn in Hell first. You know what? Scratch that. I'll burn a school down first! I'll burn every school down first, before I accept the loss of even one more job!"

The clip ended abruptly, the picture frozen on the speaker's angry, contorted face.

"Who is that guy?" Devereaux stared at the computer screen. "Does anyone know?"

"He looks familiar." Garretty slid back into his seat. "I've seen his picture before, somewhere. In the paper, maybe. Kevin Russell. That's his name."

"Right." Hale closed the computer. "Russell's the leader of the public services union that includes school janitors, amongst others. That was a speech he gave. Four weeks ago. And since then, ten more jobs have been cut. One of them was at Jones Valley Middle School. One was at Inglewood."

"Where did the video footage come from?" Irvin was still on her feet.

"Anonymous tip." Hale touched the side of her nose. "On a thumb drive. Someone mailed it in."

"Well, wherever the video came from, it looks like this Russell's worth a conversation. Let's find out where's he at." Devereaux winked at the lieutenant. "Maybe we can get him to jump ship. Imagine that guy heading up the police union. There'd be no more problems with overtime then."

Chapter Twenty-three

Monday. Morning.

IT HAD BEEN SO MUCH EASIER WHEN HE WAS A LITTLE GUY.

There had actually been a time when Daniel *liked* coming to the newspaper with Diane. When it had been fun. He'd liked pressing the buttons on the security doors. He'd liked the mesmerizing buzz they could feel in the air as they made their way through the office. And he'd liked stopping to chat with Diane's co-workers, lecturing anyone who'd listen about the latest scientist to catch his imagination. Then, when he'd exhausted his audience, he'd demand a thick pad of paper and a set of colored pens. He'd plant himself in the corner next to Diane's desk. And amuse himself for hours by sketching out designs for the laboratories he'd be in charge of when he was older, and listing the breakthroughs he'd make on the way to his first Nobel Prize. No wonder the other journalists used to call him *The Little Professor.*

Diane hadn't needed to worry about what would happen if Daniel realized they were teasing him, in those days. But that wasn't all that had changed. Proximity locks had been brought in, which were activated automatically by a chip in the ID card that each staff member was required to wear around their neck on a branded corporate lanyard. They were convenient, but they'd replaced the keypads Daniel had enjoyed so much. Swathes of empty, dusty desks had replaced the ranks of busy, boisterous reporters who used to generate such a lively atmosphere. And anyone who knew Diane had also learned to find something urgent to do, somewhere else in the building, anytime they saw Daniel approaching. As a result, he hated the place.

Normally Diane tried to avoid bringing him, but that morning she'd been caught in a complete jackpot. Daniel had stuck to his threat to quit school. He'd point blank refused to go. And to make a bad matter worse, he'd also refused to stay at the house on his own. He said he'd been *abandoned* too many times recently. He demanded that Diane stay home with him, *like a caring mother would*.

Diane did care about Daniel. She cared about him desperately, but staying home simply wasn't an option. She'd lose her job, for sure. And she simply couldn't face that. Her sanity was hanging by a thread as it was. Without the *Tribune* there'd be nothing left between her and the abyss. So summoning all her powers of persuasion, she convinced him that if he wanted to spend the day with her, the newspaper was the only place that could happen.

Pretty much the only practical benefit of the downsizing the industry had suffered through was the couple of private offices that had been left empty. It was no good trying to move into one permanently—a few people had tried but Facilities had busted each of them inside a week, evicting them as if they were trespassing on the White House lawn. Taking over the one near her desk for a single day was another story, though. And keeping Daniel out of circulation was worth a little risk. So, after giving a wide berth to the few people who were already there when they arrived, Diane ushered Daniel all the way across the main floor. She told him the room was the Supervisor's Office— temporarily vacant due to maternity leave—and made sure he was set up with a stack of science magazines and a power outlet for his laptop before closing the door and checking that it had latched.

For a couple of hours it seemed as though her prayers for a quiet, uneventful day had been answered. She managed to handle all her work via phone or email and avoided taking any bathroom breaks, which saved her from having to leave Daniel's room unattended. But just as she was setting her sights on an early lunch—and wondering how soon she could get away with leaving after that—Daniel came out.

"This is lame." He sauntered over close to Diane's chair and leaned down to read what was on her computer screen. "I'm bored. I want to— Seriously? This is what you work on all day? Who wrote this garbage? Not you?"

"Keep your voice down!" Diane made her own voice into a low hiss, and she quickly closed the document about the school fires that she'd been reviewing. "And don't be so rude."

"I'm not the rude one." Daniel straightened up. "I didn't drag anyone to this indoor graveyard against their will. And talk about rude? You're being rude to the entire English language, writing crap like that. And rude to the truth itself. How could you know all those details about what happened at the schools? You're basically lying. You lie for a living. You're a—"

"Diane, have you got a minute?" It was Kelly Peterson. Diane's editor. She was a small, thin, bird-like woman with prematurely gray hair and a famously short temper. She'd come up behind Daniel without Diane noticing. And it was clear from her tone that she wasn't making a request.

Chapter Twenty-four

Monday. Morning.

"Dave, we know."

Devereaux leaned back in the unyielding metal chair and stared across the table at Bateman. He was unshaved. What was left of his hair was greasy, and it was sticking out from the sides of his head like an unkempt clown's. He was wearing an orange jumpsuit that was at least two sizes too large. And yet he looked a million times better than the last time he'd been in that interview room. He seemed calm. Relaxed. Even happy.

"We know." Devereaux didn't elaborate. He let the silence build, like a physical presence in the room. He'd learned over the years how much the guilty hate silence. Used properly, it's like a vacuum that sucks the truth right out of them.

Bateman said nothing.

"Listen to me." Devereaux leaned forward, finally losing patience. "We know the real story. About what you told us yesterday. It's all over, Dave."

Bateman still said nothing. But he did react this time. He smiled. Then the penny dropped for Devereaux. *He still thinks we believe him.*

"OK, rewind." Devereaux straightened up. "What we know is that you're lying. We know you didn't start that fire. Or put another way, we know you're full of shit."

"No." Bateman shook his head. "I'm not. I told you the truth. I did start the fire. I burned the place down. It was *me*."

"No it wasn't, Dave. Because last night, while you were tucked up snug as a bug in here, do you know what happened? Another school was attacked. Set on fire, just like Jones Valley was."

"So?" Bateman shrugged.

"So it couldn't have been you."

"The second school? Right. I never said it was. Someone else must have set that fire. But Jones Valley, that was me all the way."

"It wasn't." Devereaux crossed his arms. "And you're missing the point, Dave. The two fires? They were identical. Same method. Same materials. Same person."

"Why does that make it the same person?" Worry and confusion creased Bateman's face. "It must be a coincidence. This other guy, he must have used the same kind of container as me. Or bought his gas at the same place. Fire isn't exactly a recent discovery, you know, Cooper. Everyone knows how to make it. Humans have known since the Stone Age, or whenever."

"Maybe." Devereaux leaned forward. "But what about napalm, Dave? Do you know how to make that? Have you ever even heard of it, you dope?"

"Don't insult me." Bateman's shoulders started to sag. "Of course I've heard of napalm. I've seen *Apocalypse Now*. But who cares if I know how to make it?"

"I care, Dave." Devereaux nodded. "I care very much. Because the fires? They were started with homemade napalm. Not gasoline, like you told me yesterday."

"I knew that." Bateman raised his chin again. "I just didn't want to give away my secrets. I was afraid people would copy me. And that's what must have happened. Word must have gotten out—maybe one of the firefighters blabbed, or maybe a cop—and someone thought it was a cool idea. It's been in the paper, right? All the details?"

"Name the ingredients in napalm, Dave."

"Let me think." Bateman looked up at the ceiling for a moment. "No. I can't bring them to mind right now. Not all of them. You're putting me under too much pressure."

"OK. Name one ingredient."

"Stop it!" Bateman covered his eyes. "Stop going at me."

"I'll stop when you cut the crap."

"It's not crap!" Bateman flopped forward on the table with his head on his outstretched arms. "But you're going at me, and I'm tired, and you won't stop, and I can't remember, and I just need a break."

"You need to tell me why you lied, Dave." Devereaux lowered his voice. "You could be in a lot of trouble here. You gave a false statement. You obstructed an investigation. And that led to a second school getting destroyed. People could have been hurt. Kids. They could have been killed. Which means you're looking at jail time, if you don't start helping yourself."

Bateman wrapped his arms around his head and let out a long, low moan.

"It's not too late, Dave." Devereaux leaned in close. "I can still help you. But you've got to play ball. Admit you didn't set the fire. Then tell me why you lied. Do those things, and I can make the charges go away. But if you don't get ahead of this before we catch whoever really did it, and we're very close now, there'll be nothing I can do. You'll get locked up for real."

"I did it." Bateman's voice was muffled by his sleeves. "I did. I did. I did."

"You didn't." Devereaux added a little steel to his voice. "You lied about the fire. And that makes me wonder: What else did you lie about? What you said about Principal Oliver? Did any of that really happen?"

"Yes!" Bateman pushed back from the table, arms locked, eyes wide. "Every single thing I told you. Actually, more than that. He . . . He . . ."

"OK." Devereaux held up one hand. "Then consider this. You didn't like what Oliver did? Then wait till you're in jail. It won't be a middle-aged high school teacher doing things to you, believe me. And it won't be just one guy. The things you told me about, in the principal's office? They'll seem like a picnic in Railroad Park. You'll be wishing you were back in school."

Bateman sat in silence for a moment, then his face contorted and he sank down in his seat, his head lolling forward and his arms hanging limply by his sides.

"You didn't set the fire, did you, Dave?" Devereaux lowered his voice until it was barely audible.

Bateman shook his head.

"Why did you say you did?"

Bateman opened his mouth, then closed it again without saying a word. Another moment passed, then his shoulders twitched in an exhausted shrug.

"Were you covering for someone?" Devereaux tried to catch Bateman's eye. "Did someone pay you to take the fall? Or threaten you?"

"No." A small, single tear broke free from the corner of Bateman's right eye and trickled slowly toward his stubble.

"You sure? You're not lying to me again?"

Bateman shook his head.

"What about other victims? You said maybe Oliver had picked on some of the other kids at the school. Can you give me their names?"

"No." A second tear appeared on Bateman's cheek, and then a third. "I'm useless. I can't do anything right."

"All right, cut that out." Devereaux got to his feet. "You're not useless. And don't worry. I'll sort this out. I'll get you released. The charges'll be dropped. You'll be home before the end of the day. Just promise me one thing."

"What?" Bateman looked up at Devereaux, wide-eyed, like a kid who was desperate to redeem himself after a scolding.

"Get yourself some help. You're a mess."

Devereaux sat back down after Bateman had been led away to the cells, and thirty seconds later Agent Irvin tiptoed into the room.

"What do you think?" Devereaux held his hands out as if weighing two similar objects. "Are we in fruitcake territory?"

Irvin sat in the chair Bateman had been using and tried to shift it forward, forgetting that it was bolted to the concrete floor. "Not at all. What he did was perfectly understandable."

"Understandable how?" Deep furrows appeared on Devereaux's

forehead. "The guy confessed to something he didn't do. You heard him. I've never had to work so hard to make someone admit they *didn't* commit a crime."

"You've got to take it in context." Irvin clasped her hands together. "Answer me this. What if Principal Oliver had tried to make you do some of those things Bateman talked about? What would you have done?"

"He wouldn't have tried that with me. He didn't. I was in his office a million times, and he never even gave me a sideways look."

"Hold that thought." Irvin held up her hands like she was on traffic detail. "And work with me. Imagine he had . . . touched you. What then?"

The thought brought the calm clarity down on Devereaux, and he couldn't help but smile. "Let's just say it would have been a mistake he didn't make twice."

"Exactly." Irvin stood up and started to pace from side to side, gesticulating as if she were giving a lecture. "You'd have reacted with violence, and you'd have gotten closure. Because you'd have felt in control. To a degree, at least. But Bateman isn't like you. I'm sure he wanted to do something. To stop Oliver. To fight back. To take revenge. But he couldn't. He failed. And in turn, the failure compounded the humiliation of the actual attacks. So he did what I've seen other hopelessly inadequate personalities do in this type of circumstance. He claimed to have done something that for the longest time he'd wanted to do. That he'd been desperate to do. So you see, it wasn't so much a lie as a catharsis."

Devereaux didn't respond, though a frown started to spread across his face.

"What?" Irvin stopped moving and put her hands on her hips. "You don't believe me?"

"That's not it." Devereaux shook his head. "I just wish Bateman had told me all this at the time. I could have saved him a lot of pain, back then. And the city the cost of a new school now. I remember seeing him waiting outside the principal's office a couple of times, crying. I should have known something was up. Did I tell you he used to make up nicknames for himself, to sound more interesting? He—"

There was a loud knock, and Garretty's head appeared around the side of the door.

"Cooper, you're needed. You, too, Agent Irvin. We've found Russell. The union leader."

"This should be entertaining." Devereaux got to his feet. "Where is he?"

"In a car." Garretty held the door open. "He's on his way here. And he's bringing his lawyer."

Chapter Twenty-five

Monday. Late morning.

ALEXANDRA HAD NEVER WANTED TO KNOCK ON FOLKS' DOORS AND RUN away when she was a kid. She hadn't thought it was funny, even back then. So when she broke off from Nicole's algebra lesson, went to answer the bell, and found no one there, she wasn't amused. She felt a sudden anger flare inside her. And dissipate just as quickly when she noticed the envelope that had been left on the step.

It was letter paper–size. Thick. Heavy. Stiff. And there was no name or address written on it. No marks or writing of any kind. Could it be some new kind of junk mail? Designed to snag your interest so you'd want to open it, rather than throw it in the recycling with all the rest? If so, she reluctantly admitted to herself, the ploy was working . . .

"How are those problems coming along, Pumpkin?" Alexandra walked back into the kitchen, kissed the top of Nicole's head, and took a surreptitious glance at the worksheet her daughter was battling with. She was only halfway through. "Need another few minutes?"

Alexandra refilled both their iced tea glasses, grabbed a letter opener from the stationery drawer, then took the seat opposite Nicole. She slit open the envelope. Reached inside for the contents. Pulled out a stack of shiny paper. Turned it over. And felt her stomach contract. Her heart begin to race. Her breath catch in her throat. Her hand begin to shake. Her eyes lock on to the fuzzy black-and-white image on the first page. And refuse to budge.

The table disappeared from her consciousness. The kitchen disappeared. The house. The whole city. Even Nicole ceased to exist to her. All that was left was the photograph. And the nausea. Which only grew when she turned to the second picture. And the third. Her stomach twisted a notch tighter with each new image, all the way through to the final one. She didn't count how many there were. She didn't notice how long it took to examine them all. Though she must have retained some kind of brain function because when a vague awareness of her surroundings eventually came floating back to her, she found that at least she'd been holding the pages upright, with only their blank sides facing her daughter.

Alexandra jammed the papers back into the envelope and forced herself out of her chair. She moved to the sink. Started to thrust the envelope toward the garbage disposal, but pulled it away at the last moment. What if it jammed? She didn't want the pages getting stuck with their vile contents on permanent display. No. Fire would be a better option. She turned to the stovetop. But stopped again. What about the smoke alarm? And how would she explain the flames to Nicole? It was hopeless. She started to sag, ready to slip down onto the floor, but got ahold of herself just in time. Pulled herself upright. Half walked, half ran to the living room. Crossed to the old writing desk beneath the window. Opened the top flap, knocking over a Murano glass bowl and sending a shower of sweet-scented potpourri onto the floor. Took out a small key. Unlocked the bottom drawer on the left. Yanked it open. Dropped the envelope inside. Locked it. Returned the key. Took a minute to control her breathing. Then returned, slowly and calmly, to the kitchen.

"So how about those problems, Pumpkin?" Alexandra forced a cheery note into her voice. "Are you ready for me to check them?"

"Not yet, Mommy." Nicole looked up, smiling sweetly. "I'm not quite done."

"Well, let me see them, anyway." Alexandra snatched the worksheet out from under her daughter's outstretched forearms, and the slight giddiness she was feeling was replaced by disappointment. Nicole had made no progress since the last time she'd looked. None at all. She was still stuck on the exact same calculation.

Chapter Twenty-six

Monday. Early afternoon.

FRIENDS CLOSE. ENEMIES CLOSER?

Devereaux couldn't think of any other reason for Captain Emrich to volunteer his office for an interview with a suspected arsonist. An arsonist who, according to the Internet, was being touted as a potential future rival for the mayor's office . . .

Two minutes after Devereaux joined Hale and Garretty around Emrich's chrome and steel meeting table, the door opened again and Emrich's assistant ushered two more people into the room. One of them was a defense attorney called Bubsy van Erran. Devereaux had never crossed swords with her, but he'd seen her around the courthouse on a couple of occasions. And he'd been warned not to be fooled by her eccentric *favorite aunt* persona, with her baggy cardigans, long shapeless skirts, and ruffled, graying hair. The word was, all that was a ruse to lure unsuspecting witnesses within range of her steel-trap mind, defenses down, ready to be crushed and left bleeding on the stand.

The man with van Erran was presumably Kevin Russell, though he looked nothing like the firebrand who'd been seen ranting and raving on Hale's computer screen. This guy seemed slimmer. His face was shaved. His hair was neat. He was wearing a flawless navy blue suit. A crisp, open-collared white shirt. And his black dress shoes were polished to a deep, even shine. *This guy's more like a banker than a union leader,* Devereaux thought as he caught a whiff of Russell's soft, flowery cologne. Although Devereaux wasn't certain about that. He avoided bankers, whenever possible. He preferred the kind of criminals he had a chance of arresting.

Captain Emrich emerged from behind his desk, his hand extended and a photo-op-worthy smile clamped across his face. He greeted the visitors like they were old friends, and showed them to their places around the table. Russell ended up facing the shiny black samurai mask, like Darth Vader but with ears and horns, that Emrich had brought back from Hitachi, Japan. Birmingham's oldest sister city. Emrich claimed it was one of the things that was presented to him by the chief of police when he'd been posted there as part of a six-month cultural exchange. *A coincidence, the seating arrangement?* Devereaux doubted it.

Emrich made small talk with Russell and van Erran until his assistant returned with a tray and set it down on the table. It was clover-leaf-shaped, inlaid with sky blue and jade green flowers, and had a small but fierce-looking white dragon guarding the center. Arranged around it were six short, handleless cups and a black iron teapot, which Emrich picked up and started to pour from. *Enough of the Japanese trinkets,* Devereaux thought. *You have a passport, and you know how to brown-nose. We get it . . .*

"Thank you for thc tca, Captain." Van Erran took a tiny sip. "It's excellent. But we know you're a busy man. We don't want to take up any more of your time than we have to. Now, here's the thing. The reason we thought it would be worth sitting down with you fine folks for a while this afternoon is that a disturbing rumor has reached our ears. A rumor about my client here, Mr. Russell. About a video of him. An illegally-taken, clandestine video."

"I see." Emrich set his cup back on the tray.

"Is there such a video?"

"There is *a* video." Emrich refreshed his and Russell's cups. "I'm not in a position to comment on its legal status. Or on the progress of any criminal investigation that may or may not be linked to it."

"I understand. But in any case, we'd like to see it."

"I thought you might." Emrich pulled out his phone, hit a couple of buttons, and a screen unrolled itself from a long rectangular box on the ceiling in front of the opposite wall.

No wonder there's no money left to fix up the conference room, Devereaux thought as the video began to play. Then he turned his attention to Russell, who didn't flinch or betray a single emotion from beginning to end. Not even when Emrich seemed to fumble the controls on his phone, leaving the enlarged image of Russell's sweaty, distorted face displayed on the screen for way longer than strictly necessary.

"Oh." Van Erran dropped her hands into her lap. "Is that it? Is there perhaps another video you're not telling us about?"

"No." Emrich took another sip of tea. "This is the only one."

"Really? Then I must apologize, Captain. For wasting your time. You see, I'd heard a whisper that the tape you had could land Mr. Russell in some pretty hot water. But what we've just seen? It was a master class in public speaking. He could use it on his résumé."

"I disagree." Emrich set his cup down again. "Your client is on tape threatening to commit a felony. A felony that has, in fact, been committed. That's something we have to take seriously."

"You're talking about the fires at the two schools?"

"Obviously."

"Well, bless your heart, Captain. Your case must be going very badly if you're scraping this low down the barrel, so soon. And no wonder, with all the kids I've seen out there, roaming the streets, too scared to go to school. All the desperate parents, lining up to sue the city. Dear me. I'm glad I'm not in your shoes, truly I am. But here's the thing. The words you heard come out of my client's mouth? Hyperbole. Rhetoric. That's all they were. No part of anything he said formed a serious or credible threat. And I think you know that."

"That depends on what kind of man your client is. Whether his word counts for anything." Devereaux turned to face Russell. "You stood up in front of those guys, and you promised to save their jobs. You failed. You weren't embarrassed by that? Ashamed? Pissed? You didn't feel obliged to follow through on some of those grand-sounding threats you made?"

"Who says I failed?" Russell laced his fingers together and rested his chin on his knuckles.

"I do." Devereaux's eyes narrowed. "Or did ten more of your guys not just lose their jobs?"

"Yeah, they did." Russell couldn't stop a smug grin from spreading across his face. "That was a terrible shame. But membership is up. Dues are up. And my personal approval rating is through the roof. You see, Detective, people don't mind if you hit the canvas. They can relate to it. Who hasn't been knocked down a couple of times in their lives? Just as long as you go down fighting. That's what wins their hearts."

"Oh, and one other thing." Van Erran shook her head and looked up at the ceiling, as if cursing her forgetfulness. "My client has an alibi for two hours either side of the time when each of the schools was attacked. If you need statements or whatever, I'll he happy to provide them. Just say the word."

All of a sudden Devereaux was very glad that Russell was nowhere near the police union. And he had a feeling that sometime very soon the IRS would be receiving an anonymous tip about the state of the guy's finances . . .

Emrich steered the conversation back to safer waters, and after a round of smiles and handshakes from everyone but Devereaux he escorted Russell and van Erran out of the room.

"Here's an idea." Devereaux opened the door a crack and peered into the corridor. "Why don't we take the stairs."

"Hold on a minute, guys. Stay put. The captain will want to speak to me when he gets back. Meantime—" Hale gestured toward the miniature Japanese garden that Emrich kept on the corner of his desk. "Cooper! Stay away from that sand thing. No more writing rude messages in it. But as I was saying, in the meantime, I want your thoughts."

"We'd have done better to bring a tape measure." Garretty slumped back onto the Barcelona-style couch. "Give it to Emrich and Russell and let them get on with it."

"You're right." Hale kept one eye on Devereaux. "Probably would have been quicker, too."

"That Russell asshole wasn't involved in the fires." Devereaux moved back and took the spot next to Garretty. "Maybe in five years I'd look at him, if he'd just lost an election or something. But not now. Not when he thinks the world's spread out in front of him."

"Agreed." Hale stayed on her feet. "So what else have we got?"

"Not much right now." Devereaux started to check the points off on his fingers. "We struck out on the physical evidence. Napalm sounds exotic, but the ingredients in the homemade kind are too common to trace. You don't even need special expertise to put it together because the instructions are all over the Internet. No one showed up at the hospital with interesting burns. Nothing came back from the gas stations and hardware stores. We expanded the canvass to include movers and packaging suppliers, given the Styrofoam angle. Still nada. Nothing useful came from residents at either scene. And my old school buddy turned out to be a basket case. One hare we still have running is the chance that Joseph Oliver, the principal, might have left more victims out there. They could be pretty highly motivated to take revenge. No luck yet, but we'll keep trying."

"We got nothing off the interviews, either." Garretty frowned. "Yet. They're still ongoing, too. I've got half the squad involved. Colton, Levi, Denise, P.J., they're all on it. Have you been downstairs recently? It's like a zoo. Teachers. Pencil pushers. Students. And you know what? We've even had extra kids showing up, who should be way down at the bottom of Irvin's list. Word's spread, and evidently you're not cool if you're not a suspect."

"Only to be expected, I guess." Devereaux shrugged. "Who hasn't wanted to burn down a school, sometime or another."

"Um, me!" Hale put her hands on her hips.

Garretty winked at Devereaux. "Maybe we should head down there? Round up some delinquents? Sounds like they'd feel more comfortable talking to you."

Before Devereaux could respond there was a loud knock and the door swung open. It was Agent Irvin.

"Good. I've found you." She was a little out of breath. "I've got something."

Chapter Twenty-seven

Monday. Afternoon.

A DAY DIDN'T GO BY WITHOUT DIANE MCKINZIE FEELING THE LOSS OF her father. But that morning was one of the occasions she was glad he at least couldn't see what she was doing, and how low she'd sunk.

One of the increasingly frequent occasions . . .

Frederick McKinzie had been a legend at the *Birmingham Tribune.* For decades, cub reporters wanted to be him and seasoned pros were in awe of him. He worked at the paper his whole career, and literally died at his desk. The word was he could have had any management job he'd named, but he turned them all down. The only things he wanted were the chance to chase down any stories that interested him—that he thought were important to the people of Birmingham— and the freedom to report them however he saw fit. He covered the 16th Street Baptist Church bombing in 1963. He interviewed Martin Luther King in Birmingham Jail, the same year. He documented the civil rights marches throughout the decade. He reported the shooting of Governor Wallace in 1972. So what would a man with that pedigree have thought of being asked to write for the paper's new Big City Nights blog? Diane knew exactly how her father would have reacted. He'd have burned the building down before agreeing to it.

Diane struggled to make her fingers hit the keys, even though she'd been able to type over a hundred words a minute since she was twelve years old. It was just so demeaning. *Local housewife suspected of running a brothel.* Big deal. And no one would have turned a hair if the woman had lived in Woodlawn instead of Mountain Brook, which should have been the real story. *Shenanigans reported involving Auburn football players.* There's a shock. Although there might have been an actual shock, if someone had dared scratch the surface of the big schools' recruitment practices. *Teens hide grandmother's body in Social Security scam. Rats found feasting on her corpse!* Why wasn't she investigating the lack of oversight for the city's most vulnerable citizens instead of regurgitating such gratuitous nonsense? This was all total garbage. Pure gossip. No sources. No fact checking. No analysis. It wasn't reporting. And it certainly wasn't what she'd become a journalist to do. What she'd worked for ever since she was a little girl, sitting on her father's lap and writing practice articles under his critical eye.

To think she'd actually encouraged her son to follow in her footsteps! Diane rolled her chair back from her desk. She must have been crazy. Thank goodness he'd had the sense to find his own direction. She just hoped that he wouldn't have to put up with this kind of nonsense if he could make it as a scientist. She hoped *his* work would be appreciated, at least.

Her father would have hated pretty much everything about the industry these days. The management-by-spreadsheet approach. The increased commercialization. The technological changes. Diane hated these things, too. They made it hard for true quality to shine through. For going the extra mile to be noticed, let alone appreciated. And given those difficulties, Daniel's little incident couldn't have come at a worse time. Maybe that was the reason she'd been demoted to the blog? It made sense. And it could be fixed. All she'd have to do was find a way to explain the circumstances to Kelly. To make her understand that what she'd seen wasn't Daniel's usual mode of behavior. It was only the stress talking. School was hard for him. And he'd just been disqualified from an important science competition because his entry was too advanced for the idiot teachers to comprehend . . .

Chapter Twenty-eight

Monday. Afternoon.

"WE'RE LOOKING FOR AARON WHITE."

A balding, heavyset guy in his mid-thirties peered at Devereaux from around the side of a long, shiny, chrome-plated cappuccino machine, then went back to polishing it with the corner of his apron. "Sorry. Whitey's not here."

"I just called." The café was the first place Devereaux had tried after Irvin gave him White's name and employment details. "I was told he was around today."

"He was." The guy wouldn't meet Devereaux's eye. "But he went out."

"When will he be back?" Devereaux leaned on the counter, planting his hands between display boxes of cookies and cake bars.

"I don't know." The guy shrugged.

"Let me tell you about a guy I once met." Garretty stepped up alongside Devereaux. "He was very unhelpful. Wouldn't give straight answers to even the simplest of questions. Thought he was really clever. Then, one day he cracked wise with the wrong two people. And you know what? He took the ass-kicking of his short and worthless life that very afternoon."

"I'm being honest with you here." The guy stopped his polishing. "It's impossible to say when Whitey'll come back."

"Any reason to believe he won't be coming back?" Devereaux leaned farther forward. "Did he say anything to you?"

"No. I swear."

"Where did he go?"

"If I was forced to guess, I'd say the clinic."

"Which clinic?"

"It's a little embarrassing for him. Whitey has this problem, you see, with his—"

"Hey, jackass!" Another man emerged through the swing door at the back of the serving area, also wearing a black apron. He was a little older but thinner, and he had a broad smile on his face. "Knock it off." He gave the first guy a playful smack across the back of the head, then turned to Devereaux and Garretty. "Don't listen to him. I'm Aaron White. How can I help you gentlemen?"

Devereaux showed White his badge, then gestured to an empty table at the rear of the café. "Let's sit and talk for a minute. You can have your hilarious buddy bring us some coffee. On the house."

Devereaux waited until the three of them were settled then got straight down to business. "Mr. White. A question. Where were you yesterday?"

"That's easy." White smiled. "Here. I was working."

"All day?" Devereaux frowned.

"No." White loosened his apron strings. "Three to eleven. I don't mind working Sundays, but I hate early mornings. I slept till around noon, hung out at home, then came here. Arrived maybe ten minutes early. Why? What's this about?"

"What time did you leave?"

"I don't know. Eleven-fifteen? Eleven-twenty? It doesn't take long to close up."

"I mean earlier in the day. When you took your dinner break."

"Oh, no. I had dinner here. In the back. I can eat for free that way. And the food's pretty good. Why would I go out?"

"So you didn't leave until your shift was done? Not even for a minute?"

"No. I stayed until the last cup was clean and the last square inch of floor was mopped. Maybe if you told me what this is all about—"

"Can anyone vouch for you being here, uninterrupted, until after eleven?"

"Of course. It was busy yesterday. Not everywhere's open on a Sunday. It was a mob scene. We had a ton of customers. They'd all have seen me. And then there's Beth. Beth Renaldi. My co-worker."

"Where's this Beth now?"

"At her other job, I guess. Something at the university. She only works here weekends."

"Write down her address and phone number." Devereaux slid his notebook across the table, open at a blank page.

"I can't." The smile on White's face faded a little. "I don't know it. Our boss will, though. Want me to write her details instead?"

"Can't hurt."

"What about Saturday?" Garretty gestured to the guy at the counter to hurry up with their drinks. "What were you doing then?"

"The same thing." White finished writing and passed the book to Devereaux. "Another three to eleven. But guys, listen. You're making me nervous, not telling me what this is about. Can you clue me in? Or let me get back to work?"

"We'll let you go in a second." Devereaux slipped the book back into his pocket. "Just one more question. I want you to cast your mind back a little. OK, quite a lot. To when you were a kid. At school. You were at Jones Valley for a while. Then you transferred. Finished seventh and eighth grades at Inglewood. Why was that?"

"My dad's job moved." White's face fell further when he saw a customer drop a five-dollar bill by the register, which went straight into the first guy's pocket. "Can I go now?"

"Where did his job move to?"

"The airport."

"That's hardly the other side of the world. You could have stayed at Jones Valley if you'd wanted to."

"I guess. But it was a hassle, the extra travel time."

"That was the only reason? Nothing bad happened to you at Jones Valley? Nothing that made you want to leave?"

"You can tell us in confidence." Garretty leaned in and lowered his voice. "Or we could go somewhere more private to talk?"

"I don't know what you guys are driving at. Jones Valley was fine. Inglewood was fine. They were both just schools. What do you want from me?"

"Do you remember the principal at Jones Valley?" Devereaux waved the first guy away as he finally tried to deliver their coffee. "Joseph Oliver?"

White half closed his eyes for a moment, then shook his head. "Nope. Can't say I do. Why? Should I?"

"No. Actually, I'm glad you don't." Devereaux gave White a business card then got to his feet. "You can get back to work now. And if that other guy doesn't give you half the tips from while we were talking, call me. I'll see to it he gets fired."

Chapter Twenty-nine

Monday. Afternoon.

ALEXANDRA HAD NEVER BEEN SO DISTRACTED. NOT WHEN SHE WAS waiting to see if she'd gotten into Notre Dame, for her undergrad. Or Duke, for law school. Or waiting for the jury to return in her first trial. Or while she was nursing her sick mother. Even when she was waiting to see if she really had gotten pregnant by a cop who'd just shot a fourteen-year-old boy. But as Nicole rocked rhythmically back and forth on her creaky wooden chair, reciting her irregular French verbs, Alexandra simply could not concentrate.

"All right, then, Pumpkin." Alexandra felt light-headed. "That's enough French for today. Time for our break. Do you want to play in the yard for a little while?"

"No thanks, Mommy." Nicole hopped down from the chair and headed toward the hallway. "Not today. I want to draw."

Alexandra waited until she heard her daughter's footsteps reach the top of the stairs, then made her way to the living room. She crossed to the desk and unlocked the bottom drawer on the left. Took out the thick white envelope. Flicked a few stray pieces of potpourri out of her way and sank down until she was sitting with her back to the wall. Took out the papers. And started to leaf through the stack.

She could hardly bring herself to look at most of the images, but she didn't have to focus on them too closely. There was one in particular she wanted to find, and it had a very distinctive format. It was a color photocopy of an old Polaroid photograph, with its pastel, three-inch-square image all at sea in the surrounding expanse of plain paper.

The photo's composition was simple. It showed a man standing outside a plain brick house with his arm around a little boy. Alexandra recognized both people. The caption—written in a shaky, hesitant hand on what would have been the lower border of the original picture—read *Daddy and Cooper (age 4)*. But something was wrong. Something that had been gnawing at Alexandra's subconscious since she'd worked her way through the pages this morning.

The man in the photograph wasn't Cooper's father. He was the man who'd *killed* Cooper's father. Raymond Kerr. One of the most notorious murderers in the history of Birmingham. What could the two of them have been doing together? And who could have been stupid enough to mislabel the picture that way?

Chapter Thirty

Monday. Afternoon.

CAPTAIN EMRICH STRODE INTO THE CONFERENCE ROOM AND FLUNG A folded newspaper onto the table, sending it skidding the length of the battered and pockmarked surface. "Have you all seen this?"

"Seen it." Devereaux picked up the paper and started to leaf through it. "Haven't read it yet."

"It's a disgrace." Emrich stalked around to the head of the table, staring in turn at Hale, Irvin, and Garretty. "We look very bad. And there's worse online, in their *blog*." He almost spat the word out. "Patrol's up to its ass in petty complaints, with so many kids roaming around while their parents keep them out of school. The switchboard's jammed with callers. Half the businesses in the city aren't happy because employees with young children aren't showing up to work. And we're being painted as the bad guys. Which needs to stop. Immediately."

And in other news, water is wet, Devereaux thought.

"We need to catch this arsonist." Emrich emphasized his point by chopping the air with the side of his hand. "We need more effort. *Maximum* effort. I want everyone giving a hundred and ten percent, until we get this job done. Is that clear?"

Devereaux wondered which buttons Russell had pushed after the meeting, to get Emrich so riled up. And whether maybe Russell wasn't such a bad guy, after all, if he could have such an effect.

"We all understand, sir." The frustration was plain in Hale's voice. "I briefed you on progress this morning, and since then, in concert with the Bureau, we've followed another line of inquiry."

"Where did this line of inquiry lead?" Emrich's chopping hand had balled itself into a fist. "To an arrest? A credible one this time?"

Hale took a deep breath. "It's only a matter of time, sir."

"Time is the one thing we don't have." Emrich banged the table. "I want more effort. More ideas. Come on, people. Think!"

Hale and her detectives had seen the captain in this kind of mood before, so they kept their heads below the parapet.

"Honestly, Captain?" It was Irvin who finally broke the silence. "Unless we get something from the interviews, which is doubtful as we're more than halfway through and the list was carefully prioritized, we don't have many options left. We may have to wait for him to strike again, and hope he makes a mistake this time."

"And hope that no one dies in the process?" Emrich banged the table, harder. "Unacceptable!"

"Will he strike again?" Devereaux pushed the newspaper to the side. "If this is about revenge, and the guy had a grudge against these two specific schools, then maybe he's done?"

"It's impossible to be sure." Irvin frowned. "But I doubt it. If he'd stopped after one school, then maybe. But hitting two suggests he has a broader grudge. Plus he's shown he's good at it. He knows he can get away with it now. He's probably enjoying it. And here's the key. Each fire might give him temporary satisfaction. But if it doesn't deal with his fundamental, underlying anger, he'll keep going until we stop him. He may even escalate, and start targeting inhabited buildings at some stage."

"You keep saying *he*." Hale frowned. "Do we know it's a man setting these fires? Couldn't a woman do it?"

"I say *he* because statistically arson is overwhelmingly a male crime." Irvin looked at Hale. "But you're right, Lieutenant. It's possible we're dealing with a female perpetrator. And if we're right about the motive being a lack of professional recognition or respect, that tips the scale back a little in the female direction, because women, as we know, are far more likely to be underappreciated in the workplace."

"We're going off-point here." Emrich clapped his hands. "Male or female, I don't care. I just want the asshole stopped before someone dies. And I'm not prepared to wait for him—or her, Lieutenant—to destroy another school. So. Come on. Ideas, people. We need a game-changer here."

"I actually agree that it's better not to wait." Irvin placed her hands flat on the table. "If we wait, we leave the odds stacked in the arsonist's favor. We put all the power in his hands. We let him decide where to attack, when, and so on. And there are a lot of schools in Birmingham for him to pick from. Even with the extra uniforms you've got on patrol and all the security guards the Board of Ed's paying for, we can't watch every inch of every one, twenty-four/seven. But we do have another option. Something we haven't talked about yet. A way to take back the initiative, and hopefully catch the guy in the act. It's something that at the Bureau we call a proactive strategy."

"Proactive." Emrich nodded. "I like that. Tell me more. What? How? Where? When?"

"There are two stages." Irvin gripped the index finger on her left hand. "First, we select the school *we* want the arsonist to target next, and we harden it. We exclude all civilians, mount the necessary surveillance, and flood the area with police and Bureau personnel." She gripped a second finger. "Second, we draw the perpetrator into the open, and arrest him when he attempts to make his attack."

"How do you know you can pull the guy's strings that way?" Hale spread her hands. "How do you know he won't just do his own thing, regardless?"

"We know because we use his own psychology against him." Irvin spoke slowly. "He's trying to show the schools, the Board of Education, the city, the world at large, that they were wrong to undervalue him. He's doing it in an impersonal, but very public way. In other words, he didn't go to his old boss's house when no witnesses were around and punch him in the stomach. Instead, he set fires that people for miles around could see. Which means the public exposure angle is crucial to him. He'll be hanging on every word, online, and in the press. So what we do is plant a story of our own. We disparage his efforts to date. And we include what amounts to a dare to attack the school we've already selected."

"That could work, I guess." Emrich scratched his temple. "If it's worded carefully enough."

"We have plenty of precedent to guide us. The Bureau's used this technique many, many times. We've always had a successful outcome, so we're not breaking new ground here. We're not crossing our fingers and hoping." Irvin cleared her throat. "We could start by saying that the arsonist's performance isn't very impressive. That he or she got lucky at Jones Valley, stumbling by chance on one of only two schools in the whole city without upgraded sprinklers. And that the failure to cause any serious damage at the second school, Inglenook, demonstrated a ridiculous lack of technical prowess and basic research skills. We'll put in a quote from a suitable city official to subtly point to the school we want to use as a target, saying it's under renovation and so will soon have a new style sprinkler system fitted. Then we'll close by saying the police think that having been so comprehensively thwarted by technology and his own incompetence, the arsonist wouldn't dare try again."

"I'm not convinced." Garretty narrowed his eyes for a moment. "I had a girlfriend once, when I was fresh out of college. A health freak. From New York. She took it into her head that I ate too much 'cue. She wanted me to switch to salad and that kind of crap. So she left all kinds of magazines lying around, open on pages with articles about how awful slaughterhouses are and the like. Do you know what I did, every time I saw one? I headed straight down to Johnny Ray's."

"I'm guessing the relationship didn't last long." Devereaux winked at his partner.

"So your behavior was totally consistent and predictable?" Irvin smiled, then turned back to Captain Emrich. "Now, obviously the wording can be tweaked until everyone's happy with it. And the Bureau's a little more sophisticated than Tommy's ex-girlfriend. I'm not pulling this stuff out of the air. The approach is tried and tested. I could give you five examples off the top of my head where this technique has worked. Take one from the Chicago office. It's a famous case. A guy was tampering with pharmaceuticals. People were getting killed by them. The perp was running around the city at will, hitting whichever drugstores took his fancy. Until the agent on the case planted an article in the local paper, just like the one we're talking about, goading the guy and guiding him without his realizing it to a particular store. It was full of agents, naturally, and the guy was caught that same day."

"All right." Emrich got to his feet. "Enough talk. Lives might be at stake. How quickly can we make this happen? I want a plan on my desk by close of play today."

Chapter Thirty-one

Monday. Afternoon.

HALE, DEVEREAUX, AND GARRETTY HELD THEIR TONGUES UNTIL EM-rich had retrieved his newspaper and left the room, but their expressions spoke volumes. And they all had their eyes focused firmly on Agent Irvin.

"What?" Irvin waited until she heard the door slam behind her. "It's a good plan! It'll work. If it's implemented right."

"Then we better implement it right." Hale turned to Irvin. "And we don't have much time. Captain Emrich wants it to happen, so there's no point discussing whether it's a good idea or not. Right now we need to focus on logistics. I want a list. Actions. Timescales. Responsibilities. Go."

"No problem." Irvin got up and crossed to the sheet of paper hanging on the wall. "There are three main bases we need to cover. First"—she took out a pen and wrote *(1) Press Contact*—"we need to identify a journalist who'll cooperate with us, and who we can trust. We'll need him to place our article under his byline, to avoid it standing out as a plant. And we need him onside before lunchtime tomorrow. Could the department's PR guys help with that? Or would you prefer me to go through the Bureau?"

"Neither." Garretty scrawled in his notebook. "Cooper and I have unofficial contacts with a few local journos. We'll find someone who'll play ball. It'll be quicker that way. And easier to control."

"Good. Thanks." Irvin added *(2) Identify Target Location* to the list. "Now, in parallel, we need to figure out which school to use as the trap. I guess someone at the Board of Education would be the best place to start?"

"We'll take that, too." Garretty made another note for himself. "I'll cross-reference with the results of the interviews. It makes sense to approach someone who's already been cleared."

"Right. It does. And finally . . ." Irvin wrote *(3) Finalize Article.* "This one speaks for itself. I'm happy to take it. I'll pull something together, let you guys see it, and run it by my mentor at the Bureau, as well."

"Those points all sound fine." Hale stood and took the pen from Irvin. "But I'm adding a fourth." She used all capitals for her entry: *INCREASE SURVEILLANCE ON ALL OTHER SCHOOLS.* "You know. Just in case."

"Good idea." Irvin nodded. "I agree. You can't argue with *safety first.*"

Devereaux's phone chirped in his pocket. He pretended to be absorbed by the list on the wall.

"Are you going to check that, Cooper?" Hale glared at him.

"I'll check it later." Devereaux shrugged. "It's just a voicemail. The signal's garbage in here."

"It might be Chris Lambert again."

"That's why I'll check it later."

"Cooper!" The intensity of Hale's stare increased tenfold. "Check it now!"

Devereaux sighed. He fished out his phone, glanced down, and his expression immediately clouded. "It's from Alexandra. That's weird. She never tries to call when I'm working. Give me a moment?" He listened to the message, then got to his feet and started making his way around the table. "Something's wrong. I couldn't make sense of it, exactly, but there's a problem. And it sounds urgent. I need to duck out for a minute and call her back. Lieutenant? Is that OK?"

Hale didn't answer right away because her attention had been taken by her own phone. An email had arrived, marked urgent. There were photos attached. She scanned the images, then stepped sideways to block the door. "Cooper, you can call Alexandra from the car. Tommy, you can do the same for the journalist and the education guy. We're leaving right now. That message was from Chief Young. He's found something at Jones Valley Middle School. Something we need to see."

Chapter Thirty-two

Monday. Late afternoon.

FREDERICK MCKINZIE WAS ALWAYS A CALM, LEVELHEADED KIND OF GUY.
Diane McKinzie only saw her father lose his temper once in the
whole of her childhood. But boy, that one time, did he blow his stack!
It was at a dinner party at their house to celebrate the latest journalism award that Frederick had won. And one of the guests—another
reporter—made some comment suggesting that Frederick had been
lucky.

When the last of the guests had left, and his blood pressure had returned to normal, Frederick sat Diane down to explain why he'd gotten so angry. "You see, sweetheart, in journalism, there's no such thing
as luck. There's only hard work. Take this award I won as an example.
Regular folk might think, wow, that McKinzie fella, he sure fell on his
feet! Happening to be outside the mayor's house at midnight just as
the guy who won the contract to supply the city's electricity showed
up, carrying a shiny metal briefcase crammed with C notes. Now, regular folk don't know about all the years I spent cultivating my sources.
Or all the nights I spent sweltering in my car, watching the house, till
the electricity guy showed up. But a fellow newspaperman? He should
know what it takes. So for him to say I was *lucky,* that meant one of
two things. He's a fool, and I can't abide fools. Or he doesn't respect
my work. Which is worse."

Frederick's words stayed with Diane as she grew up, and when she
reached college she turned them into a kind of mantra. Whenever she

was behind with an assignment, or later as a cub reporter if she was struggling to hit a deadline, she'd print *N L - O H W* across the top of her page. No Luck - Only Hard Work. The initials floated back into her head just as she was finishing the last piece for the paper's blog, and was worrying about how to patch things up with Kelly. It was as if her father was sending her a message: You want to fix the relationship? Then make it happen. Don't wait for something to fall into your lap.

Diane gave her piece a final read-through, then picked up the phone and called Gianmarco's. She got through to the maître d'. Asked him for a favor—hold a table for her for 6:00–6:30ish, but when she arrived with two guests, pretend they were fully booked and he was giving her a table they usually hold back for VIPs. Next she released Daniel from the office he'd been using. Ushered him out to the parking lot. Bundled him into her Mini's passenger seat. Told him not to open the door on pain of death until she gave him the green light. Then she let all the air out of both her rear tires.

Kelly Peterson appeared after twenty minutes—ten minutes later than usual—heading toward her Mercedes convertible, arms bulging with two briefcases, a purse, and a box of files. "Are you OK, Diane? Two flats? That sucks. Have you called the auto club?"

Diane crossed her arms tight across her chest. "Yes. A minute ago. And you know what they said? They're short staffed right now. Half their mechanics are on some new federally mandated training course. Another bunch are out with a bug. Blah blah blah. I didn't honestly listen to all of it. But the bottom line? I could be here for hours. And I have Daniel in the car."

"That's awful! Do you guys want to ride with me? Your place isn't far out of my way."

"Well, if you're sure it's no trouble, Kelly, that would be wonderful. And how about this? Let me treat you to dinner on the way. I absolutely insist. Would Gianmarco's be all right with you? They're pretty popular, but hopefully they'll have a table left when we get there."

Chapter Thirty-three

Monday. Late afternoon.

Devereaux had strapped the mask on tight around his nose and mouth, but the stench still got through to him. So did the taste. And that brought with it an unnerving physical sensation, like he was sucking raw decay straight into his lungs.

Chief Young met Hale and the detectives at the front entrance to Jones Valley Middle School and led them into the main corridor. The roof was missing in that part of the building and the afternoon sunlight flooded in, throwing crazy shadows across the smoke-blackened walls and debris-strewn floor. The reception counter and one set of lockers had been smashed by a jumble of giant steel girders that looked like they'd been flung down by a petulant giant. Other lockers had twisted in the heat, their doors buckled open and their contents reduced to ash. A shoe had somehow survived and now lay on the floor, mixed in with jagged chunks of roof tile and lengths of shattered door frame. And at the far end, sticking out from the wall about eight feet above the ground, the melted remains of a TV screen clung to the twisted stub of its mounting bracket. Devereaux thought it looked like something Salvador Dali would have created if he'd survived into the twenty-first century.

"This way." The chief was wearing heavy gloves, so he didn't offer to shake hands. "Follow me. But be careful." He pointed to a line of four yard-square metal plates on the ground near the remains of the reception counter, where the scorching was at its darkest. "Sections of the floor are missing. They're at the lab. We took them for analysis."

The floor was crunchy underfoot as they strode down the corridor behind the chief, and Devereaux noticed that where it had dried, the surface of the wall had become dusty and flaky. He reached out to touch an inch-long strip of charred plaster that had separated from the cinder block, but when his finger made contact it just disappeared into a puff of fine gray powder.

The chief stopped at a pair of wide blue doors at the far end of the corridor. The smoke damage was minimal in that area, and the white stenciled word *GYMNASIUM* was clearly legible. "OK. Are you folks ready?"

Hale nodded, and the chief pushed through the doors. Devereaux took in the scuffed wooden floor with its multitude of overlapping colored lines. The basketball hoops, cranked up out of the way, with their baseboards parallel to the floor. The climbing bars on the walls. The honor boards, higher up. The inevitable badminton birdie stuck way up in the rafters. And in the center, two guys in dark blue coveralls. They were standing next to a piece of lighter blue plastic sheet, about six feet square, which was weighed down at each corner with a brick.

"This is where we took one of the control samples from, for comparison with material from the seat of the fire." The chief started toward the two guys, and nodded when they drew close. The pair kicked away the bricks and pulled back the sheet, revealing a three-feet-square hole in the floor. "The other places were totally standard. But here you can see why I sent you the pictures."

Hale looked down through the gap and scanned the scattered, moon-white remnants without saying a word. Garretty made the sign of the cross. Devereaux stepped back for a moment as a flood of memories from his childhood fought for a way into his head. He closed his eyes. Focused on breathing until the unwelcome thoughts were back at bay. Then he pulled out his flashlight, knelt down, and peered as far into the crawl space as the beam would allow.

"This is very strange." Devereaux switched off the flashlight and stood back up. "I can count four skeletons. But only one skull."

Chapter Thirty-four

Monday. Early evening.

DIANE SET DOWN HER DESSERT SPOON AND ALLOWED HERSELF A DIScreet smile of satisfaction.

The maître d' at Gianmarco's had been suitably theatrical when she'd arrived with Kelly and Daniel, throwing up his hands and grimacing with despair at her request for a table. Once they were seated the food had been magnificent, particularly the Chicken Francese. But the best thing of all had been the conversation. Daniel really can be very personable, if kept on a narrow-enough path. Diane was wilting a little from the effort of subtly steering him—at times like that she felt like a puppet master, constantly wrestling with invisible strings— but it had been worth it. Kelly had listened sympathetically as Daniel described his disappointment at not getting a place at either Ramsay or Carver high schools, where the city's specialty engineering academies were based, and which would have been the best match for his particular skill set. He kept his language moderate when he outlined what he thought of the science curriculum at Vestavia Hills, his fallback school, and his worries about the implications for his career path. She even laughed at some of his physics jokes. And as an added bonus, Kelly also said nice things about Diane and her work.

Who knew? Maybe Daniel would start to appreciate what his mother did for her living a little more, in future. And recognize that *she* might actually be the smart one in the family . . .

Chapter Thirty-five

Monday. Early evening.

Tyler Shaw's left hand was shaking.

Stop it! He glared at his reflection in the bathroom mirror, and noticed that his chin and neck were starting to reappear from under the thin layer of watery foam. *Calm down! You've got to do this. Before it's too late. Stick to the routine. Everything must be the same way. Or nothing will work!*

Shaw lifted the razor and tried again.

When he was safely shaved and daubed with his favorite cologne, Shaw made his way to his bedroom, still naked. He pulled the curtains—the ones covering the alcove at the foot of his bed, not the window—knelt down, and clasped his hands together. He needed guidance. What he was about to do was harder than anything he'd ever tried before. And more important. So should he go through with it? The real thing? Right away? Or would a trial run be better? To make sure he was ready. Shake off any remaining rust. Iron out any kinks he might have left. After all, he'd been out of the game for quite a while.

Screw it. Shaw got to his feet and reached for his lucky dragon print shirt. *I'm doing it.* He continued to get dressed, pulling on his Wranglers and lizard-skin boots, and assured himself he'd been wrong to ever worry. The black coroners' vans he'd seen lined up outside the school weren't of any significance. Nor were the extra police who'd been poking around. He could safely ignore them. It stood to reason. Because if he was going to be stopped, why hadn't he been caught a long time ago?

Chapter Thirty-six

Monday. Early evening.

ALEXANDRA'S RANGE ROVER WASN'T ON THE DRIVE WHEN DEVEREAUX reached the house. The front door was locked. And when he tried to use his key, it wouldn't fit in the slot.

The shock hit him like a punch to the gut, just like it had eight years ago. Only that time Alexandra hadn't even tried to leave a message. She'd just changed the locks, gone away, and then sold the house. Moved, without telling him. Although then it was because she was pregnant and hadn't wanted him to find out. Could that be the answer again? Devereaux started running back through his mental calendar, checking off the dates, figuring the odds, and feeling a tiny bloom of excitement begin to grow in his chest. Then he reached for his phone to listen to her message again. And saw the key, still in his hand. It was the one for his apartment, at the City Federal. He had the key for Alexandra's house on a separate ring. Maybe it was time to do something about that, he thought. As long as he hadn't been cut adrift again . . .

Devereaux called out for Alexandra from the hallway, and when he got no response he tried her phone. There was no reply. Feeling his heartbeat quicken, he moved to the kitchen. No one was there. There was no sign of disturbance, either, thankfully. Just Nicole's schoolbooks piled neatly to one side of the table. He checked the living room. The dining room. There was nothing in either place. He took the stairs three at a time and checked their bedroom. It was empty, the bed neatly made. Nothing was spilled or broken in their bathroom. The other bathroom was clear, too. Which left one last room. Nicole's. Devereaux pushed the door. It opened two inches, then caught on something. The tip was protruding beyond the edge of the door. It was metal. Shiny. Sharp.

"Whoever you are, I'm coming in on three." Devereaux drew his gun. "One . . ." He drove his shoulder into the door, which easily cleared the pair of craft scissors it had snagged on and continued on its arc, thudding into the wall where its handle left a crescent-shaped dent in the paintwork. Devereaux stepped into the room, gun raised. And found himself confronted by two dozen Barbies. Nicole had them laid out across almost every flat surface.

Devereaux sank down onto the bed and tried Alexandra's phone again. This time she picked up.

"Cooper? Where are you?"

"At the house. I got your message. It was messed up somehow so I couldn't understand it all, but I came home as soon as I could. Where are you? What's going on?"

"I had to get out for a while. Something happened. It freaked me out a little, so I brought Nicole to the diner. For a change of scene, you know?"

"What was the problem?"

"It's hard to explain. We can talk about it later. Face-to-face."

"But everything's all right? You're OK?"

"I guess."

"Well, good then. Hey, how about this? I could come over there. Meet you guys. Maybe grab a slice of pie."

"There's no point. We had to wait to get seated because there are all kinds of kids in here for some reason, but we're almost done now. I'll be home soon. Want me to bring you a slice back?"

"No. Don't worry about it. Take your time. Feel better. I'll see you when you get here."

Devereaux picked Nicole's scissors up from the floor and took them to the little desk with the folding lid she kept in the corner of the room. It wasn't like Nicole to leave her stuff lying around, Devereaux thought. Alexandra must have dragged her out of there in a hurry. He wondered what could be bothering Alex so much. What aspect of English grammar or American history could be so upsetting that she had to race off to the diner. And how that would compare with the recent sight of four skeletons. Of which three were missing their heads.

The corner of a piece of paper was just visible, peeping out from under the desk lid. Devereaux was curious to see what Nicole had been working on, so he raised the lid and saw that she'd cut a series of holes in the paper. Four rectangles about an inch by an inch-and-a-half. One, around an inch-and-a-half by three. And another, near the bottom and not as straight as the others, around an inch-and-a-half by three-and-a-half.

The medium-size rectangle had been thrown into the trash. It had been folded in half, stapled around three sides, then crumpled up. Devereaux fished it out, flattened it, and then an idea came to him. He crossed to Nicole's Barbie house and swung it open. He checked the doormat. The dining room table. The study. There was no sign of what he thought he might see, so he was about to close up and head downstairs when he noticed that the dolls' desk wasn't level. Something had been jammed under the left-hand pedestal. He squeezed his hand into the small space, tipped the desk back, and flicked a small homemade envelope out from under it.

Devereaux sat back on the bed and looked at the dainty envelope. Should he open it? Why not. It wasn't like he'd be reading his daughter's mail. Dolls have no expectation of privacy. And he was intrigued to see what Nicole had made. Alexandra got to see to their daughter's work every day, but he hardly ever did. What would be inside? He wondered. A birthday card? A love letter? An alarm schematic for an upcoming bank job?

Very carefully, using just the tips of his fingernails, Devereaux extracted the four tiny pieces of paper. Nicole had drawn on each one. Very neatly, and in great detail.

Devereaux pulled out his phone and hit redial.

"Alexandra. You need to come home."

"We'll be leaving in ten minutes." Alexandra sounded like her mouth was still full.

"No, Alex. You need to come home right now."

Chapter Thirty-seven

Monday. Evening.

"ARE YOU SURE YOU WANT TO DO THIS?" HALE DREW HERSELF UP straight and looked down at Irvin. "Because you know I'm going to seriously kick your ass."

Irvin was certain that she didn't want to do it. She had no interest in racquetball as a sport. She'd had to borrow an outfit, which didn't fit properly. And she was cursing the cousin who'd convinced her that signing up for the "friendly" interagency league would be a good way to break the ice with the people she'd be working with in her new city. She'd certainly never have agreed if she'd known that her first match would be against this enormous, and apparently furious, lieutenant.

"Of course I want to." Irvin tightened her grip on the racquet. "But listen. You're not mad about the initiative I suggested in the meeting earlier, are you? Because I wasn't trying to cross you in front of your boss. I honestly think it's the best way to go."

"No." Hale allowed half a smile to ghost across her face. "I'm not mad. I just want to blow off a little steam. You ready?"

"Sure." Irvin shifted her weight onto the balls of her feet. "What I suggested isn't some fly-by-night scheme, you know, Lieutenant. I didn't make it up on the spot. It's tried and tested. And you know Special Agent McMahan, right?"

Hale nodded. Larry McMahan—the special agent in charge of the Bureau's Birmingham Field Office—was an old friend of hers. "Ready?"

"Absolutely." Irvin raised her racquet a little higher and looked nervously at the length of Hale's reach. "So you know you can trust McMahan's judgment. He got involved personally when that little boy went missing, back in June, didn't he? And he's going to get involved again now. He's going to review every step with Captain Emrich. And if he's not totally satisfied he won't—"

Hale launched the ball, Irvin lunged, but she was too slow to come close to making the return.

"That's *one*." Hale strolled across the court to retrieve the ball. "But listen. Tell me something. You heard about what Fire and Rescue found at the school?"

Irvin nodded.

"And you don't think that's reason enough to abandon tomorrow's operation?" Hale adjusted her wrist tether. "The game's clearly changed. This is a multiple-homicide investigation now. And don't worry. This place is soundproof. You can speak freely."

"OK." Irvin kept her eye on Hale's hands. "I will. The answer's *no*. We shouldn't abandon. And I don't agree with your assessment, either. The arson investigation hasn't changed. The multiple homicides should be treated as a separate case."

Hale drove in another serve and this time Irvin got her racquet to the ball, but without enough strength to carry it back to the wall.

"*Two*." Hale picked the ball up again. "Why separate cases?"

"Lots of reasons." Irvin risked pushing her eye shield up for a moment. "If there'd been one fire, and the murders were recent, and evidence of the killings had been close to actually getting destroyed, I might buy the arson as a secondary crime. But why set the fire in the wrong part of the school? And why was there a second fire in another school? And why now? There are no matching missing persons reports in the last five years. I checked. And the business with the missing heads? That suggests a whole different can of psychological worms, which will almost certainly be at odds with the personality of an arsonist. The crimes are at opposite ends of the spectrum."

Hale launched the ball, deflecting it off the side wall this time, and it had bounced twice before Irvin even moved.

"*Three*." Hale let the ball roll away. "So why not this scenario? Joseph Oliver, pervert principal of Jones Valley, whereabouts currently unknown, hears that Cooper's old buddy has finally grown a pair and is telling unsavory stories about his time at school. Now, Oliver had other victims. Four of them were a little feistier than Cooper's buddy, back in the day, so Oliver didn't feel safe letting them leave the premises with breath in their bodies. Maybe that's why he switched to younger targets, who knows? But the point is, Oliver doesn't want his retirement spoiled by a lethal injection if word spreads and we take an interest in the school. So he reaches out from wherever he's hiding and pays someone to torch the school, thereby burning up any evidence that remains. Only, the guy he hires is incompetent and sets the fire in the wrong place. Or Oliver's marbles are going, and he gives them the wrong information. Then finally, to deflect suspicion further, he goes for a twofer and has Inglewood hit, as well."

"That's possible, I guess." Irvin stepped to the side and put her foot on the ball to stop Hale getting it. "But regardless, one case or two, catching the arsonist has to be the priority right now. The fires are where the present danger lies. Catch the torch, and if *you're* right we're halfway to solving the murders, too. If *I'm* right, we at least know where we stand. And if the guy takes the bait the way I think he will, we'll know which it is by this time tomorrow."

Chapter Thirty-eight

Monday. Evening.

DEVEREAUX LAID THE FOUR TINY DRAWINGS OUT ON THE KITCHEN TABLE and waited for Alexandra to come downstairs after tucking Nicole into bed.

She appeared after ten minutes, walking slowly and looking down at the floor. She slid onto the seat next to him without saying a word and forced her eyes to survey each of the images. She noted the composition. The use of perspective. The pen control. The use of color. Black. Blue. Yellow. Green. Brown. Pink. And red. Lots and lots of red.

"What the hell are these, Alex?" Devereaux struggled to keep the anger he was feeling out of his voice. "Where did her ideas come from? What on earth kind of filth are you filling her head with?"

Alexandra got to her feet and left the room. She returned a minute later with the white envelope from her desk. She shuffled through its contents. Selected a photograph. And laid it on the table next to one of Nicole's drawings. Both were versions of the same scene. A man lying on his back on a tiled floor. One of his arms had been hacked off and dropped on the wrong side of his body. His legs were twisted upward at an unnatural angle. A cleaver was lodged in his abdomen. And his corpse was surrounded by a vivid slick of fresh crimson blood.

"What are those?" Devereaux snatched the stack of papers from Alexandra. "Where did you get them from?"

"See for yourself." Alexandra dropped the empty envelope on Devereaux's lap then backed away to the far wall. "The other three are in there, somewhere. The originals, I mean. Our sweet little daughter's apparent inspiration. And don't stop till you reach the end. Take a good look at the last one. Then get back to me about who's the filthy one."

Devereaux felt as if a rope had been tied around his chest, and that it was being pulled tighter with every fresh page he looked at. He saw pictures of stabbing victims. Men who'd been shot to death. Dismembered. Bludgeoned. In one case, garroted. But he knew it wasn't just some sicko's random collection of murder porn. It was his family's history. Ending with the Polaroid of him and his dad. Which Alexandra had seen.

The evil genie was out of his bottle.

"Where did you get this from?" Devereaux struggled to get the words out.

"Why does it say Raymond Kerr's your father?" Alexandra kept her distance. "What aren't you telling me?"

"I can explain." Devereaux focused on his breathing. "And I will. But please. First things first. The envelope. Where did you get it?"

"It was left on the doormat."

"Here? When?"

"This morning."

"And I'm just hearing about it now?"

"What? Like you get to set the timetable for my day? I was shocked! I didn't know what to do. And I did call you. I can't help it if you put your precious job first and me and Nicole second."

"Who left it?"

"I don't know. The bell rang. I opened the door. No one was there. Only the envelope. It wasn't addressed. I figured it was a mailshot or something. So I opened it."

"Did you see anyone? Running away? Or in a car?"

"You think I'm stupid? You think I wouldn't have mentioned something like that?"

Devereaux held his hands up.

"OK." Alexandra levered herself off the wall. "Your turn. Spill."

"I will." Devereaux covered his eyes. "Just give me a minute. I need to think."

A question had started to whisper inside Devereaux's brain while he was talking with Alexandra, growing louder and more insistent until he could no longer ignore it: *Why are there no demands?*

"Was there anything else with this?" Devereaux turned the envelope over, rechecking for marks or symbols. "A note? Another envelope? A phone message? Or anything else weird delivered at a different time?"

"You don't think I'd have mentioned it, if there was?"

Devereaux's cynical mind was screaming *blackmail,* but could there be any innocent explanation for the envelope showing up? If there was, he couldn't see it. Someone was looking to hurt him. With his job. In the press. With his family. *Father and son. Guilt by association.* The problem was, the asshole hadn't shown his whole hand yet. Which was no doubt part of his plan. He was trying to ratchet up the tension so that when he made his next move, Devereaux would jump all the higher. Which left him with an immediate choice. Wait. Do nothing. And surrender the initiative to the other guy. Or take preemptive action to close the asshole down.

There wasn't much to work with, but two things did stand out to Devereaux. Timing. And content. The envelope had appeared in the early stages of the arson case, when the main suspect was Dave Bateman. Bateman, who was making allegations against Principal Oliver. Oliver, who Devereaux had crossed swords with many times nearly thirty years ago. And the photographs? They were incredibly rare. Devereaux had never seen most of them before, despite all the research he'd done into his father's crimes. They weren't the kind of things you could put your hands on anymore. They must have been collected a long time ago. By someone with a reason to think that one day they might need some leverage.

"Honey, we will talk." Devereaux swept Nicole's drawings into the envelope along with the other papers. "I promise. And I'll explain everything then. But first I've got to check on an old acquaintance. He's about to be in a lot of trouble."

Chapter Thirty-nine

Monday. Late evening.

ALEXANDRA DOUBLE-LOCKED THE FRONT DOOR FOR ONLY THE SECOND
time since she'd bought the house. The first time was on the day she
moved in, when she was paranoid that Devereaux would somehow
find out where she was and try to force his way back into her life.

She turned out all the lights, as she'd done that first night, and sat
alone in the dark. Only this time she was haunted by a different vision.
It wasn't a newspaper photograph of the boy Devereaux had shot. It
was the four snapshots of Hell on earth, so painstakingly re-created
by her innocent little girl and laid out in a neat square on her kitchen
table.

Alexandra didn't move for . . . she didn't know how long. Eventually she dragged herself to the cupboard where she kept her bottles
and poured herself a generous slug of Blanton's. Then another. And
another. And finally, with her world starting to spin for a different
reason, she clumsily retreated to her bedroom.

It was a warm night. Alexandra didn't like the air to be on while she
slept. But she pulled the comforter tight around her, anyway, right up
to her chin. *It's funny,* she thought. *Last night I'd have given anything
for Devereaux to come home. Tonight, I'd give anything for him to
stay away. Is that ever going to change back again?* And while she was
still pondering that question, other thoughts hit her. *I keep calling him
Devereaux. But who is he really? And do I even want to know?*

Chapter Forty

Monday. Late evening.

DEVEREAUX STILL DIDN'T LIKE THE FERRARI, BUT HE TOOK IT, ANYWAY.
He figured it was suitable for what he had in mind. It would set the
right tone. And he wouldn't care too much if it ended up getting damaged.

There were more direct ways to get back downtown, but Devereaux
found himself cutting across to 18th Street South and sticking with it
as it became Arrington Boulevard. That was the route with the best
views of Vulcan. The first place Devereaux would go as a kid, whenever he ran away from a foster home. The statue looked a little different in those days. The giant was holding a torch, instead of a spear.
And the column was clad in marble, concealing the rough limestone
that was now exposed again. One thing that hadn't changed, though,
was the god's lack of underwear. As a kid, whatever was going wrong
for him—whether he was cold, or frightened, or hungry—Devereaux
could always look up at that enormous bare ass and feel himself start
to smile. He wished it had the same effect on him that night. But instead, he was imagining a design for a new statue. One where the god
of DNA was pounding Devereaux's head into an anvil with an enormous club of cursed double helixes.

The sign on the roof was painting the white terra-cotta cladding of
the upper floors its nightly red as Devereaux approached the City Federal. He liked that. It reminded him of the iron ore in the soil that had
fueled his city's magical growth. But after he parked in the building's

underground parking lot and rode the elevator to the twenty-fifth floor, his mind turned to more practical matters. He entered his apartment. Crossed to the bookcase in his living room. Removed all the books from two shelves, then lifted down the shelves themselves. Prized open the detachable panel this revealed. Reached into the opening. Took out a package. Checked the contents. Returned everything else to the way it had been when he arrived. Then headed back down to retrieve his car.

The half-dozen brick warehouses on Hollingworth Boulevard, just east of East Lake Park, had been abandoned for decades. Ever since the airport expanded and bigger, more efficient units had been built closer to the terminals. No one used the old ones anymore. Not officially, anyway. And not obviously. Devereaux hoped his information was correct as he eased the Ferrari past the line of dark, hulking structures, trying to keep the rumble of the engine to a minimum as he searched for signs of occupation.

The roof had collapsed on the building farthest from Fifth Avenue so Devereaux was about to discount that one when a detail caught his eye. It was hard to make out in the gloom, but something was snaking its way out of the ruined steel framework. It was a jury-rigged cable, leading to a nearby power line. And when Devereaux was turning at the end of the street, ready to take a run from the opposite direction, his headlights picked up movement. Very slight. A figure, dressed in black, stepping back and disappearing into the shadow of a crumbling buttress. It was enough.

Devereaux pulled up out of sight on Fifth and reached for his portable radio. "Detective to Central. 10-31. Unit 6, Hollingworth Business Park."

The 10-31 is a police radio code for Crime in Progress, as every self-respecting criminal knows.

Thirty seconds later he heard the roar of a high-powered engine, being driven hard. A black Lincoln Navigator sped past him. A blue Escalade followed hard on its heels. Then two red Suburbans. A white Range Rover. A silver Lexus SUV. And a navy blue Tesla. An electric car. A smart choice for a crook, Devereaux thought, easing away from the curb and adding the Ferrari to the end of the convoy. Let the big V8s make all the racket. Attract all the attention. Meanwhile you just slip silently away in the other direction.

The Navigator was still thirty feet shy when a door opened in the side of the warehouse and two men ran out. They started to slip and slide their way across the deep strip of gravel separating them from the street, and were soon followed by maybe ten more guys. Devereaux didn't pay them too much attention, though. He was watching the Tesla. It slowed before the rest of the vehicles, and turned to head off-road between the central two buildings.

Devereaux followed, struggling to keep the Ferrari straight on the slippery surface and crouching low in his seat in case the Tesla driver decided to loose off any shots. They reached the far side of the ware-houses without any gunplay and swung to the right, bringing them parallel with the street again. Devereaux backed off the gas, allowing a gap to open up. He kept the car rolling slowly until the Tesla reached the last unit. A door opened in the back wall of the building and three men emerged. One was holding a briefcase. The other two, shotguns. Both weapons were pointing at the Ferrari. Devereaux surged forward and spun the wheel hard right, sliding the rear around one hundred and eighty degrees. He hit the gas again, spinning the wheels and spraying the trio with a sudden hail of sharp, pointy stones. Then he dived out of the car, sprinted forward, and grabbed the briefcase guy around the neck.

"You have the advantage in numbers. I'll give you that." Devereaux tightened his grip. "Firepower, too. But time? That's on my side. Unless you think you can outflank me inside two minutes without turning your boss into a pepper pot. Because that's how long you've got before the police get here."

Nobody moved.

"OK. Or we could try this, instead." Devereaux produced the package he'd retrieved from his bookcase and held it out, keeping one arm around the briefcase guy's neck. "Here. Take it."

"Throw it on the ground." The guy's voice was calm. "One of them can open it."

Devereaux pitched it forward, but it didn't travel far.

The right-hand guy lowered his shotgun, picked up the packet, and cautiously peered inside. "It's full of hundred-dollar bills. At least twenty. Maybe more."

"A gesture of good faith." Devereaux let his guy go. "I need a minute of your time."

Devereaux nosed the Ferrari between the stained concrete pillars that carried I-59 above the divided section of First Avenue North and rolled to a stop in the debris-strewn no-man's-land at the side of the bridge. He climbed out, avoiding a heap of dead flowers that were periodically refreshed by crazy people who thought they could see the Virgin Mary's face in the supporting cement wall. The Tesla pulled up next to him, and a moment later he was joined by the guy whose neck he'd grabbed.

"People call me Frank." The guy held out his hand. "It's not my real name."

"I know." The guy's real name was Slobodan Dzerko, but none of his original running buddies could pronounce it properly. Plus, when he was starting out on his chosen career path and had yet to attain his current level of sophistication, he thought it was cool to adopt a faux-friendly demeanor before putting the fear of God into anyone who crossed him. He liked to start with, *Let me be frank with you . . .* And the nickname stuck.

Devereaux shook Dzerko's hand.

"You're Cooper Demonbruen. No. Devereaux. I remember you. You always had a flair for the theatrical. Like when you set up that guy Giggs, with the French Maid's costume and the Poodle? Then shot him down in flames in front of his whole crew? That was priceless. The guy was such an asshole. So, here. Take your money back. Tell me what you need."

"Thanks." Devereaux put the cash back in his pocket. "Now, here's my problem. I'm a little out of touch these days. Say I wanted someone to take a permanent vacation. Who would I talk to? If I wanted the job done right?"

Chapter Forty-one

Tuesday. Early morning.

THE DAWN SNEAKED UP ON ALEXANDRA UNDER COVER OF THE PREVIOUS night's whiskey haze, and the alarm jolted her awake before she realized she'd even been asleep.

She shot out a tired arm to silence the clock then rolled over and reached across the bed, searching for Devereaux. Hoping he hadn't left early for work again. Craving his arms around her. The sound of his soothing, not-ready-to-get-up-yet voice. And then the memory hit home. He hadn't left that morning. He'd left the night before. When she'd pressed him for answers about those ghastly photographs. And that appalling man. Surely he couldn't really be Devereaux's father?

The shower did little to invigorate her, and the coffee machine never got the chance. She was too distracted to deal with tamping down the espresso grounds or fitting all the fiddly little parts back together. She should have bought a different system, like the kind with the pods. She should have done a lot of things differently. Like with Devereaux. She was beginning to think she hadn't handled the situation very well the night before. Was it likely he had a reasonable explanation for the contents of that envelope? No. Or for why he hadn't told her before? Probably not. But she hadn't even given him the chance. Isn't that what trusting someone is supposed to be about? Giving them the benefit of the doubt?

Non, je ne regrette rien started spontaneously playing in her head. It had been her favorite song in college. Her statement of intent. A blueprint for her adult life. And now Edith Piaf was mocking her across the decades from a half-forgotten South Bend dorm room. How disappointed her teenage self would be. Her very existence had become a festival of regrets. If only she could go back and change everything. Start over with a clean slate. And get Devereaux to start over with her.

But then again, would there be any point? Can anyone ever really change?

A CASE OF TWO STEPS FORWARD,
ONE STEP--ANOTHER DAY!

The temperature may have been high in the Magic City last night, but none of the heat came from a fire. Not at a school, anyway. That may have come as a surprise to the good people of Birmingham. Many of you may have expected the genius to keep up the momentum, and take the third consecutive step on the path to inevitable triumph.

This reporter has been chosen to reveal the truth: In the genius's original plan, another devastating inferno <u>had</u> been scheduled for last night. But, for reasons that cannot yet be revealed, the genius chose to change the plan! However, as the keenest observers amongst you will already have noted, the key word is <u>change</u>. It wasn't a stumble. And it wasn't a defeat. It was a case of the genius showing yet another extraordinary facet: tactical flexibility. Presented with an unforeseen circumstance, the genius adapted, and in the process threw the authorities yet another curveball . . .

Chapter Forty-two

Tuesday. Morning.

DIANE MCKINZIE HAD KNOWN THE DETECTIVES ON-AND-OFF FOR YEARS. She liked them well enough. She trusted them—as far as you can trust cops. She was intrigued by the older one, Devereaux, because she knew that her father had written a piece back in the day about his father getting murdered. But it was the FBI agent who really interested her. She was new to town. Probably had no friends yet. According to the phone message she was a *profile coordinator*. But what Diane heard was *opportunity*. This might be someone she could cultivate. *Mine for information. Get an inside track from, into the arson case . . .*

Detective Garretty had left his message requesting the meeting the previous evening, after she'd crashed out for the day, so Diane had to start her Tuesday with a hustle. She had to call Garretty back, confirming the arrangements. Get to the office. Book a meeting room. Scare up coffee and cookies. And most importantly, deal with Daniel. He was still refusing to go to school, and she'd had no more luck in persuading him to stay home on his own.

There was hardly anyone around these days who might even theoretically want to stop them and chat, so Diane was able to smuggle Daniel through the sea of vacant desks and into the empty Supervisor's Office without dropping too much time.

The only meeting room available at such short notice was, of course, the least popular. It was really a ten-by-fifteen section of the main reporters' floor hived off with a glass door and glass panels for walls. The newspaper employees called it the Goldfish Bowl, because anyone moving around the office was drawn to stop and stare in at its occupants. The journalists hated it from the start, and only ever used it as a last resort. To add insult to injury it always seemed to be too hot inside because the *Tribune*'s master craftsmen had built it without enclosing a single air-conditioning outlet, and it was furnished with uncomfortable, mismatched castoffs from other parts of the building. Diane was almost embarrassed to show her guests into it, but they didn't seem to mind. Although she thought they did look a little pompous with their gold shields on display, rather than wearing the standard building visitors' tags.

Devereaux got the ball rolling with the introductions, and then left Irvin to run through the details of what they wanted the *Tribune* to do. Diane listened attentively, smiling and nodding and doing everything she could to send friendly vibes to the newly arrived agent. Irvin was thorough. And by the end of her pitch, there was only one question left in Diane's mind. If she said *yes,* what kind of leverage would it buy her? Putting her name to something she hadn't written didn't bother her. Nor did the fact that the story wasn't strictly true. She was more than happy to flex her journalistic ethics in order to help the community and stop a criminal—just as long as she could rely on a little quid pro quo, not too far down the line.

"So we're agreed?" Devereaux was surprised that Diane had rolled over so easily. He'd been expecting to hear all kinds of Woodward and Bernstein type bullshit, and maybe have to throw around a few threats about the IRS or late-night breath tests from the traffic detail. "You'll do it?"

"Absolutely. I just—" Diane caught sight of Daniel. He'd come out of the office and was standing next to her desk.

"Ms. McKinzie?" Devereaux tried to see what she was staring at. "We're agreed?"

"Of course." Diane tried to pull her attention back into the room. "Yes. I just need to run it past my editor, and we'll be good to go."

"Is there any way we could go ahead without involving anyone else?" Devereaux lowered his voice. "Secrecy's a major concern. The fewer people who know what we're doing, the lower the risk."

"I get that. But—" Daniel was moving again. He was heading in

Diane's direction. "I'm sorry, Detective, there's nothing I can do. I have to tell my editor. It'd be my ass, otherwise. But only her. She's very professional. Very discreet. And very experienced. I wouldn't be surprised if she's dealt with something like this before."

"OK. Just her, then. And I need you to emphasize the secrecy angle. Really hammer it home."

"No problem." Daniel was going to barge into the room. Diane could feel it, and she was willing him not to. "I'll handle it."

"Good. So, Agent Irvin will email you the final wording inside the next couple of hours. All I need you to do then is let me know when it's live on the website."

"Perfect." Daniel was right outside the door now, gesturing for Diane to hurry up. "I'll let you know the second it goes up."

"If we don't get a bite tonight, we'll go for the print edition tomorrow. And—"

"Mom?" Daniel took two steps into the room. "Are you nearly done here? I need your help. My computer keeps dropping off the stupid Wi-Fi."

Diane got halfway out of her seat, then sank back down. She simply could not summon any words. Devereaux turned to Garretty and shook his head. Garretty rolled his eyes in reply.

"Hello, there." Irvin twisted around to face Daniel, figuring that someone ought to break the silence. "Now, don't worry. We just need your mom for a few more minutes. We'll wrap things up as fast as we can, and then get her back to you, OK?"

It took Diane a few minutes, but she recovered a little of her composure on the way back to reception. Then she took Irvin's arm and slowed her down slightly, allowing a gap to open up between them and the detectives.

"Thanks for stepping in, back there." Diane's voice was still a little uneven. "With my son."

"No problem." Irvin patted Diane's hand. "What is it—Bring Your Kid to Work Day?"

"Oh, no. This is nothing official. I'm just keeping him out of school right now because he's working on a special project, for a competition—

he's a very keen scientist—so it makes more sense for him to come here and use the paper's reference resources. I guess he just got a little carried away. He can go all tunnel-visioned when he's near the end of something really complicated."

Diane stayed downstairs shooting the breeze with the receptionists until she saw Irvin and the detectives pull out of the parking lot. Then she stepped outside and walked around to a small concrete alcove near the loading bay. The few remaining members of the paper's smoking community often used it because it fell in a blind spot between two security cameras.

Diane didn't smoke, but she did carry matches. She took a book of them out of her purse and separated one. She struck it and watched, entranced, as the flame crept rapidly up the flat cardboard stem. All the way up to the tips of her fingers.

She felt it sear her flesh.

And she didn't even flinch.

Chapter Forty-three

Tuesday. Morning.

WAS IT THE POLICE?

The blows rained down on Tyler Shaw's front door, but they didn't give way to a battering ram. Or to bullets. They showed no sign of stopping, either, so eventually Shaw risked taking a glance through the peephole. And relaxed. It was only Mr. Quinlan. His blowhard boss at Hawkins & Leach, where he worked.

Shaw straightened his robe, tightened the cord, and slowly opened the door a crack.

"What the hell do you think you're doing, son?" The tip of Quinlan's nose bobbed up and down when he yelled, and Shaw couldn't take his eyes off it. "Why aren't you dressed? And what are you staring at?"

"Sorry, Mr. Quinlan." Shaw managed to look down at the ground. "I've been working real hard these last few days, and it's wiped me out. I must have slept through my alarm."

"You have *not* been working hard." Quinlan's voice gained another decibel. "Not nearly hard enough. You were OK your first couple of weeks, but it's been all downhill since then. You've been coasting. Showing up late. Going home early. Don't think I haven't noticed."

"I'm sorry." Shaw risked glancing up. "I didn't mean to. I'll turn it around."

"You better. Because I don't care who vouched for you, or how high up they are at the Board of Ed. I'm not going to carry you. Here's the way it goes. Strike one: You get a warning. And that's what this is, in case you're too dumb to realize." Quinlan paused. Shaw had let the door swing open a little wider and a sickening, disgusting stench was starting to billow out into the street. Unless it was coming from the fire-damaged school across the street? "Strike two: You're fired. Get it?"

"I guess." Shaw stifled a yawn. "But what about strike three?"

"There is no strike three." The smell was definitely coming from inside the house, and it was getting even stronger. "Are you clear about that, son? Because you need to be. One more screwup like this morning, and you're out on your ass."

"Got it." Shaw nodded. "Work harder. Don't screw up. No problem. I can do that."

"You better." Quinlan took a step back. "I'm docking you a day's pay for today, but I want you at the depot inside half an hour, anyway. Understand? And I have one more question before I go. What in the name of all that's good and holy is that smell? What have you been doing in there?"

"Oh." Shaw fiddled with the hem of his robe. "Is it that obvious?"

Quinlan crossed his arms.

"To tell the truth, sir, I'm ashamed." Shaw shook his head. "Two weeks have gone by, I guess. Or maybe three? No, two. It was because I was so excited. About starting my new job. Anyway, I must have forgotten to feed them, because they all died. The fish. Twenty-four of them. I found them all one morning, just floating in their tank. Not moving. I know I should have buried them or something, or flushed them down the toilet, but I just couldn't bring myself to do it. So they're still there, right in my living room. And the water? The water's the real problem, I think. It's gone all green. And a bit brown. And—"

"Get rid of them, you moron." Quinlan turned and started back toward his truck. "And get dressed. Be at the depot. Half an hour. And remember: no strike three."

Shaw watched Quinlan's truck turn onto 31st Street, then closed his front door. It hadn't been the police, but it was still a close call. The smell had almost been the end of him. Because the truth was, he'd forgotten how strong it was.

And how much he liked it.

Chapter Forty-four

Tuesday. Late morning.

THE BIRMINGHAM BOARD OF EDUCATION'S TWO-STORY BUILDING STRAD-
dles a fine line between elegant and austere. Its plain concrete façade
is reserved and understated. Its rows of rectangular windows are perfectly proportioned. But the line of pillars supporting its horizontal
canopy are a skinny, unadorned departure from the classical norm.

The building is located on Park Place. It's right across the street
from the actual park, a block-size square of bare soil, spindly trees,
scrubby paths, and four dried-up pools; a reality unable to embody its
designer's grand vision in the face of the hot Alabama sun. Devereaux
had often gazed out over it from the windows of Jefferson County
Courthouse, which stretches along its east side. The Museum of Art is
on the north side, between a concert venue and the county jail. But of
most interest to Devereaux in that area was Sneaky Pete's Hotdogs,
half a block to the west. He was thinking that if the timing worked
out, he might be able to grab an early lunch . . .

Devereaux dropped the Charger in a space outside the building and
immediately a guy appeared from behind the rusting, backward C-
shaped sculpture in front of the main entrance. He was tall and pain-
fully thin, and his neck protruded from the collar of his smart green
shirt like he was a turtle. His hair was neatly parted, he had small
round glasses, and his pants were immaculately pressed.

"Are you the detectives?" The guy held out his hand. "I'm Keith Barent Johnson. I spoke to one of you on the phone. Pleased to meet you."

Devereaux was pleasantly surprised. He'd been expecting an earful from the guy about leaving the car in a no-parking zone.

Johnson led Devereaux, Garretty, and Irvin to a small office on the second floor. He asked them to wait while he rounded up another chair, and Devereaux spent the time examining the items that were neatly lined up on the walls. There were educational qualifications behind the desk. Pictures of sailing boats on the left-hand wall. Certificates Johnson had won in chili cooking contests when he'd been in college in Texas on the right. And a giant, immaculately clean whiteboard to the side of the door.

With the chair in place and Johnson's offer of refreshments refused, Irvin launched straight into her explanation of the plan. She ran through the theory behind it just as she had at the *Tribune*'s office, but changed tack when it came to the logistics. "That's the *what*, the *how*, and the *when*, Mr. Johnson. We have those things covered. But we still need help with the *where*. That's where you come in."

"Wow." Johnson pushed his glasses a little higher on the bridge of his nose. "You guys actually listened. When you pulled me in after the Jones Valley fire, I was expecting the usual police strong-arm bullshit. But what I tried to explain is, I *care* about this stuff. I've worked this job my whole career. I've literally poured my life and soul into the fabric of the city's schools. It kills me to see someone harming them. So I said to the woman who interviewed me that I'd be happy to help, any way I could. I never thought you'd take me up on it, though."

"So what do you think?" Irvin shuffled closer to the edge of her chair. "Looking across the Board's entire estate, where would be the best place? Does anywhere stand out?"

"Yes." Johnson nodded. "Absolutely. One place does. Roundwood school. It's in Zone Two, out past the airport. Only half the property's in use right now due to ongoing refurbishment. But best of all is its layout. I'll print you out a map in a second, but it's on a self-contained, triangular site. The school's in one single, rectangular building in the middle. And it's set back from the road on all sides by a wraparound parking lot. There's no way anyone could cross it and enter the school without you spotting them. Not unless they dug a tunnel!"

WHITE FLAG? OR CALL FOR REINFORCEMENTS?

Has the Birmingham Police Department conceded defeat?

That would be a reasonable expectation for the people of the city to harbor. After all, the genius is clearly way too hot for them to handle alone. However, in a startling new development, this reporter can reveal that an expert from the FBI has been brought in to assist the struggling detectives and breathe new life into an investigation that was dangerously close to flat-lining.

The addition of a specialist player to the team is a sure sign that the authorities are finally starting to take the genius more seriously. This can only be a good thing for Birmingham. But what the desperate and terrified public is clamoring to know is, will this measure be sufficient to stop the fires? Or are there more to come?

Only time will tell . . .

Chapter Forty-five

Tuesday. Late morning.

THERE WAS TO BE NO VISIT TO SNEAKY PETE'S FOR DEVEREAUX THAT DAY. He hadn't even set foot out of the Education building when his phone buzzed with an incoming text from Lieutenant Hale:

> You + TG. My office. Bring Irvin.

Devereaux cut down 20th Street North and turned right onto First Avenue, arriving moments after a grocery truck had broken down, blocking the street. It only took a minute or two to work around it, but the delay was enough to leave Hale seething with impatience by the time they reached headquarters.

She gestured for Irvin and the detectives to sit, then pulled a piece of paper from the heap on her desk. What stopped the whole lot from sliding off? Devereaux wondered. Or the desk from collapsing? He'd heard that Julia Child's kitchen had been reconstructed at the Smithsonian after her death. Maybe the museum would claim Hale's office, as evidence of a scientific miracle? Or maybe Stephen Hawking would want it to help with his work on how black holes are formed.

"This," Hale brandished the page, "is from Crime Scene. They removed the skeletons from Jones Valley last night, and here's what they found when they got them to the lab. The victims were male. Three were early- to mid-twenties. One was significantly older. Possibly in his forties or fifties. That goes for the bones, anyway. The one skull that was left, they had problems aging because—get this—it had been seriously damaged by heat-treatment. Plus it, and the bones, had been in contact with acid."

"So they weren't the remains of students?" Devereaux took the page from Hale and scanned the information. "That pretty much takes Principal Oliver out of the frame, with victims that age."

"It could still be him." Garretty shrugged. "Your buddy said Oliver let other adults watch, sometimes. Maybe these ones threatened to tell tales out of school."

"Maybe the older one *was* Oliver." Hale took the paper back. "That'd be hard to confirm, though. They weren't able to retrieve any DNA."

"I could possibly buy Oliver as one of the victims." Irvin shuffled her chair a few inches forward, dislodging a loose carpet tile as she moved her feet. "But not as the killer. Using the school as the dump site would make absolutely no sense for him. Especially when you factor in this new detail about the acid treatment. Oliver lived alone when he was principal. I checked. So the lowest risk option for him would be to dispose of the bodies at his house. How would he hide an acid bath at the school? How would he lift the gym floor? At all, let alone without being seen."

"Good point." Hale set the paper down. "How would anyone do that?"

"Here's what I'm thinking." Irvin brushed her hair behind her ears. "We know the school was rebuilt in 2011. The perp must have had access to it during the construction. He could have worked there. Could have delivered stuff regularly. Or could have just lived nearby. That's a real possibility, because his living arrangements are key. Like I said, the school was a high-risk dump site. There must have been a strong reason he couldn't use his home, or yard, or whatever. I think it's because he was living with someone. A wife. A girlfriend. A parent. A grandparent. It doesn't really matter which. We don't have any reports of similar crimes post 2011, so I think that after he finished at Jones Valley he either got locked up for something unconnected, died, or moved away."

"That makes sense." Hale nodded. "We'll need to start pulling sentencing records and mortuary lists. See if we can put a name on this guy." Hale checked the time on her little robot-shaped desk clock. "OK. Hold that thought. We've got the go/no-go call for the school arson op. It's time to dial in."

Hale keyed in her access code, spoke her name, then put the phone on Speaker and hit the Mute key. Captain Emrich was the next—and last—to join, before Agent McMahan of the Bureau Field Office took up the reins. He kept things brief and to the point, asking each delegate to state their field of responsibility and confirm their readiness. They heard from the team leaders assigned to watching Roundwood school. The shift commanders tasked with covering the other schools in the city. Chief Young from Fire and Rescue. Representatives from Airborne Surveillance. CCTV. Traffic division. And finally, SWAT. Each voice sounded calm and confident. No one dissented.

"So we know what we'll all be doing later on, I guess." Hale hung up the phone. "Now, back to the guy who put those bones under the floor at Jones Valley. Sentencing records. And mortuary lists. We need them."

"Could you guys handle that?" Irvin stood and pushed her chair back. "I need to go and square the circle with that journalist."

"No problem." Garretty nodded.

"Most importantly, check the release dates." Irvin paused in the doorway. "With a profile like his—particularly the head removal, which indicates an extreme degree of psychosis—he won't just stop killing on his own. Something compelled him to do it. If he's alive and out of jail, he'll do it again. You can bank on it."

Chapter Forty-six

Tuesday. Early afternoon.

"HERE'S ANOTHER THOUGHT." DEVEREAUX WATCHED AS GARRETTY filled out the online requests for the records they needed. "This guy. What if he didn't go to jail, or die? What if it was his parents or wife or whoever who died? He could have inherited their place. And gotten real good at picking victims who won't be missed."

"I'm hoping he died." Garretty continued to type.

"Or what if he moved away? Went to BFE and started picking off hobos? Who'd ever know?"

"Let's just make sure he's not doing that here." Garretty didn't look away from the screen. "And that he never gets the chance to, if the asshole's not already in the ground."

"Amen to—"

The chorus from "Paradise City" started to blare from Devereaux's pocket. He pulled out his phone, checked the screen in case it was Chris Lambert, then answered.

"Detective Devereaux? It's Diane McKinzie. I'm just calling to let you know the article is up and live."

"It is? That's great."

"I'm sorry I didn't call sooner. I did try Agent Irvin after I uploaded her file, but I couldn't reach her."

"No problem. I'll make sure she finds out."

"Thanks." Diane coughed. "I tried her a couple of times. And then I got hauled off to write a post for the dumbest-ass blog you ever heard of. Big City Nights, it's called. Don't ever read it, please. It's mortifying. Today's inanity? A bunch of total nonsense about a possibly missing college professor with a weird name who may or may not be secretly gay. It's like I was dragged back in time to the 1950s. Anyway, you don't need to hear about my problems. I just wanted to confirm that we're all set."

"Well, we appreciate your help. You had no issues with your editor?"

"My editor. Yeah. She's quite the operator. She pushed back a little more than I'd expected, actually. I had to kind of promise her that we'd get first bite at the cherry, once the case breaks. I hope that's OK . . ."

"I don't see a problem."

"Excellent. Actually, there's nothing you could give me right now, is there? Just to keep her off my back? A little snippet no one else knows?"

"When there's news, you'll be the first to know. I promise."

"Oh, come on, Detective! I know how you cops work. There are always things you hold back. I'm not asking for anything super sensitive. Nothing that could derail the case. Just a little *you scratch my back*, you know?"

"Ms. McKinzie—"

"Come on. Diane. Please."

"OK, Diane. I don't have anything for you. But thinking about it, here's an idea. Roundwood school's going to be staked out around the clock for the foreseeable future, but we're expecting the arsonist to make his move this afternoon. This evening at the latest. Do you want to head down there with me? Ride along? Maybe be there when we collar the guy?"

There was silence on the line for twenty, maybe twenty-five seconds.

"Detective, thank you. I'd love to. But I don't think I can. I have a previous commitment with my son. It means I actually need to be at my house this evening. So how about this? Meet me for breakfast in the morning, instead. As early as you like. Give me what you can then."

Chapter Forty-seven

Tuesday. Early afternoon.

THE SPACE UNDER THE VIRGIN MARY BRIDGE WAS NO MORE PLEASANT IN daylight than it was at night. It might even be worse, Devereaux thought. You could see what you were stepping in. But it did make sense to meet there. It was neutral ground. You could see the other person coming from a good long distance. It would be impossible for anyone to eavesdrop without being spotted. And it was too close to the airport for surveillance helicopters to fly overhead.

The navy Tesla arrived two minutes after Devereaux parked the Ferrari and Dzerko—aka Frank—climbed out and offered his hand.

"Sorry, Devereaux." Dzerko leaned back against his car. "It's a no."

"What do you mean, a no? What's the deal? Is your guy angling for more money?"

"That's not it. The target's the problem."

"Why? Does he discriminate based on old age? Because that's against the law."

Dzerko smiled weakly. "You don't understand. You see, my guy said he'd been hired to stop this particular clock once before, in the past."

"So Joseph Oliver's already dead?"

"No. Which is part of the problem. The way you wanted to structure the deal—a quarter for finding Oliver, the rest for the other part—it made him uneasy. The other time with this target, my guy had the hit all lined up, but the clients aborted. Now, those guys paid up front, and he kept their money, obviously. But it still pissed him off.

He takes pride in his work. When he says he's going to do something, he likes to do it. It really bugged him, quitting partway."

"So here's his chance to go back and put it right."

"No. He has a strict policy. Do it once. Do it right. Or don't do it at all. And he's the best. It's not like he has a shortage of work. He can afford to pick and choose."

"You're sure he didn't pass because of me? What I do? Because if it's a trust issue . . ."

"It's not that. He did say one weird thing about you, but it had nothing to do with his decision. He'd already said no by then. And anyway, he's worked for cops before. Cop dollars spend the same as civilian dollars, right?"

"What weird thing did he say about me?"

"It was nothing. I shouldn't have mentioned it."

"Frank . . ."

"OK. It was after he started to balk. I said you were a stand-up guy, thinking this might just be a case of first-date nerves between you. But he said, no, period. And then asked if you were one of those school guys. There was one in particular he seemed to have a dislike for. And he said assholes, not guys, but you get the picture."

"I do."

"So, look. This doesn't have to be the end of the road for this thing. I could try someone else. The number two guy on my list is still pretty good. Maybe better, in some situations. Want me to hook you up?"

"No, Frank. It's OK. You've given me an idea. About another way to get what I need."

Chapter Forty-eight

Tuesday. Afternoon.

A QUOTATION WAS FLUTTERING SOMEWHERE AROUND THE EDGE OF AL-exandra's conscious memory, but she couldn't quite pin it down. Something she'd read somewhere? Or that someone had told her? It was to do with finishing a book. Yes. The idea that if you finish a book, the book's different from when you started it. Or words to that effect.

Alexandra's pedantic, lawyer's brain had objected to the idea when she'd first come across it. How could the book change, unless you were talking about something superficial like the spine getting bent? Surely it should be the other way around. If it was a good book, then the person who finished it would be changed. The book would just be the catalyst. But whichever way it was, Alexandra was wondering if there could be something similar with people and houses. Once a person had finished living in a house, could the house be changed? Take her place as an example. Devereaux had gone. And it felt like he'd taken part of the house with him. It seemed smaller now. Less welcoming. Less like a home.

A wave of raw emotion surged inside her as she thought about Devereaux, but Alexandra realized it wasn't anger, like when she'd confronted him over the photographs. Or fear, like when she'd discovered she was carrying his child. It was sadness. She didn't want him to be gone. She wanted him back. She just didn't know if there was room for him. Or his family secrets.

Chapter Forty-nine

Tuesday. Afternoon.

THE HI-FI STORE MANAGER SAID HE'D FIRED DAVE BATEMAN FIRST THING that morning. And he made a point of stressing that he'd done it personally.

He didn't have to sound so damn gleeful about it, Devereaux thought. People lose their jobs. It happens. But it shouldn't be something you gloat about. Unless you're a complete asshole. Devereaux took a long look at the guy, memorizing every detail of his face in case he ever spotted him running a red light or rolling through a stop sign. Then he went back to his car and called Dispatch to get Bateman's home address.

Devereaux was still in the Ferrari, which was terrible on slow city streets, so he nursed it northeast on Third Avenue, temporarily heading in the wrong direction for Bateman's home, then swung north for a half mile on Stevens before getting on I-20/59 and burying the accelerator for the eight minutes it took him to reach the Hueytown intersection.

Bateman's miserable little house was isolated next to a vacant, weed-filled lot at the end of a street of run-down bungalows that put Devereaux in mind of terminal patients on a geriatric ward. Pushing aside a flutter of guilt as he realized that the Ferrari he'd carelessly left at the curb would be worth more than two, maybe three of the properties, Devereaux trudged up the crumbling pathway and knocked on the door.

Devereaux had to knock three times—hard, insistent, ignore-me-at-your-peril knocks—before he heard a sound from inside the house. Eventually the door was dragged open, binding on the scuffed wooden hallway floor, and Bateman peered out, blinking weakly against the afternoon sun.

"Cooper?" It took Bateman a moment to focus. "What are you doing here?"

"I came to see you, Dave." Devereaux attempted to smile. "How about you let me in? It would be good to chat for a while. See how things are going."

"Things are going terribly." Bateman hauled the door open the rest of the way and stepped back. His hair was messed up, like he'd been wearing a hat. He had on a wrinkled blue Oxford shirt with an embroidered logo of a smiling CD player on the pocket, thick blue socks, but no pants. "Come in if you want. I got no beer or anything, though."

Devereaux stepped inside, and tried to breathe through his mouth. "Do you have cats, Dave?"

"No." Bateman led the way down the short narrow hallway and turned left into a square living room. There was a patch of threadbare Turkish carpet in the center, with a jade green velvet couch on one side and a pair of eggplant-colored vinyl armchairs on the other. In the far corner a TV from before the days of flat screens was balanced on an ancient sewing-machine table. "My mom did. This used to be her place. I took it over when she passed, a few years back. Why? Do you like cats?"

"I don't know." Devereaux weighed up his seating options, trying to figure which piece of furniture was least likely to do terminal damage to his clothes. And how to avoid whichever one Bateman had just been sitting on, without his pants. "I never had a pet. And to be honest with you, Dave, I didn't come here to talk about animals. I came because there's another problem. You could be in a lot of trouble. Now, I want to help you. I think I can make everything all right again. But only if you're absolutely truthful with me. Are you clear on that?"

Bateman sank down into the corner of the couch and pulled his knees up to his chest. "How can I be in more trouble? I don't understand. I didn't do anything."

"Let me tell you what I know, then we can make a plan." Devereaux perched on the arm of one of the chairs. "We've received information that a group of guys took out a contract to have Joseph Oliver killed. What do you know about that, Dave?"

"Nothing."

Devereaux got up and headed toward the door.

"Cooper?" Bateman let his feet flop down onto the floor. "Where are you going?"

"You've got to understand, this is a time-critical situation." Devereaux paused in front of the crud-encrusted window. "We know who the hit man is, who was hired for the job. We're closing in on him. Detectives are out there right now, with dogs, hunting him down. He'll be in a cell in a matter of hours. Minutes, maybe. And this guy? He's wanted for some pretty heavy stuff. We're talking lethal injection territory. So the minute he's a collar, he's going to start talking. Trying to cut a deal. But who do you think he'll give up first? Powerful people? The kind of guys who could say one word and have his tongue cut out with a rusty spoon, even in jail? Or you and your buddies?"

"It wasn't me."

"Shall I go, then?"

Bateman didn't answer.

"Because here's the thing. We know the contract was taken out by a bunch of guys who'd been to Jones Valley school together. Now, your next problem is that shit rolls downhill. First the hit man will give you and your buddies up. But maybe he won't know all your names. Maybe one of you took the lead in setting the thing up. Or maybe one of you stands out more, for some other reason. So he's the first of you to end up in the cells. And what does he do? He also cuts a deal. He gives the rest of you up for a walk."

Bateman still said nothing.

"It's human nature, Dave." Devereaux softened his voice. "There's nothing you can do. You can't fight it."

Bateman leaned forward and wrapped his arms around his head.

"I'm giving you a chance to get out ahead of this thing." Devereaux moved closer to the couch. "Tell me the others' names. Then I can protect you. I bet I can keep you out of jail altogether. But you've got to tell me. Right now."

"I can't." Bateman's voice was muffled by his sleeves. "We promised not to."

"Not to tell about the contract?"

"Not to tell about one another." Bateman half straightened up. "The thing is, we all have the same reason to hate Oliver. And we didn't want anyone else to know. We were all hoping to get married. Find jobs. Live normal lives. Funny, eh? Just look at me now. But anyway, it's all moot. We never went through with the hit. We called it off. We chickened out."

"Hiring a hit man is still a serious crime. I still need your buddies' names. But how about this? Write them down. That way, technically you didn't *tell* me. You can even destroy the piece of paper after I've looked at it. OK? No one will ever know the information came from you."

Devereaux passed Bateman his notebook. Bateman took his time, but eventually scrawled four names at the top of the page. Presumably the four had all been to Jones Valley school at the same time he and Bateman were there, but Devereaux didn't recognize any of them. "When did this contract thing happen, by the way?"

"Five years ago. Maybe six. And that was the end of it for me. I cut ties. I haven't seen or spoken to any of them since then."

"Probably a smart move in terms of these school guys. But go back to the hit. I'm a little confused. Because I've been doing some checking, myself. Joseph Oliver dropped out of sight eleven years ago. How did you know where to tell the hit man to find him?"

"One of the guys—the last name on the list—he's rich now, like you. And obsessed. He spent whatever it took to keep tabs on Oliver, wherever he went. And whatever he changed his name to. It drove him out of his mind when we called the whole thing off. He kept saying he'd pay for the hit on his own if we wouldn't chip in. But honestly? I think he was full of shit."

Chapter Fifty

Tuesday. Late afternoon.

TYLER SHAW STOOD IN FRONT OF HIS MIRROR AND SHOOK HIS HEAD. He'd never thought he'd see the day, but the dragon shirt would have to go. Routine or no routine.

He turned to the bed and stared down at the other three nice shirts that he owned. The black one with the tiny white skulls. The lion one. And the psychedelic one, where the fruit are changing shape and eating people. He had to be honest. None of those were much use, either. He was in serious trouble here. His wardrobe—a key tool of his trade—was in danger of betraying him.

Although, to be fair, it wasn't the clothes' fault. It was the upper crust–type guys he was having to mingle with these days. They didn't give you any wriggle room. They were too spoiled. Too fussy. Too used to getting exactly what they want, when they want it. Take last night, as an example. When that asshole violin player he'd set his sights on got cold feet over his *lack of sophistication*. He'd nearly struck out as a result. *Nearly*. Luckily he'd lined up a fallback option. A snarky academic guy. A much easier target, as it turned out. But still. He'd come mighty close to disaster.

Actually, maybe it was a good thing, what had happened. It was a warning shot. No harm *had* been done. But he'd been left with no doubt he'd have to raise his game.

Chapter Fifty-one

Tuesday. Late afternoon.

DEVEREAUX PULLED OUT HIS PHONE AS HE WALKED TO THE CAR AND called Dispatch to have them check the four names that Bateman had given him.

It turned out that one of the guys was dead, following the accidental discharge of a firearm four years previously. One had emigrated to New Zealand around the same time. And two still lived in Birmingham. Including Bill Adama. The well-off guy Bateman had described as being obsessed with Joscph Oliver's whereabouts.

Next Devereaux called Garretty, who confirmed that all was quiet on the Roundwood school front. He also said he'd be happy to cover for Devereaux while he made one more stop on his way to the stakeout. The school site was well covered, Devereaux figured. He wouldn't make a great deal of difference by showing up a little sooner. But if he could locate Joseph Oliver, that would make an enormous amount of difference. To his chances of snuffing out the guy's blackmail scheme, anyway.

Devereaux started out by retracing the route he'd taken from Bateman's former workplace, but instead of leaving Stevens at Third and returning downtown, he continued up and over the Red Mountain until I-280 peeled off to the east, toward the classy neighborhoods that nestled in its lee.

The first thing Devereaux saw when he pulled onto Adama's sweeping block-paved driveway was a red Ferrari, identical to the one he was reluctantly driving. It was parked near a giant fountain that was shaped like a wedding cake, and beyond it was an intricate white lattice gazebo complete with climbing pink roses and a faux wrought-iron weather vane.

Devereaux climbed the steps to the front door, rang the bell, and craned his neck to survey the apparent acres of flawless white render.

"Nice, huh?" Bill Adama opened the door himself and joined Devereaux for a moment in admiring the façade. He was dressed for tennis, minus the shoes, and a rose gold Apple watch stood out against his richly tanned forearm. "I'm Bill. You live around here?"

"We have a mutual, let's say, acquaintance." Devereaux studied Adama's soft, unwrinkled face and tried in vain to summon a recollection of him from high school. "*Friend* would definitely be the wrong word. I need to find him, and I'm told you're the man who can help."

"Does this acquaintance have a name?" Adama shoved his hands into his shorts pockets.

"Joseph Oliver."

"Doesn't ring a bell." Adama's top lip curled itself into a tiny sneer. "And my dinner's about ready, so I'm going to say goodbye. Whoever you are."

Adama stepped back into the house but Devereaux shot his foot over the threshold before he could slam the door.

"Move your foot." Adama was making no effort to conceal his annoyance anymore. "Or I'll crush it."

"That would be your second mistake of the night." Devereaux flashed his badge. "Now. Joseph Oliver. I want his address. And the name he's currently using."

"Who told you I would know?" Adama let go of the door and folded his arms. "Because they're full of shit. I have no idea what you're talking about."

"You do, Bill. And you're going to tell me. That's not up for debate. The only question that remains is how much you're going to piss me off in the process. Because right now I'm annoyed. But not too annoyed to have the rest of the conversation here on your doorstep. Irritate me any further, and you'll spend the night in jail."

Adama stepped back outside and pulled the door closed behind him. "You'll take me to jail, for what? Having that pedophile scumbag euthanized? Allegedly."

"I know you didn't have Oliver killed. You and your buddies didn't have the stones for it, so you chickened out. But you do know where he is. Tell me, and I'll take care of the problem for you. Put *him* in jail. Think about it. Imagine what'll happen to him when the other lifers find out he likes little boys."

"Screw you. I don't need you to take care of anything. Or those other losers. You want to find Oliver? Fine. Do it yourself. You think I really don't remember you? Of course I do. You're Cooper Devereaux. And you know what I remember most? How you didn't help me when I needed it, at school. So I'm not helping you now. You can bite me. And then you can get the hell off my property."

"One last chance, Bill. Tell me where Oliver is. Or you *will* spend the night in the cells."

"Really?" Adama held out his wrists. "Go ahead. I'm calling your bluff."

"OK, then." Devereaux reached into his pocket, pulled out a business card, and slipped it between Adama's fingers. "Take care of that. Don't lose it. You'll need it in the morning. Think of it as a magic key. Because calling me is the only way you'll be able to get out."

Chapter Fifty-two

Tuesday. Early evening.

IT WAS ONLY KRAFT MAC 'N' CHEESE. AND SHE SUSPECTED THAT THE MILK may not have been one hundred percent fresh. But it was the best meal Diane had ever eaten in her life. Because it had been cooked by Daniel.

Diane hadn't asked him to do it. She'd actually been apprehensive about what the evening might have in store, after he'd turned down her offer to stop for a milkshake or ice cream on the way home from the newspaper. But once they'd walked into the house, her mood had turned on a dime. He hadn't just offered to cook. He'd insisted. He said he wanted to do something special for her, to make up for the way he'd let his anxiety get the better of him a couple of times recently.

When she'd finished eating, she moved to the couch—taking a second bottle of wine with her—and allowed herself a moment of self-congratulation while Daniel dealt with the cleaning up. She'd been so right to turn down Detective Devereaux's offer of a ride-along to the school. She'd figured it would be better all around for her not to cancel another evening with Daniel. But the time they'd just had together? It was worth a million head starts on a million stupid stories. And sure. Yes. She'd had her fair share of wobbles along the way. But all things considered, she'd done a pretty good job of bringing up her son. Ever since her selfish, narcissistic, cheating asshole of an ex-husband had left her and run off to . . . where? She couldn't remember. Couldn't remember when he'd gone. What his name was. Where she was. What she was doing . . .

Chapter Fifty-three

Tuesday. Evening.

DEVEREAUX KEPT HIS SPEED DOWN ON THE WAY TOWARD ROUNDWOOD school to give himself time to make a couple of phone calls. Then he parked three streets away, figuring he was no longer in the kind of neighborhood where the Ferrari would work well as an undercover car, and walked the rest of the way.

The school site looked just as it had on Johnson's plan—a long, wide triangle, like a slice of cheese. Appropriate, Devereaux thought, given that they were using it as a trap. The Bureau was watching the short end and one of the long sides, and the BPD was responsible for the other. Devereaux saw the department's surveillance vehicle as soon as he turned the last corner. It was fitted out to look like a telephone company truck, complete with a dummy cable leading from a hatch to a nearby utility pole and a host of fake microwave dishes scattered across the roof to disguise its array of infrared cameras.

Inside, three cushioned stools were fixed to the floor, positioned to give good access to the banks of monitors and equipment racks along both walls. Lieutenant Hale was perched on the farthest one from the door, and Garretty moved up next to her to give Devereaux room to slide in.

"I didn't expect to see you here, Lieutenant." Devereaux wasn't too happy about finding an extra body taking up space in the already confined interior.

Hale shrugged. "I've got nothing better to do. And this is better than fielding more calls from that Lambert guy. I told you to call him back!"

"I will." Devereaux tried to focus on his breathing, but that wasn't easy with the lingering odor of coffee and Chinese food that was overwhelming the inadequate supply of air. "I'll do it later."

"Make sure you do. I'm sick of hearing his voice. He wants your help with some gardening project now. Or something like that. If he calls tonight, you're answering. His whining's all I need, on top of this madness."

"You know, if you're not behind this operation, Tommy and I can handle it." Devereaux was pretending he hadn't noticed the crisscrossed strips of Velcro that had been stuck to most of the flat surfaces, for securing portable items of equipment. Velcro's flammable. It can spontaneously combust. Apollo One's capsule had been full of Velcro . . .

"I'm not behind it." She flashed a lukewarm smile. "But if it's going to be a clusterfuck, I don't want to have to read about it in a report."

"No sign of our guy yet, then." Devereaux tried closing his eyes.

"Two false alarms." Garretty stifled a yawn. "A guy on a bike. And two in a pickup. But nothing for over an hour now."

The three of them settled down to wait. The stakeout slumber, some cops called it as a reaction to the mantra that was drummed into them at the Academy: *brain alert, body inert.* The human version of *lock and load* was how Devereaux preferred to think about it. He was happy to wait any amount of time, as long as there was the prospect of some action at the end of it. He'd just have preferred not to do the waiting in such an enclosed space.

Forty-five minutes drifted by, then Garretty pointed at the center screen. "Movement."

"A Ford Pinto?" Hale leaned forward. "I haven't seen one of those in years. I thought they'd all exploded."

The rusty old car entered the school's parking lot, coasted around the side of the building, and rolled to a stop next to an emergency exit. A guy got out. He looked to be in his early twenties. He was wearing jeans, a red T-shirt, white sneakers, and he had an Atlanta Braves baseball cap jammed down tight on his head. He glanced around, then opened his trunk and took out a crowbar and a white twenty-gallon container. He took a step forward, started to line up the crowbar, then the fire door burst open. Two agents in FBI windbreakers and hats charged out. They grabbed the guy, threw him facedown on the asphalt, and zip-tied his wrists behind his back.

"OK, then." Hale shook her head. "Maybe I owe Agent Irvin an apology."

Devereaux and Garretty could hear the guy screaming for his rights from across the street. They slipped through the line of low trees at the edge of the parking lot and started toward him, but one of the agents gestured for them to slow down. He picked up the white container from the ground, then came forward to intercept them.

"I think we might have a problem, guys." The agent took the cap off the container and turned it upside down. "It's empty. Plus we've searched him, and he doesn't have any matches or a lighter. Nothing flammable at all."

Devereaux walked over to the guy, who by now was sitting propped up against the school wall with his hat lying upside down on the ground next to him.

"School's a strange choice of place to be on a fine Tuesday night." Devereaux poked the guy with his toe to make sure he had his attention. "And not a very wise choice. So let me offer you a couple of alternatives: Home, wherever or whatever that may be. Or the station house, answering a million questions."

"I want to go home." The guy's voice was quieter now.

"OK. You've got one chance to make that happen. Tell me what you're doing here." Devereaux picked up the guy's crowbar. "And don't lie."

"Toluene." The guy nodded at the container that the agent was still holding. "It's a kind of chemical, right? I figured they have some in the school lab."

"You were trying to steal toluene?"

The guy nodded.

"And drive away with it in a Ford Pinto?"

"Yeah . . ." The guy looked confused. "Why? I'm not going to leave my car behind . . ."

"Forget the car. Why did you want the toluene?"

"To sell it. I know a guy who buys it. For making meth."

"You're an idiot. You need to give us this guy's name. And then you need to stop this bullshit. Clean yourself up. Get yourself a job. And a new car. Because if I ever see you again . . ." Devereaux hooked the sharp tip at the curved edge of the crowbar under the guy's chin, lifted it an inch, looked him in the eye, then turned and walked away.

Devereaux turned back after two steps. "Actually, one more question. Why pick tonight to steal the toluene?"

"Tonight was my last chance." The guy tried to rub his chin on the neck of his T-shirt. "They're getting a new alarm tomorrow."

"What makes you think that?"

"I saw it on the *Tribune*'s website."

"It's a new fire alarm they're getting, you cretin. And if anyone else asks about that, keep your mouth shut."

The detectives did rock-paper-stone on the way back to the surveillance truck to see who would break the news to the lieutenant. Garretty won. He declined the honor. But after they climbed inside and closed the door, Devereaux didn't even get the chance to open his mouth.

"I just got off the phone with the captain." Hale's expression was grim. "Green Acres Middle School's on fire."

Chapter Fifty-four

Wednesday. Morning.

WHERE WAS SHE?

Diane McKinzie opened her eyes. She tried to move her head, but her neck was too stiff. So she moved her eyes, instead. She saw tall bookshelves. A pair of framed *New Yorker* cartoons on the wall between them. A chandelier with a missing shade. It was her own living room! She was on the couch. And she was under a blanket. She didn't remember fetching one from the cupboard. She didn't remember deciding not to head for the safety of her bedroom. Didn't remember anything she'd done after dinner, the previous night.

She checked the time. Eight o'clock. She was late! She'd have missed her meeting with Detective Devereaux! This was a disaster. She had to fix it before Kelly Peterson found out. Where was her phone? She fumbled around until she found it, and saw it was on silent. Which was weird. And that she had a voicemail. She played it as she hurried upstairs to change her clothes.

Unsurprisingly, the message was from Devereaux. But he wasn't chiding her for not turning up. He was canceling on her! And apologizing. Something about unforeseen developments. And asking for a favor. For her not to stress the link when she wrote the story. What *link*? What *story*? What on earth was going on?

Chapter Fifty-five

Wednesday. Morning.

"DID YOU MENTION YOUR FERRARI TO ANY OF THE GUYS IN HERE?" Devereaux took a sip of coffee and smiled at Adama across the dented metal table.

Adama didn't reply.

"No?" Devereaux took another, longer sip. "That's probably wise. You see, mine's a loaner. But you chose yours. People might start to wonder why . . ."

"This is it?" Adama's voice was hoarse. "You're here to insult me? To gloat? After you totally framed me?"

"The insults are a bonus. A kind of karmic payment-in-advance for the thing I have to do next, this morning, which is really going to suck. I'm actually here to find out if you're happy to stay, or if you want to be released."

"I'm *going* to be released, asshole."

"You probably are, yes." Devereaux frowned, as if weighing a complex problem. "But when? The courthouse is swamped, these days. Cases drag and drag. And while you're in here, I may decide to look into the charges against you myself. I'm a very good investigator. Did you know that? I'm actually so good, I can find evidence even when none exists . . ."

"All right! Then I *want* to be released. Right now."

"Then you know what to do."

"Yes. OK. I'll tell you about Joseph Oliver. His address. His alias. Everything."

"That's good. But it's no longer good enough. Circumstances change. Prices rise. You're a businessman, right? You understand these things."

Adama closed his eyes. "What else do you want?"

"I found out some interesting things after our little tête-à-tête last night. Like for example that you own the store Dave Bateman used to work at."

"Right. I gave him that job. I was trying to help the guy."

"Give it back to him. Give him a raise. And make sure the manager knows that whatever Bateman does—even if he comes to work naked, craps on the carpet, and sets the place on fire—he doesn't get fired. Ever again."

Adama scowled. "OK. But that's it, right?"

"Just a couple more things. You're going to buy Bateman a new car. Nothing fancy like yours, just something decent. American. You're going to pay for him to have a cleaning service at his house. Say, twice a month. You're going to send him on a nice, weeklong vacation, once a year. Somewhere in the United States. And you're going to have him to dinner at your house, once a month."

"Not dinner."

"Twice a month."

"Once a month." Adama held up his hands. "But only if my wife doesn't have to be there."

"Deal. Now, they don't allow sharp implements in here, but you have my details. Email me the information about Oliver the minute you're home."

Adama rolled his eyes, then nodded.

"And Bill? I'd like to think we now have a relationship built on trust and understanding. But if by any chance your email doesn't arrive? Or the information it contains turns out to be inaccurate—"

"I know. I'll be back here on some other bullshit charge."

"Oh, no. You misunderstand. See, I'm going to find Oliver, even if you don't help me. And when I do, let's say he has some kind of accident. For sake of argument, an extremely painful and ultimately fatal accident. Now, if I was pissed with you, what good would it do me if you had an alibi?"

ANOTHER ENTRY IN THE SAD LITANY OF FAILURE?

The voyage of the *Titanic*. The flight of the *Hindenburg*. The launch of the *Challenger* space shuttle. The FBI's attempt at catching the genius. What do these things all have in common? They were all complete disasters!

People throughout the city are shaking their heads, and many are laughing out loud at the so-called experts and their doomed, feeble-minded strategy to outwit the genius. What will they do next? the people ask. And whatever they try, will it make a difference?

A resounding NO is this reporter's prediction. How can anyone compete with the genius's superior intellect? It was too much on its own for the dullards in public service to cope with. And now that a source of inside information has been added to the mix? There's only one possible outcome. Crushing defeat for the FBI. And inevitable triumph for the genius. If this was a game, the only detail yet to be established would be the margin of victory!

Chapter Fifty-six

Wednesday. Morning.

DEVEREAUX WAS THE LAST TO ARRIVE.

Captain Emrich was standing behind his desk holding the little rake from his Japanese garden, and he used it to punctuate the air as he spoke. "This tardiness had better be related to the case, Detective."

"Absolutely, Captain. I was just brushing up on my Arthur Miller." Devereaux nodded to Irvin and Lieutenant Hale, then took the seat next to Garretty. "I thought a working knowledge of *The Crucible* might be a good thing, this morning."

"If I may, Captain?" Hale flashed Devereaux a look that said *not another word*. "OK. First thing. Chief Young sends his apologies. He can't make it this morning due to the aftermath of last night's incident. But he has sent me some information. He says the damage at Green Acres was severe. Worse than at Jones Valley."

"Was it the same kind of device?" Emrich set the rake down on his desk and took his seat. "Homemade napalm again?"

"He believes it was." Hale nodded. "But the real kicker this time? Green Acres had an updated sprinkler system. Someone had disabled it. Presumably, the arsonist."

"Smart move," Garretty said. "Maybe he learned from Inglenook."

"Maybe he learned from history." Devereaux thought back to the movies he used to watch with his father. "In World War II, for the big bombing raids in Europe, the first thing they'd do was pound the hell out of the places in the cities with water mains running through them.

Then when they followed up with the incendiaries, there was nothing to put out the flames."

"Or maybe, back in the twenty-first century, he read the article the Bureau planted on the *Tribune*'s blog." Emrich was back to brandishing his rake.

"It's possible that the perp read the blog and adapted, yes." Irvin kept her hands clasped on her lap. "But it's more likely that word of the operation leaked. There are at least three people we're aware of outside the department and the Bureau who knew of the plan. Diane McKinzie and Kelly Peterson at the *Tribune*. And Keith Johnson at the Board of Ed. I know that McKinzie's and Johnson's backgrounds were already checked, and that Johnson was actually interviewed after the Jones Valley fire. My boss had them checked again this morning. I'll email all of you the results, for the file. Following on from that, I think our next move should be to talk to each of them."

"Did you find anything we missed, on the backgrounds?" Devereaux asked.

"No." Irvin shook her head. "We just noticed one thing, and it's new. One of them picked up a traffic ticket. Ran a red light. Last night. Diane McKinzie. It's a surprisingly cool car, hers, actually."

"Then are we agreed? Interviewing them's the way to go?" Hale glanced at each person. No one objected. "OK. Which of them first?"

"I'd start with Johnson," Irvin said. "He's worked across the school system his entire career, and three fires suggest someone's carrying a pretty broad grudge."

"Makes sense to me." Devereaux got to his feet. "What are we waiting for? Come on. Let's get started."

"Cool your jets, Detective." Emrich got up and moved around his desk. "Doing some more interviewing is all we've got? After a third school has gone up in smoke? Give me something more proactive!"

"A minute ago you implied that doing something proactive was what got the third school burned down." Devereaux made a show of rubbing his chin. "And now you want us to do something more proactive. What's the story, Captain? Are you in a sweep to see which will be the next school to go up?"

"OK, guys." Hale held out her arms. "We just need to find the right balance. It certainly makes sense to regroup right now. Make sure we're covering the basics. That way we can prepare the ground for more . . . proactive . . . ideas as soon as possible after that. Right?"

"Right." Irvin nodded. "And I actually have one other idea that'll help bridge the gap. I think it's time we start to consider the possibility that there might be more to these fires than just revenge. There might be something deeper, psychologically. And in case that's true, I think we should launch a tip line. Invite the public to call in and help."

"Why?" Emrich sneered at the idea. "You think someone's going to call in and give up the arsonist, but only if there's a special number?"

"No." Irvin stuck out her chin. "Based on the pattern that's starting to emerge, I think the arsonist himself will call."

Chapter Fifty-seven

Wednesday. Morning.

DIANE HAD INTENDED TO CALL HER HOPEFULLY SOON-TO-BE NEW BEST friend, Agent Irvin, so she was surprised to see that her fingers actually dialed Detective Devereaux's number. She spotted the difference in time to hang up before he answered, but decided to go with it, anyway. Let fate be her guide. *Everything happens for a reason,* she told herself.

"Detective! It's Diane McKinzie. I'm so glad I caught you. I wanted to tell you in person how sorry I am about what happened at Green Acres school last night."

"Don't worry about it. It wasn't your fault. We knew from the get-go there were risks. It comes with the territory."

"I get that. But still. I feel just awful that a plan I helped to set in motion went so horribly wrong. I hope you didn't get in any trouble with your job?"

"Me? No. And anyway, me and trouble with the job are old friends. We go way back."

She had heard stories . . .

"I'm glad, Detective. And I hope this doesn't put me in your bad books. I know how superstitious some of you cops are."

"Not me."

"That's good. Did you see my column this morning, by the way? I did like you asked and kept the focus away from any link between the fire and that last piece you guys had me post."

"I saw it. You did a great job. Very subtle."

"Thanks. I had to cover Green Acres, obviously. And keeping away from the link wasn't easy. It's the kind of thing readers can quickly catch on to on their own. I figured the best way to keep them off the scent was to bury them with details about the new fire. I'm pretty much out of material now, though, is the problem. So about that fire, Detective. Is there—"

"Are you trying to hustle me, Diane?"

"No! Absolutely not. I could just use a little help, is all. If there's anything you could give me . . ."

"Tell you what. How about this? I have something to attend to right now. It'll either take all day, or I'll be in and out in five minutes. Assuming it's the latter, I could drop by the newspaper as soon as I'm done. We could sit down, put our heads together, see what we can come up with."

"Brilliant idea, Detective. I'll see you soon."

Diane was surprised by how much she was starting to like Detective Devereaux. She'd known *of* him for years, of course. But she'd only really thought of him as a faceless cop. Well, a faceless cop with more than his share of skeletons, if the local scuttlebutt was to be believed. How much of that could be true? Maybe she could write an article about him. Come at him sideways, and uncover the truth that way. Her father had written about Devereaux's father. She could write . . .

Wait. First things first. She needed information about the fire. Devereaux seemed to play his cards pretty close to the vest, so she'd have to be right on her game when he arrived. Was there time to go home and change? No. But that didn't matter. Finding somewhere private to talk was much more important. Not the Goldfish Bowl again, though. What about the Supervisor's Office? Maybe Daniel would agree to swap it for her desk? She'd only need to trade places for an hour or so . . .

Chapter Fifty-eight

Wednesday. Morning.

"THERE'S STILL NO ANSWER FROM HIS EXTENSION." THE RECEPTIONIST at the Board of Education building—Brenda Lee, according to her name badge—didn't seem too concerned, though. She pulled a dog-eared beige ring binder from a nook near her right knee and started to leaf through its pages. "Why don't you gentlemen take a seat? I'll soon track him down, I'm sure. He is expecting you?"

"He certainly is." Devereaux leaned on the counter, which he thought looked more like a fireplace. It had a broad marble top in place of a mantel and a square-edged grooved pillar at each side. Behind it Brenda Lee keyed in another couple of numbers without getting an answer, then shot out a plump arm.

"Hey, there's Julie." She waved frantically. "Julie! Come here a minute!" Then she turned to Devereaux and Garretty and lowered her voice. "Julie works on Mr. Johnson's floor . . ."

A short woman in her forties with a neat plaid skirt and brown cardigan made her way over from the base of the stairs.

"Hey, Bren." Julie tried to surreptitiously check out the two visitors. "Do you need something?"

"Yeah. I'm trying to find Mr. Johnson. These gentlemen have an appointment with him but he's not answering his phone. You haven't seen him, have you?"

"Keith Johnson?" Julie looked surprised. "Sure I have. He left."

"Are you certain?" Devereaux shot a glance at Garretty.

"Absolutely. I saw him go."

"When was this?"

"Twenty minutes ago. Twenty-five, max. I heard him slam down the phone, and then he came racing out of his office looking like he'd seen a ghost. He took the back stairs. And he was running so fast I was half frightened he was going to fall. Probably heading for his car. He likes to park on that side of the site."

Devereaux and Garretty stepped away from the counter.

"And it looks like we have a winner." Devereaux reached for his phone. "We need his plates out over the air. And let's get a radio car to his address, just in case."

"That prick." Garretty scowled. "I really believed he was on the level. *I poured my life into those schools.* What an asshole."

"Excuse me, Detectives!" Brenda Lee was waving her arm again. "Look." She pointed to the corridor that ran down the side of the stairwell. Keith Johnson was standing there, bent almost double, his hands propped against his knees, his hair astray, and his glasses in danger of slipping off his nose.

Upstairs in his office Johnson retreated behind his desk and pulled a bottle of water out of a drawer. "Do either of you guys want one?"

Garretty shook his head. Devereaux took a moment to check his email. Nothing from Adama.

"OK, Keith." Devereaux waited until Johnson had sucked down half the bottle. "Want to tell us what that was all about?"

"Nothing." Johnson set the bottle on a round Birmingham in Bloom coaster on his desk and looked down at the floor. "And I'm here now. So shall we get started?"

"Skipping out on an appointment with two BPD detectives is not *nothing*, Keith. Do you realize how much heat you almost brought down on yourself?"

"I'm sorry." Johnson's face turned scarlet. "It's embarrassing. Look, I got pranked, OK? By my neighbor. We use the same housekeeping service. They come every Wednesday, and he called and told me that one of the women told him that there'd not been much to do in my house today—which is true, it was very tidy when I left for work this morning—so she'd taken my cavies outside to the back yard so the little guys could have a change of scene and somewhere new to explore. Can you imagine? Long-haired Peruvians? Guinea pigs? Outside? In this climate? They'd all be dead! It's crazy, but I was halfway to my house before I realized he was pulling my leg."

"He's a funny guy, your neighbor." Garretty leaned back until the front legs of his chair were off the ground.

"Maybe we should have his car taken to the pound?" Devereaux suggested. "See how amusing he finds that?"

"Oh." Johnson looked from one detective to the other, trying to figure out if Devereaux was serious. "I'm not sure we need to actually do anything . . ."

"It's your call. Think about it." Devereaux took out his notebook. "In the meantime, let's get back to business. The operation at Roundwood school, yesterday. I need to know who else you told. It's very important."

"I'm sure it is. You need to figure out if someone warned the arsonist, and that's why he attacked a different school. Believe me, guys. I want the asshole caught as much as you do. But I can't help you." Johnson spread his hands. "I didn't tell anyone. Not a word. Not a whisper. Nothing."

"Not your boss? An assistant? A heads-up to an onsite security guard?"

"No. No one. I guarantee."

"Let me tell you about a guy I knew once, Keith." Garretty straightened his chair and leaned forward. "His neighbor went on vacation and left him to watch her house. When she came back, she found the house had been burglarized. He swore to the local police that he hadn't told anyone it was vacant. But he hadn't mowed the grass in the yard. He hadn't emptied the mailbox every day. And he left a package on the stoop for a solid week after it was delivered. So while he technically hadn't told anyone, he'd kind of *told* a lot of people."

"Detective, I'm not stupid." A note of irritation had crept into Johnson's voice. "I see where you're going with that. And no. I didn't leave any trails of bread crumbs. And I didn't leave any dots to join. If the arsonist got his hands on inside information, it wasn't through me."

*

Devereaux nodded to Brenda Lee on the way back through reception, then turned to Garretty. Their conversion with Johnson had reminded him of a book he'd read as a kid about a guinea pig that dreamed of dancing the role of the Sugar Plum Fairy, but before he could mention it his phone buzzed. An email had arrived. From Adama.

It confirmed Joseph Oliver's new name: James Owen.

And it gave an address for him. In Miami.

Chapter Fifty-nine

Wednesday. Late morning.

ALEXANDRA WAS IN THE KITCHEN WHEN SHE HEARD THE BELL.

She dropped the box of chamomile tea bags she'd been struggling to open and ran to the door. Clawed it open. Saw the back of a man as he jumped into a white SUV. Raced down the path, trying to get a look at the plates. Failed, because the vehicle moved away so fast. And was left with a problem.

Lying on the mat, between her and the way back into her home, was another white envelope. It looked identical to the first one. Except for one thing. Even from twenty feet away, Alexandra could see it was thicker. Which meant it would contain more photographs. More appalling, grotesque images. She didn't want to sully her eyes by looking at them. Didn't want to be anywhere near them. Didn't even want to step over them, to get inside the house. But she couldn't leave the envelope lying there. Someone else could find it. Nicole could find it . . .

Alexandra hid the envelope behind her until she'd made sure Nicole was still playing in the back yard. Then she went upstairs and locked herself in the bathroom. She sat for a minute with the envelope on her lap. Told herself that really she had to open it. Not out of morbid curiosity. But because there could be more photos of Devereaux inside. Photos that could answer the questions that had been spinning in her head since he'd left, driving her to the verge of craziness.

She took another minute to summon the courage. Then she lifted the flap. Took out the contents. And studied every detail of every page.

Chapter Sixty

Wednesday. Late morning.

One of the receptionists at the *Tribune* remembered Devereaux and Garretty from the previous day. Diane had sent word that they were expected, so she was happy to escort them to the meeting room while her partner covered the desk.

The Goldfish Bowl was empty when they arrived but Devereaux spotted Diane at her desk at the far end of the office. She was hunched over her keyboard, so wrapped up in her work that she didn't even hear when the detectives approached. She was creating a Word document, and using a font that looked like an old typewriter's. Devereaux disliked the conceit of it, but was fascinated by how quickly her fingers moved. He found the rhythm almost mesmerizing as the vowels and consonants danced across the screen, banding effortlessly together into words. It was diverting to guess what they'd say before they were finished. Until he saw the final letters of his own name pop up at the end of a sentence.

Devereaux scanned up to the top of the screen. McKinzie was writing total gibberish. A ludicrous, childish story about how a daring young investigative reporter had played a key role in capturing a school arsonist—a character so cunning and elusive that the police could never have cracked the case on their own. He nudged Garretty and gestured toward the screen. Garretty started reading from the beginning, and snorted out loud when he read the description of the two dim-witted detectives. Diane heard him. She jumped, shrieked with surprise, and hit a couple of keys to switch the screen to a different document. Then she swiveled her chair around, leaned forward, held her head in her hands, and groaned.

"Oh my goodness." Her voice was ragged. "I'm so embarrassed. I can't believe you saw that. Please. Let me explain."

"We're all ears." Devereaux perched on the corner of the desk.

Garretty folded his arms. "Just don't use long words. Nothing too hard for us to understand."

Diane straightened up and fanned her face with her fingertips. "Time to get a grip, Diane. OK. First thing. Have you heard of Frederick McKinzie?"

"The name rings a bell," Devereaux said.

"Not for me," Garretty countered.

"Well, he was my father." Diane paused for a moment. "He was basically *Mr. Tribune* back in the day. Long story short, I wanted to be just like him. All I ever did as a kid was play newspapers. He'd help me. He taught me shorthand. Bought me my first typewriter. I still have it. I used to write stupid articles on it, about things I imagined my stuffed toys doing while I was at school. He loved them. Kept every one in a special binder. Called it *Diane's Daily Dispatch* and even designed a cute little masthead for it. Anyway, writing those stories for him is one of my fondest memories. It reminds me of when I thought anything was possible. Like having a career, instead of churning out crappy blog posts until they find someone cheaper to replace me with. So now, when I'm pissed off or stressed, I write a little story for my dad. Only he's dead now, of course, so I can't give it to him. But you get my point."

"I guess." Devereaux pushed himself away from the desk. "Whatever gets you through the day."

Diane checked over her shoulder as she stood up. The door to the Supervisor's Office was closed—almost all the way. Had Daniel been listening? Diane was embarrassed at the prospect, but only a little. Daniel had grown up the same way she had. He knew the deal. Everything would be fine as long as he didn't disrupt her meeting again. *Stay inside,* she thought. *Stay inside!* Then she took Devereaux's arm and ushered the detectives back toward the Goldfish Bowl.

*

Diane listened to Devereaux's questions and Garretty's allegory, and gave them an answer without hesitation.

"I told one person. Kelly Peterson. My editor. I cleared that with you beforehand, remember? And I did nothing that could have tipped anyone off. I don't even talk in my sleep. And anyway, if I did, there'd be no one there to hear me." Diane noticed that Devereaux wasn't wearing a ring.

"We're going to need your editor's contact details." Devereaux reached for his book.

"No need." Diane held up her hand. "She works right here, in the building. I'll take you to her office as soon as we're done."

"That's convenient, having her so close."

"Not all the time, believe me." Diane half smiled. "We'll head over there in a second. But before we wrap things up, you said on the phone you'd sniff out some details for me to use in my next piece on the fires?"

"Right." Devereaux scratched his chin. "I did say that. And I tried. I wracked my brain. There's not much you don't already know, is the problem. Though there is that one thing . . . No. It's probably no good. Leave it with me. I'll keep digging."

"What thing?"

The door opened and Daniel stepped into the room. "Mom, when are—"

"Can I help you with something?" Devereaux's glare was not remotely friendly.

"I'm talking to my mom. She needs to—"

"You can talk to her later. She's working right now. You need to respect that. Now get out, and don't interrupt her again."

Daniel attempted to lock eyes with Devereaux but gave up after six or seven seconds and slunk out of the room, not bothering to close the door.

"I'm so sorry!" Tiny red dots were spreading upward from Diane's neck. "He's not normally like that, but he's working on a major project right now for—"

"Don't worry about it." Devereaux got to his feet. "Shall we head for this Kelly's office?"

"Sure." Diane stood, after a moment. "In a second. You were telling me about a *thing*? To do with the fires?"

"Oh, that. It's probably nothing. And we're not even supposed to know about it. Remember that agent from the Bureau? Linda Irvin? She's decided to take their side of the investigation in a different direction. Appeal directly to the public. Launch some kind of help line. I think it's a mistake, personally. And not very useful for you, probably?"

"No, no, I could definitely do something with it." *Agency Rift Threatens School Safety? Investigation Hits the Skids? Desperate G-Men in Public Plea for Help?* Diane's reporter's brain was spinning. "When's it going live? Have they got a phone number set up? What about email? A website? Social media tie-ins? What hashtag are they using?"

"Good questions." Devereaux shrugged. "I guess I could find out. If you promise to keep my name out of it."

Chapter Sixty-one

Wednesday. Late morning.

IT DIDN'T MATTER WHAT MR. QUINLAN SAID. HE COULD BE OUTSIDE THE front door with a sledgehammer and a megaphone and it wouldn't change a thing. A whole army of bosses could be lining up out there. Tyler Shaw wasn't moving. He just didn't have it in him.

Shaw's body may have been stranded in his bed, but his mind was elsewhere. It was floating between Charlotte and Roanoke. Cincinnati and Toledo. Des Moines and Omaha. Rapid City and Denver. Salt Lake City and Bakersfield. Tucson and El Paso. San Antonio and Baton Rouge. All the places he'd been to in the years after his mother died. After he could no longer bear the loneliness in her quiet, empty house. While he traipsed around the country, desperate to latch onto a relative. To make a friend. To find a lover. To somehow connect with someone. Anyone!

It had all been in vain, though. He should never have left Birmingham. Because the story was the same wherever he went. Whenever he found someone—as soon as he started getting close—they left him. They walked out. Changed the locks. Moved away. Got a restraining order. Died. One way or another, he always ended up alone.

There are billions upon billions of people in this world, he thought. What did he have to do to make just one person stay with him? Of their own free will?

Chapter Sixty-two

Wednesday. Early afternoon.

DIANE McKINZIE TOOK DEVEREAUX'S ARM AND STOPPED HIM ABOUT ten yards short of Kelly Peterson's office door.

"You guys won't want me in there with you, I guess, so I'll get out of your hair. There is just one other thing, though, before I go. A favor I need to ask."

Here it comes, thought Devereaux. "Your traffic ticket?"

"What? No. It's about Kelly. When you're talking to her it would really, really help me if you didn't tell her about Daniel coming into our meetings those two times. She heard him saying some stuff the other day that she took all out of context, and I think I've got her back on my side again but I wouldn't want there to be any new misunderstandings. She's great, Kelly, but she can jump to conclusions sometimes. Be a little judgmental. Especially where other people's kids are involved. She doesn't have any of her own, you see, so she doesn't quite get it."

"No problem. We won't bring him up, and it'll be *Daniel who?* if she asks us anything. And I'm sorry that *I* jumped to a conclusion there. Usually the first thing people ask for help with is their traffic tickets."

"That's not a bad idea. Luckily I haven't had any lately, but I'm going to keep your number, just in case."

"What about last night? I heard you picked one up then."

"Really? I did? I didn't even realize. It must have been one of those automatic cameras. I guess I'll be seeing it in the mail pretty soon, then."

"I thought you stayed in last night? That's why you passed on the stakeout?"

I thought I did, too, Diane thought. *What's happening to my memory? Maybe I should back off the pills a little . . .* "Yeah, well, I basically did. I just had a quick errand to run. Not worth mentioning, really."

"I hear you have a cool car, if that's any consolation?"

"Really? My Mini's nice enough, I guess. It's no Porsche, though." Diane gave Devereaux's arm a playful punch. "That's right, Detective. I keep my ear to the ground, too . . ."

Kelly Peterson kept two desks in her office. One was a standard size, and had a computer, a telephone, and a couple of reference books on it. The other was larger, and was covered with neatly organized stacks of paper, each one weighed down with a different large, metal initial. Three of her walls were plain, but the one facing the desks was hung with six large wooden trays. Each one was broken into thirty-odd unevenly-sized sections, and many of the divisions between them were partly worn away and stained a deep black. More metal initials were distributed throughout the compartments—these standing upright— and Devereaux realized that they spelled out a name. Ezekiel Peterson.

"They're typesetters' trays." Peterson noticed Devereaux staring at them as he took the visitor's chair next to Garretty's. "They were my grandfather's."

"Interesting." Devereaux turned and took a second look. "Is he the reason you got into newspapers?"

"No." Peterson sat behind her computer desk. "That's a coincidence. But he is the reason I can read upside down and backwards, so you might want to take care if you write anything down today."

"Thanks for the warning." Devereaux took his notebook out, anyway. "But if I do write anything, it'll just be a name. Or names, maybe. What we're doing is pretty simple. The piece that you guys posted for us was supposed to lead the arsonist who's out there into attacking Roundwood school last night. Instead, he attacked Green Acres. We need to find out if that's because he got wind of the trap. We're not for one minute suggesting any kind of wrongdoing here. But if you mentioned the real purpose of our article to anyone, for any reason—management reports, accounting for use of web space, anything like that—we need you to tell us."

"I understand. It's a logical question. And the answer's no. I didn't mention it to anyone, because I didn't have to. I didn't need anyone else's authority to run the story, and Diane McKinzie told me that you guys had stressed the need for secrecy—which was pretty obvious, really—so I made a point of not making any notes or records that could give it away."

"That's excellent." Devereaux closed his notebook. "Thanks for being so cooperative. And thanks for laying off the speculation angle, too, linking the article and the choice of target. That would have been embarrassing. And the negative publicity could have put people off coming forward with information, hurting the investigation. We appreciate it."

"No problem. We're obliged to report the facts, but we don't want to see other schools going up in flames any more than you do. I can't guarantee that angle'll stay off the front page for long, though. We've already had one letter complaining about our failure to highlight the connection."

"That was quick." Garretty raised his eyebrows. "The fire only happened last night. Your coverage was this morning. Was it an email, this complaint?"

"No. It was an actual letter." Peterson rolled her chair across to her other desk, took a piece of paper from the top of one of the piles, and passed it to Garretty. "You don't see these very often anymore."

Ms. K. Peterson.
Birmingham Tribune.

Dear Ms. Peterson,
I am writing to express my disgust at your newspaper's shoddy
and incompetent coverage of the fire at Green Acres school.
Your inept reporter described the event as if its location had
been chosen at random, and completely failed to note the connection with the article you published the previous day, which
was nothing more than a crude and thinly-veiled attempt, presumably by the FBI, to lure the genius who has been orchestrat-
ing this extraordinary campaign into a trap. Please correct
this misconception immediately. The public of our great city
deserve better!

Sincerely,
J.R.O.

Garretty read the letter, holding it gingerly by the edges, then passed it to Devereaux.

" 'J.R.O.'?" Devereaux looked at the others.

"Means nothing to me," Peterson said.

"I'll check with Intell." Garretty scribbled a quick note. "Have them run it against known aliases."

"The letter itself. It must have been hand-delivered, given the time-scale." Devereaux looked around for a trash can. "Do you still have the envelope?"

"My assistant opens the mail." Peterson picked up her phone, asked for the envelope to be brought in, then listened for a few seconds. "Very weird. Apparently Sarah didn't open it. She found it in her in-tray. She brought it in with the rest of the mail, figuring it had gotten opened somewhere else by mistake, but none of the other assistants she's spoken to since then know anything about it."

"You know, Ms. Peterson, don't waste too much time on it." Devereaux suppressed a smile. "We'll just take the letter, if you don't mind, and have our lab check for prints and so on. I'm sure that'll be enough."

*

"What were you smirking about in there?" Garretty pulled Devereaux aside as soon as they reached the corridor leading back to reception. "And why didn't you press harder for the envelope?"

"Because there is no envelope, Tommy. And I know who sent the letter."

"You do? Who?"

"Diane McKinzie. It's brilliant, actually. You heard her bullshit. *You better give me the inside track so I can stop the public seeing the link to your article.* This is her insurance. If we don't play ball, she'll say *Oh dear, Detectives. Look. Some bright spark's figured it out. Now you* really *better give me some juicy info so I can stop it happening again!* You can't blame her for trying. She thinks she's fighting for her job."

"I guess. The typeface is like the one she had for that crazy story she was writing for her dead dad. And that was totally over-the-top, too. *The genius,* my ass!"

WITH TWO LIFELINES GONE, IS IT REALLY
TIME TO PHONE A FRIEND?

We all know about the Japanese Kamikaze pilots in World War II. The plane crash survivors who ate the corpses of the dead passengers in the Andes Mountains. The rafts full of refugees crossing the ocean from Cuba. And now we have the Birmingham Police Department tip line!

Attempting to enlist the public's help to catch the genius only shows the depths to which the authorities have sunk--and how high their level of desperation has risen! It also reveals their stupidity. The genius will simply use it against them. To inside information will be added: mis-information!

As a strategy, it's doomed to fail from the outset. Ask yourself this: How many morons does it take to outweigh one genius? No one knows for sure. But this reporter would happily wager that it's more than there are in the whole of the United States!

Chapter Sixty-three

Wednesday. Early afternoon.

Devereaux called Irvin from the car.

"McKinzie went for it." He eased up the ramp onto I-20/59, then hit the gas and smiled at Garretty's terrified expression as the car surged forward like a plane tearing down a runway. "She's going to run the help-line story. Shoot me over the details as soon as you have them, and I'll pass them on."

"Thanks, Cooper. They'll be with you inside the hour."

"No problem. But while I've got you, help me settle a bet with Tommy. Is this thing for real? Or were you just pushing Emrich's buttons?"

"Which horse did you back?"

"Let's just say I'm hoping there was more mischief in your mind than method."

"You would, though, wouldn't you, Cooper? I'm sorry. Tommy wins."

"The guy's really going to call?" Devereaux worked his way around the slower cars on the intersection with Stevens. "You're confident?"

"No. Not confident at all. And seriously? It depends on why the guy's setting the fires. If it's revenge, then no. He probably won't call. On the other hand, if he has messed-up wiring in his head, it's very likely he will. He'll probably call multiple times. The whole payoff for him will be seeing the impact he's having. Making the Bureau, the police department, Fire and Rescue, all of us dance to his tune. He'll constantly dig for details, to keep refreshing the picture in his head. He'll offer to help. He'll try anything to worm into the investigation. But however friendly he may seem, that'll be a false impression. It'll just be a way to get a seat closer to the stage."

"I see." Devereaux left Stevens at Rosedale. "OK. Well, if anyone puts himself in the frame, let us know. We'll look at him real hard."

The phone rang again just as Devereaux was rolling to a stop at the side of the street. He was tempted to let voicemail take care of it, thinking it might be Lambert calling for the nine-hundredth time, but changed his mind when he saw it was the Porsche dealer's number.

"Mr. Devereaux? Great. We have good news for you. Your 911's ready. You can pick her up anytime. How does later this afternoon work for you?"

"It doesn't work at all." Devereaux was torn. He really wanted that car back . . . "I'm right in the middle of something, and I don't have time to come over there."

"No problem, then. We can bring her to you."

"I don't have time to get home, either."

"Oh. Well, would there be someone we could leave the keys with?"

There is a doorman at the City Federal, 24/7, but leaving the keys wasn't the answer, Devereaux thought. He wanted to inspect the car. To make sure it was perfect. To check that the new speaker was balanced properly, and the whole audio system wasn't out of whack. He was about to decline when a couple of women walked by. They were in their mid-twenties, maybe. All blond hair. Crop-tops. Daisy Dukes. Tall sandals. Oversized sunglasses. And Devereaux caught the nudges and giggles that passed between them as they looked down at him and Garretty—two *dudes* wedged into a flashy Ferrari.

"Actually, yes there is. But what about the loaner? I can't get that back to you today."

"Give me one second, sir . . ." Computer keys rattled at the other end of the line. "Actually, that won't be a problem, either. No one needs it until Friday. We could send someone over for it first thing to-morrow?"

"OK. That sounds good. Let's do it."

Devereaux left Garretty in the car and crossed the street to the last in the line of hundred-year-old mansions that crested the hill. The first floor of the house had been converted to a restaurant, and two min-utes later Devereaux was standing at the upstairs window of what had been its master bedroom. To the left he watched the old parking valet harassing Garretty about leaving the car on his turf, as he'd known would happen. To the right, he could see all the way past Railroad Park as far as downtown.

"I love how we don't have a river." Devereaux turned and sank into the battered leather armchair. "You ever notice that? Most cities have a river running through the center. Not us. We have railroads."

"*Had* railroads." Tom Vernon was sprawled in the other chair, his feet—in new Versace loafers—resting on the wooden steamer trunk he used as a coffee table. "Though I'm guessing you didn't come here to talk geography."

Devereaux's relationship with Vernon spanned more than three de-cades, and had seen its share of highs and lows. They'd fought like cats and dogs when they first met, in seventh grade. They'd been the best of friends, as Vernon helped Devereaux find food and shelter dur-ing the darkest days of his foster care. They'd had each other's backs after graduation, as they landed up in the outer reaches of Birming-ham's underworld. They fell out spectacularly following Devereaux's about-face in joining the Police Academy. Ignored each other for years after that. And had only been back on the upswing for three months or so, after Devereaux had reached out for help in a recent case.

"No, it wasn't geography that brought me here." Devereaux took a sip of the Woodford Reserve that Vernon had poured for him when he arrived. "I came because I need a favor."

"Name it."

"I've got the name and address of someone in Florida. I need pictures, to make sure I'm dealing with the right guy before I head down there to see him."

"You can't go through police channels?"

"If I did that, the guy would end up in the system."

"And you prefer he ends up . . . somewhere else?"

"Maybe. Depends what he says when I talk to him."

Chapter Sixty-four

Wednesday. Afternoon.

THE MAN DIDN'T RUN AWAY THIS TIME.

Alexandra could see his silhouette through the frosted glass panel in her front door. He'd rung the bell and now was just standing there, waiting for her. She didn't know what to do. This wasn't like when she ran out of the house to chase him, and the adrenaline rush gave her courage. Now she felt like prey. And she was cornered. Should she call 911? Or Devereaux? Or hide? Suddenly she wished she had a gun . . .

The guy rang again, then rapped on the glass with his signet ring. "Mrs. Devereaux? Are you home?"

Mrs. Devereaux? What the . . .

Alexandra stormed down the hallway and yanked open the door. "It's *Ms. Cunningham*. How can I help you?"

"I just need your signature, miss." The guy stepped to the side and gestured toward the covered-in delivery truck at the side of the street, with a giant Porsche logo on its side. "Then I can let you get on with your day."

Alexandra figured she shouldn't leave the car at the side of the street. What if something happened to it before Devereaux had even seen it again? He'd go crazy. She wasn't ready to get into a whole conversation with him about it, either. There were far more important things for them to talk about, and she still needed time to digest all the details. She didn't need any stupid distractions. The best thing would be to put the Porsche in the garage. Leave Devereaux a note. Then get out of the house until he'd been and gone again.

This was another benefit of homeschooling, she thought. The rest of the afternoon's lessons could easily be switched to the Birmingham History Center . . .

Chapter Sixty-five

Wednesday. Afternoon.

"WHAT HAPPENED BACK THERE? SOMETHING BAD?"

Garretty was concerned. Devereaux hadn't said a word since he'd emerged from Vernon's restaurant, and in the five minutes since pulling away from the curb he hadn't shifted higher than second gear. He was driving so slowly that they'd just been overtaken by a hippie camper van . . .

"Nothing happened." Devereaux put his phone on speaker and hit the Play button. "Just listen to this voicemail. It came while I was in there."

"Oh, hi, Detective Devereaux. It's Diane McKinzie. I'm just calling to see if you had those details we were talking about? I'm definitely going to run with that idea. It'll be a really interesting piece, and I think it could be a major help to the investigation, too. I'd love to maybe get some feedback on how effective it is? Maybe run some follow-ups, if that works for you? And also, about the schools. Have you got anything else for me on those? Because here's what I'm thinking. We haven't really tapped into the human interest angle yet. How people have been affected. You know, the teachers whose workplaces have been destroyed. The kids. The firefighters who—"

"She goes on and on." Devereaux silenced the phone. "And she keeps calling me with more and more questions."

"So?"

"You heard Irvin. She said to watch out for someone who's trying to worm into the investigation."

"McKinzie's not worming in. She's a journalist. They ask questions in their sleep. I knew this guy once, who—"

"It's not just the questions. What about the ride-along I offered her? Most reporters would kill for a chance like that, and she turned it down. Then lied about where she was and what she was doing."

"We don't know that. The thing about the errand might be true. And if not, she might have a good reason for lying. Maybe she had an appointment at the hospital that she wanted to keep quiet. I don't know. Maybe she's sleeping with someone's husband."

"And the traffic ticket? That didn't ring true, either. You know if you've run a red light. Specially at night. You think, maybe you can make it. You hit the gas. And flash! Flash! Two of them, like bolts of lightning with a huge fine attached. There's no way you can miss it. You know you're screwed, right away."

"I guess. OK. Hold on. Let me check something." Garretty called Irvin and talked for a couple of minutes. He was frowning when he hung up. "OK. The light McKinzie ran? It's on the route Google Maps gives from Green Acres school to her house in Vestavia Hills. She got the ticket about ten minutes after Chief Young estimates the fire took hold. And get this. She wasn't driving her Mini, like she implied when we spoke to her at the newspaper office. She was in another car that's registered to her. Some ancient Volvo."

Devereaux slammed his hand against the steering wheel. *He really wanted to go home and get his Porsche back!* "Screw it. Vestavia Hills, then. You got her address?"

"Yeah, but it won't help. No judge is going to sign a warrant because of a suspect being extra helpful."

Devereaux looked across at Garretty for a moment, winked, then hit the gas. He figured he might as well stretch the Ferrari's legs one last time . . .

Chapter Sixty-six

Wednesday. Afternoon.

IT WAS TIME FOR THE WALLOWING IN SELF-PITY TO STOP.

That might have been OK in the old days, but it wasn't why Tyler Shaw had come back to Birmingham. He'd come back to make some serious changes. To stop drinking. To pull himself together. To not just stay on the same path—to move up to a whole other level.

And he was well on his way.

Two down . . .

Shaw threw the stained comforter onto the floor and stood up. He pulled back the curtains covering the alcove at the foot of his bed and gazed at his icons. They were good. They were helpful. But they weren't enough. They were yesterday. He needed to focus on tomorrow. On the achievements that were yet to come. The two targets he still had to hit. Which included an athlete of some kind. That was going to be a real challenge. Maybe he should get that one out of the way tonight? Do that, and it would be plain sailing from there on in.

Chapter Sixty-seven

Wednesday. Late afternoon.

DIANE MCKINZIE LIVED HALFWAY DOWN ONE OF THE CUL-DE-SACS THAT were laid out along the sharp, pointy reaches of Lunker Lake—a dragon's claw of still green water between I-459 and Lake Purdy. Her house had a roof made of crazy tessellated shapes like most of the properties in the area, but otherwise was a fairly standard brick box. It had a dark brown door in the center. A bulky garage protruding to the left. A bay-windowed lounge not quite balancing it out to the right. And it was separated from the street by a half-dead lawn with a withered stalk of a cherry tree trying to survive in a dried-out pocket of earth in its center.

There was no response to the bell, and the garage and front doors were both locked, so Devereaux made his way around to the back. He checked off each room in turn, making sure it wasn't occupied. The lounge. The study. The kitchen. The utility. All the way along until he reached the shallow rear window of the garage. Then he took out his flashlight and peered through the film of dust that covered the surface. He caught sight of white metal. It was the side of a car. Something sleek and low. Discouraged, he angled the beam around until he could see the hood. He focused on the front, where the badge was attached. It was a circle with an arrow pointing to the top right of a triangle that ran around the outside. And there was a surprising word emblazoned across its center.

Volvo.

Devereaux removed the laces from his shoes, tied them together, and formed a loop at one end. He took out the switchblade he always carried and pried open the thin rectangular vent that ran along the top of the window, just above its hinges. He enlarged it slightly. Then he used the tip of the knife to poke the lace through the space he'd made and lower it down the inside of the glass until the loop slipped over the handle at the bottom left of the frame. He pulled up, releasing the catch. He repeated the process for the handle at the right side. Then eased the window open wide enough to climb through.

Devereaux was floored by the car. It was gorgeous. When he'd heard the words *ancient Volvo* he expected some ratty, hipster-friendly abomination on wheels, but this was something he'd gladly drive. And it was in great shape for its age. The paintwork was flawless, and the interior—though basic, by current standards—was impeccable. He tried the driver's door, eager to slide in behind the wheel, but it was locked. Disappointed, he turned his attention to the rest of the garage. He started at the front and worked his way systematically back again, opening trunks and suitcases, and lifting boxes and packages down from shelves. He found men's clothes. Yard toys. A broken golf club. A wedding dress. An easel. Cans of paint. Hand tools. Fluid for lighting an outdoor grill. Cracked glass flasks from a kid's chemistry set. A pair of Buzz Lightyear drapes. Six empty plastic ten-gallon containers. A ladder. Boxes for six plastic gerbil houses, which looked like miniature space stations, with electronic timers to control access to the different sections. A wooden sled. A drum of benzene. A broken ironing board. A section of rubber hosepipe, balancing on pegs on the wall and stinking of gasoline. And a giant box of Styrofoam packing peanuts. Devereaux was still raking through it with a broom handle to see if anything was concealed inside when his phone buzzed.

It was a text from Garretty, who was watching the mouth of the cul-de-sac:

She's coming. You've got 30 seconds max

Chapter Sixty-eight

Wednesday. Early evening.

BLIND FAITH.

There were times when that was pretty much all Diane McKinzie had going for her. Her father had died. Her husband had left. Her job was going sideways. And her son was—Daniel. She had to find *something* to pull her through. So blind faith it was. Blind faith and vodka. And pills.

Now she had Kraft mac 'n' cheese as well. And strange as it sounds, that was better. Because for the second night running, Daniel was cooking for her. He'd insisted on it, despite Diane's offer to order take-out. He said he wanted to cook. And eat together. And sit and talk after the meal, rather than rush off to his room on his own. He wanted to hear about her day. How her important series was going, about the school fires. What it was like to work with those cops, and that FBI agent. How what she did could actually help them solve crimes.

She'd come a long way, she thought. Thanks to blind faith. It would be best not to turn her back on it just yet, though. Who knew what was lurking around the corner? But maybe she could ditch the vodka and the pills. And after last night's experience, cutting back on the wine with dinner might not be a bad idea, as well . . .

Chapter Sixty-nine

Wednesday. Early evening.

DEVEREAUX WAS ON A HIGH AFTER HIS DISCOVERY IN MCKINZIE'S GA-
rage. The buzz had continued through the conversation with Lieutenant Hale, when she signed off on round-the-clock surveillance. He'd
felt good while they waited for Levi and Colton to show up and take
the first shift. He was still smiling on the drive to headquarters, to
drop Garretty off. His mood was sunny all the way to the City Federal
Building. And then the moment he reached the bottom of the garage
ramp, the bubble burst. Because his second parking space was empty.
His Porsche wasn't there. And it was supposed to be.

The doorman swore blind that he hadn't left his post, even for a
second, so Devereaux called the dealer and demanded answers.

"I don't understand, either, Mr. Devereaux. I'm sure it was delivered this afternoon. Let me just check the paperwork. Yes, I've got it
now. Here we go. Model: 911. Color: sapphire blue. License plate:
DVRX. Delivered to: home. Signed for by . . . Looks like *A. Corin-
thian*? *Callaghan*?"

"*Cunningham*. It says *Cunningham*. And don't worry about it. The
car's not lost. I know what's happened."

Devereaux covered the five and a half miles to Homewood in a virtual
daze. How could this be? He'd woken up many times over the years
not knowing where *he* was. But that was because he'd been somewhere

strange. Somewhere new. It wasn't because he'd not known where *home* was.

The driveway was empty when Devereaux arrived at Alexandra's so he let himself in, checked the kitchen table, and found her note saying she'd left the Porsche in the garage. He was disappointed she wasn't there. He wanted to see her. To explain. To throw out a rope and pull her back to the shore. But at the same time, he was relieved she was gone. What he had to convey, he wasn't sure he had the words for. He couldn't stand the thought of screwing it up and losing her again. And it tormented him to think that with every hour he delayed, the ill tide was probably carrying her farther from his reach.

The only ray of sunshine was that at least he had his Porsche back. He smiled when he saw it sitting in the garage, gleaming, the perfect embodiment of understated power and elegant precision. He unlocked the door and slid halfway onto the driver's seat, savoring the aroma of soft leather like a cigar aficionado taking his first puff of the evening. He went to move the seat back and make room for his legs under the wheel. But he stopped before his finger touched the button. He climbed back out. Grabbed his phone. And called Lieutenant Hale.

"Lieutenant? Big problem. We're watching the wrong person."

THE FINAL CURTAIN?

Plans were made. Tests were carried out. Concepts were proven. Obstacles were overcome. On top of all that, the authorities were outwitted at every turn. And now the conclusion of the genius's mission is mere minutes away . . .

Success is inevitable, such is the peak of the genius's power. So what will come next? The miserable excuse for the city's education system will have been taught its lesson, so maybe it's time to take inspiration from the disrespectful, interfering Birmingham Police Department and their imbecilic cronies in the FBI?

In other words, maybe it's time to find out: Do police stations burn as brightly as schools?

Chapter Seventy

Wednesday. Early evening.

"HE'S GONE, BUT SHE'S STILL IN THE HOUSE." COLTON LOOKED UP AT Devereaux and Hale from the window of his Charger, a mixture of worry and anger creasing his face. "The mom's definitely in there. She's the one we were told to watch. Not the kid. How were we supposed to know you'd change your mind?"

Hale pulled Devereaux to one side. "You're sure, Cooper? Because of the position of the driving seat?"

"I had a real good look when I was in the garage. The seat was all the way back. I could have gotten straight in. No way could someone McKinzie's size have driven like that. It had to be someone taller. Plus Colton and Levi just saw Daniel drive off in that Volvo. He doesn't even have a learner's permit."

"He could be sneaking off to his girlfriend's. Diane could know about it, and be covering for him."

"True. But that kid? A girlfriend? And what about the benzene and the Styrofoam in the garage. A coincidence?"

Garretty arrived while Hale was thinking it through.

"All right, then." Hale squeezed Devereaux's shoulder. "We'll get the Volvo's plates out over the air. You go to the house. See what's happening."

*

Diane was lying on the couch in the living room, covered with a blanket. She wasn't moving, and a wine bottle lay tipped over on the floor near her outstretched arm.

"Maybe she's a functioning alcoholic?" Garretty banged on the window. "Maybe she's like this every night?"

"I don't think so." Devereaux also pounded on the glass. Diane still didn't respond, so he returned to the front door and drove his foot into the wood just below the lock. The frame shattered. Wooden splinters showered into the hallway. A six-foot length of architrave caught one of the framed newspaper articles, knocking it to the floor and smashing its glass. Devereaux kicked the debris aside and ran to the living room, with Garretty hard on his heels.

Diane flailed her arms, moaning and trying to push Devereaux away until she managed to unglue her eyes and finally focus on his face.

"Detective?" Her tongue seemed to be too big for her mouth, and her speech was slurred and indistinct. "What are you doing here? Wait. Where are we?"

"Diane—we need to know where Daniel is." Devereaux spoke slowly, but there was an urgent edge to his words. "It's very important. Where did he go?"

"Daniel's my son." Diane smiled crookedly. "He's a good boy. A lot of stress. If he said anything, it's just—"

"We need to find him, Diane. You need to help us. He's in danger. He's going to get hurt if you don't tell us where he went."

"He cooked dinner. We're going to talk. So tired . . ."

"He's gone somewhere in your car. Your Volvo. The one that was in your garage. You need to tell us where he went."

"The Volvo's Dad's." Diane shook her head. "Daniel can't drive."

"He's gone to a school, hasn't he, Diane?"

Diane tried to slump back down onto the couch, but Devereaux held her upright.

"You know it's Daniel who's been setting these fires, don't you, Diane? Somewhere deep inside. That's why you keep asking all your questions. To see if we're close to catching him."

"Daniel's my son. He hasn't done anything wrong. Leave him alone."

"Hey. What's this?" Something had caught Garretty's eye. It was the corner of a scuffed gray ring binder, peeping out from under the couch near the abandoned wine bottle. He reached down and fished it out. There was a hand-drawn shield on the front cover flanked by a lion and unicorn, and below those were the words *Daniel's Daily Dispatch* picked out in extravagant gothic script. Garretty opened the folder and started to leaf through its pages. "This is weird. It's full of stories, like pretend newspaper articles. Looks like they're written by a kid. They all talk about the same person. Some *genius*. How he's going to be the youngest person to ever be the president of Harvard. The first—"

"That's mine!" Diane broke away from Devereaux and snatched the folder from Garretty, sending a shower of more recent, loose pages fluttering across the room. "They're only stories. They don't mean anything."

"Put that down, Diane." Devereaux took her arm, eased the folder from her grip and let it drop onto the couch. "There's no time. Come with us. There's something we need to show you."

Devereaux opened the garage door and left Garretty to prop Diane upright. Then he moved to the middle of the empty space and held out his arms. "You see? The Volvo's not here. Daniel's taken it."

He grabbed the section of hose from its pegs on the wall and held it under Diane's nose, making her retch. "Can you smell that? It's gasoline. Daniel syphoned it out of the Volvo's tank."

He moved to the far corner and grabbed a handful of packing peanuts. "He took a bunch of these, too. And he added benzene, from that can over there. Which makes a kind of bomb, Diane. Think about that."

Garretty tightened his grip on Diane's arms. "Daniel's got that bomb with him, right now, in the car. And every police officer in the city's out looking for him. When they see him, they'll open fire. The car will explode, Diane. Daniel will be blown to pieces."

Diane writhed and twisted, desperate to break free, shrieking and sobbing like a tormented dervish.

"There won't even be enough of your son left for you to bury, Diane." Devereaux moved in close and grabbed her jaw, forcing her to keep her head still and look at him. "Not unless you tell us where he's going. Then we can stop him. Keep him safe. So you can see him again. But you have to tell us which school, right now. Every second you waste is a second closer to a bullet setting off that bomb."

"Wylam!" Diane stopped struggling and slumped against Garretty. "Wylam Elementary School. That's where he'll be."

FIELD REPORT

The fires are easy to start now that the genius has perfected the gadget, though there is one aspect that is slightly less than optimal. The proximity required to carry out the ignition sequence often affords the genius a poor overall vantage point. That makes it hard to watch the puppets dance, which in turn reduces his satisfaction. A new system should be introduced for the next phase of the mission.

Some form of remote ignition device would seem to be the answer, or possibly a timing mechanism. At the time of writing, the genius isn't yet sure. But have no fear! Further rounds of development and testing, in tandem with his outstanding brilliance, will undoubtedly yield the necessary breakthrough.

If this first magnificent phase has taught us anything, it's that the genius always delivers!

Chapter Seventy-one

Wednesday. Early evening.

HALE AND GARRETTY STOOD IN THE PARKING LOT BEHIND A CROOKED line of BPD sawhorses. There was a kids' play area at the top of the grassy mound to their left, with a pair of giant blue umbrella-shaped structures shielding the climbing frames from the setting sun. And ahead, across a narrow service road, was Wylam school, its brick walls almost hidden behind three enormous weeping willows. It looked like it should be some kind of tranquil boathouse on a wide, lazy river, Hale thought. A place for fun and relaxation. Or for learning and study. Not somewhere to be assaulted by pairs of cops with Colt M4s, wearing black helmets and body armor.

People from the long, low rows of houses in the nearby streets had been alerted by the sirens and were now gathering and starting to press up against the barriers opposite the school's main entrance. Others joined them as they arrived home from work. A dozen uniformed cops were in place, holding them back. Hale had one eye on the crowd and one on the sky above the roof of the school. She was concerned that an idiot would squeeze through the cordon and get himself shot. And she was terrified that she'd see fingers of black smoke start to reach up from the structure and soil the cloudless sky. She prayed the SWAT guys could wrap things up fast, before either of those things happened. And preferably without any harm coming to this boy, Daniel McKinzie.

The hands on the giant clock on the wall facing the playground had crept forward by twenty-two minutes when the SWAT commander finally approached Lieutenant Hale, his helmet in his hands.

"Is it over?" Hale stepped toward him.

The commander shook his head. "We swept the entire building. There wasn't a soul to be found. It was a false alarm, Lieutenant. Daniel McKinzie isn't here."

Chapter Seventy-two

Wednesday. Early evening.

DEVEREAUX HADN'T GONE WITH THE OTHERS TO WYLAM SCHOOL. Instead, he'd helped Diane McKinzie back inside and got her settled on
the couch. Then he'd slipped around to the back of the house and
found a spot in the shadows with a view through the rear windows.

Ten minutes crawled past, then Devereaux saw Diane begin to stir.
She started to struggle with her blanket and kept pawing at it until she
uncovered her phone. She poked clumsily at its screen, and finally
managed to place a call. She held the phone to her ear, but didn't
speak. She hung up. Tried again. And again, six, seven, eight times.
Then she flung the phone across the room and staggered out into the
hallway.

Diane reappeared in the kitchen. She took a tall beer glass from a
wall cupboard and dumped six tablespoons of salt into it. She filled it
with hot water from the faucet. Swilled the mixture around. Held her
nose, and forced herself to drink every drop. She stood for a moment,
swaying slightly, one hand over her mouth. Then she doubled over and
vomited into the sink, the long, hard convulsions wracking her entire
body.

Tears were streaming down Diane's face as she opened a drawer
and took out a handful of shiny purple pods. She fed one into her coffee machine, hit a button, and downed the espresso shot it produced in
one mouthful. She followed it with three more. Then splashed cold

water on her face, turned, fished her keys out of a wooden bowl on the countertop, and started to make for the hallway.

Devereaux reached the ruined front door just as Diane was shuffling out through the wreckage.

"Oh, Diane, I'm so, so sorry." Devereaux took Diane's hand and led her back inside. "At least I found you, so I can give you the news right away. This really is the worst part of my job. I just hate it. If only you'd not lied to us about which school Daniel was heading for . . ."

"I didn't lie. I mean, wait!" Diane suddenly shifted more of her weight onto Devereaux's arm. "What news? What do you mean? What's happened?"

"It's like I told you. The traffic cops were all looking for Daniel. You said he was going to Wylam school, so we cleared the patrols away from there. But he wasn't going to Wylam, was he, Diane? If only we'd known . . ."

"What happened to my son? Is he safe? I didn't know! I thought he was going to Wylam, when I told you that. It was only after you'd gone it hit me—maybe I remembered it wrong? It's all been so confusing. If only they hadn't stopped Daniel getting into Ramsay! Or Carver. No wonder he was mad at them. How can he climb to the top if he's trapped at the wrong school? He's a genius, my son. He's—"

"Who stopped him, Diane? Who's he mad at?"

"It's not his fault. It's the system. It's not fair. Kids at other schools, they get priority, if they're from certain neighborhoods. That's why Daniel didn't get in. If they'd only spoken with him. Seen his work. The projects he's been working on—"

"Schools like Jones Valley?"

"Right. The kid who got into Ramsay from there isn't anything special. She's not even half as smart as my Daniel. She totally didn't deserve to get that spot."

"And Inglenook?"

"Right. That boy was a hooligan. Not as bad as the one from Green Acres, though. He's nothing but pond scum."

"But the other kid was different, right? Super bright, from what I heard. Maybe the brightest kid in the state."

"The girl from Putman? Are you kidding me? They basically took pity on—"

"Stay here, Diane." Devereaux grabbed her car keys and shoved her back toward the living room door. "I'll be back with more news for you very soon."

Chapter Seventy-three

Wednesday. Evening.

DEVEREAUX WEAVED THROUGH THE RESIDENTIAL STREETS OF VESTAVIA Hills and then made a left onto Lake Parkway, figuring he could more than offset an extra couple of miles on the way to Putman school by sticking to the fastest roads. He called Dispatch to request backup units and a fire truck, pulled around a dawdling furniture delivery van, then left a voicemail for Lieutenant Hale.

The replica of the Statue of Liberty filled Devereaux's rearview mirror as he was about to cross the Cahaba River, parallel with I-459. She was high up on her stone pedestal, looming a ghostly green against the rapidly darkening sky. Devereaux noticed that the flame in her torch had already been lit. That didn't usually happen until later in the evening, he thought. And it didn't strike him as a good omen, given the circumstances.

Devereaux passed the giant sign for Hamburger Heaven then zig-zagged through the intersection from Crestwood onto Montclair before both roads dived beneath I-20. Putman school came up on the left after another third of a mile. Devereaux followed its narrow driveway through the tall, lopsided pine trees that screened the main building from the street. The neat rectangular structure was made of brick. It was two storeys high, with wide, white-framed windows and five glass pyramids evenly spaced along its roof to bring extra light to the second-floor classrooms.

There was no sign of smoke or flames, and all the parking spaces that were randomly dotted around between the trees were empty. Devereaux felt a stirring of doubt. Could Diane McKinzie have misled him again? She'd seemed sincere when they'd spoken. She may have been a little worse for wear, but she wasn't stupid. Surely she understood the consequences of not helping to find Daniel. But she was the boy's mother. She'd already gone to crazy extremes to shield him. If she somehow thought she was protecting him again now by lying, Daniel could be anywhere . . .

Devereaux rolled farther through the patch of trees, wincing as the Porsche's wheels sank down into the abrasive, pebbled surface. Then he reached for his phone, cursing himself for not having asked for someone to watch Diane's house when he'd called Dispatch earlier. But before he could finish dialing he caught sight of a pair of faint, dusty tire tracks. They led up onto the sidewalk at the far end of the lot and disappeared around the side of the building.

The area behind the school was shaped like a long, wide rectangle with one corner cut off, bordered by more tall, randomly spaced pine trees. It had previously been filled with a jumble of tennis courts, soccer pitches, and a baseball diamond, but these had all been cleared away over the summer in preparation for a new, better-organized set of facilities. It had been leveled so that the kids would still have somewhere to play, and was now covered with a temporary layer of sand and dirt. The space was empty, except for one thing. The white Volvo, which was sitting alone in the dead center, facing the building like the only car at a dilapidated drive-in movie.

Devereaux could see Daniel McKinzie sitting behind the wheel, which struck him as odd for a moment because he'd forgotten the Volvo was right-hand drive. The boy was holding something. A stopwatch. Devereaux heard a loud crash high up to his right, and almost immediately began to smell smoke. Daniel swapped the watch for a notebook and scribbled rapidly across its center pages. Then he took a pair of binoculars and began to methodically scan the rear of the building, left to right, top to bottom, until he reached the right-hand side of the first floor. Then he spotted Devereaux watching him. He scrabbled for the ignition key. Fired up the engine. Lurched forward. Snaked across to his right, and stopped twenty feet from the front of the Porsche.

Don't do it, Devereaux thought. *Don't do it!* He could see Daniel's hands jammed together at the top of the steering wheel. His knuckles were white. His arms were locked out straight. And his eyes were darting from side to side, sizing up the too-narrow gaps between the Porsche, the wall, and the line of trees.

Devereaux kept his foot on the brake and waited until he saw the tension melt away from Daniel's arms. Then he shifted into Park, climbed out of the car, and walked slowly toward the Volvo. He kept his arms away from his body, palms down, until he was level with the driver's door. Then he mimed for Daniel to roll down his window.

"It's OK, Daniel." Devereaux kept his voice quiet and low. "Your mom told me you'd be here. She asked me to bring you home. And she explained how none of this is your fault. It was the system. It screwed you. Giving places at the good science schools to those unworthy kids, but not you? Of course that made you mad. I totally get it. So there's no need to worry. I can help you. I just need you to switch off your engine and—"

The Volvo leapt forward and then peeled away into a wide U-turn, accelerating unsteadily as Daniel worked his way through the gears. Devereaux shook his head and climbed back into the Porsche, easily closing the gap but making no attempt to overtake the other car. There was no point. Daniel had nowhere to go. Devereaux just had to keep him penned in until the squad cars arrived. Then they could throw a butterfly net over the boy and hand him over to the shrinks at the UAB Hospital.

Daniel turned hard left, trying to loop around the Porsche and race back to the gap at the side of the school building. Devereaux moved across, blocking his path. Daniel kept his wheel on full lock, hoping to cut across in front and slip away down the other side but Devereaux steered right, coming up alongside him. The cars were parallel now, two feet apart, driver to driver. Devereaux glanced across at the Volvo. Daniel's body was rigid with tension. His eyes were brimming with anger. He sneered, then reached his left hand down between the front seats. He pulled something out of the gap. A gun. He moved his arm across his body, trying to aim the muzzle out of the open window.

Devereaux tapped the brake pedal and fell back, out of the line of fire. Daniel dropped down to second, hit the gas, and surged forward toward a gap he'd spotted between two trees on the border with Wild-oak Drive. He snatched third, squeezing another couple of miles per hour out of the ancient, whining engine. He adjusted his steering slightly. Pressed even harder on the gas. And slammed into the steering wheel as the Volvo snagged on the curbstone at the edge of the school yard. The solid granite block ripped the metal lip from beneath the slender chrome fender and the car's elegant curved nose buried itself deep into the dusty red soil.

Devereaux kept his distance and watched Daniel wrestle with the Volvo's stalled engine. The boy tried over and over to get it going, twisting the key and pumping the gas as the carburetor flooded and the starter motor shrieked and stuttered in vain. Finally Daniel pounded on the steering wheel in frustration, then tried to open the door. It was jammed. The impact must have distorted the car's body-work. Daniel tugged on the handle, over and over, but it wouldn't budge. He leaned across and tried the passenger door. It was stuck, too. Devereaux could see Daniel's movements growing increasingly panicked. Finally the boy twisted around and managed to squeeze out through the open window, landing in the dirt on his back but scram-bling quickly upright.

"Are you OK, Daniel?" Devereaux stepped out of the Porsche, his gun concealed behind him. "Are you hurt?"

Daniel was reeling a little, clutching his bruised ribs with his right hand and clinging to his gun with his left.

"How's this for an idea?" Devereaux took a cautious step forward. "Let's get you to the hospital. Have a doctor check you out. Make sure you didn't take a bang to the head. Your mom told me you're going to be America's top scientist one day. That's a big deal. We can't take chances with—"

"Don't listen to her." Daniel stepped away from the car. "She's a moron. She should have said, *the world's greatest physicist*. It's my destiny to be—"

A second explosion rocked the school. Devereaux glanced over his shoulder and registered the twin columns of smoke rising from two of the glass pyramids that had collapsed, and the tongues of angry red flame licking around the jagged remnants of their metal frames. And when he looked back he saw Daniel on the far side of the Volvo, running fast.

"Daniel, stop!" Devereaux sprinted after the boy. "Think about this. The entire Birmingham Police Department's out looking for you. If another officer sees you, he'll shoot. You can't be any kind of scientist if you're dead."

Daniel cleared the trees and continued across Wildoak Drive, and Devereaux lost more ground when a driver in a shiny yellow Hummer panicked at the sight of his gun and stopped dead, right in his way. By the time he shimmied around the back of the SUV he was only just in time to catch sight of Daniel dodging down the driveway between two green-painted wood and brick houses near the corner of Briar Meadow Road.

"You're supposed to be a smart kid." Devereaux paused at the mouth of the driveway that Daniel had taken. "So stop this. Come out. What you're doing is the opposite of smart. It's going to get you killed."

Daniel didn't respond so Devereaux moved forward along the broad slabs of concrete, turning sideways to squeeze between a white minivan and the wall of the right-hand house. He emerged and continued toward the flat, grass-filled yard at the back of the properties. The fence was high—too high for a teenager with sore ribs to climb?—but there were plenty of things to hide behind. A shiny steel gas grill. A kids' trampoline. A stack of garden furniture. A pile of—

Devereaux heard a dried-up leaf crunch behind him. He spun around. Daniel was running toward him from the other side of the minivan, left arm outstretched, gun in hand. Devereaux dived to his right. Rolled. Came back up in a crouch, his own gun raised. He lined up on the center of Daniel's chest. Started to squeeze the trigger.

Then relaxed.

Daniel was holding a Colt 1911. A solid weapon. A heavy one. Most adults find it hard to keep a gun like that steady, even with two hands. But this kid was brandishing it effortlessly with just his left. Like it was a toy. *A toy* . . .

Devereaux slowly got to his feet. "Nice try, Daniel. But I know that's not a real gun. Put it down. Come with me. We'll go see your mom."

"All right." Daniel lowered his arm and moved closer to Devereaux. "If we have to. But there's something I want to show you, first." He opened his right hand and held up an engraved silver cigarette lighter. "It was my grandfather's. It's old. But believe me, it still works." Then he snapped his left arm up and pulled the water pistol's trigger, drenching the front of Devereaux's shirt with gasoline.

Chapter Seventy-four

Wednesday. Evening.

DIANE MCKINZIE FELT SICK. SICKER THAN SHE'D EVER FELT BEFORE. But not because of the booze. Or the salt solution she'd made herself drink. Or whatever Daniel had slipped into her food to close her down early for the night. It was because of eight words.

"You can give your statement in the morning."

That was the last thing the policewoman had said. She'd called a guy to come and board up the front door, when it became apparent that Diane was in no state to handle that herself. She'd sat with Diane until the work was done. Reassured her that Daniel wasn't seriously hurt, as soon as the information came over the air. Promised to let Diane know the second the doctors cleared Daniel for visiting. Got her settled on the couch. Then dropped her bombshell, and left.

She could give her statement. About Daniel. About how he was her son, and yet she hadn't known what he'd been doing. Not *known*. Not had *proof.* The *Dispatch* reports he'd written didn't mean anything. Anyone could see that. They weren't serious! They were just childish make-believe. Figments of his imagination. They had to be . . .

The policewoman had been helpful. She'd been polite. But if it had been tattooed across her forehead in capital letters, her opinion wouldn't have been any clearer. She didn't believe a word Diane had said. And there was the problem. If Diane couldn't convince someone in the heat of the moment, in the midst of her wrecked home, with tears in her eyes and streaks of vomit still on her chin, how could she convince anyone else with just her words?

And how could she continue to convince herself?

Chapter Seventy-five

Wednesday. Late evening.

THE TWISTED OLD TREES DANCED WILDLY WITH THE SHADOWS THROWN
by Devereaux's headlights as he guided the Porsche along the rough,
root-lined track through the forest. He stopped in his usual spot and
covered the final few yards to the cabin on foot, and only pulled out his
flashlight when he reached the pitted wooden door.

The cabin had once belonged to Devereaux's great-grandfather—or
so he'd believed when he bought it, fifteen years previously, in an attempt to reconnect with his heritage. Following his last case, he knew
he had no family ties to the place at all. The half-derelict structure
couldn't connect him with previous generations any more than it
could keep out the rain. Its decaying wooden frame couldn't provide
him with the stability he'd thought his ancestors would bring. But that
was OK. After everything he'd learned about his family he didn't want
any links with them, anyway. All he wanted was a place to think,
where he wouldn't be disturbed. And the little cabin was still the best
place for doing that.

Devereaux took a can of Avondale Battlefield IPA—his favorite
beer—from the dwindling stack of six-packs to the side of the iron
furnace that dominated the far end of the small rectangular room,
then shoved the battered brown leather couch forward until it was
bathed in the moonlight that was flooding in through the largest of
the holes in the roof.

Devereaux slipped out of the BPD windbreaker he'd put on after the crime scene guys had taken his shirt, massaged the bruised knuckles of his left hand, and lay back on the couch. He looked up at the stars, twinkling in the inky sky above. Were they laughing at him? Could they see the irony? Lieutenant Hale had met him at headquarters after he was done with his paperwork, and said she was going to put him up for a commendation. For arresting Daniel McKinzie, and putting a stop to his arson spree.

What a bunch of bullshit. First, there was more chance of a turkey voting for Thanksgiving than Captain Emrich approving any kind of an award for him. And second, Hale and Devereaux both knew the true cause of her enthusiasm. The fact that Devereaux hadn't shot the kid, despite almost getting lit on fire. Hale saw that as progress. Devereaux saw it as fraud. The real reason he hadn't pulled the trigger wasn't that he'd grown as a person since the last incident. It was that he was afraid of Alexandra's reaction. Eight years ago, in the aftermath of similar circumstances, she'd walked away from him because he'd shot a kid the same kind of age. In that back yard near Putman school, Devereaux had been terrified of the same thing happening again. Concern for Daniel McKinzie's miserable life hadn't come close to entering the equation.

The wind picked up a little, stirring around some of the tinier fragments of wood and broken shingles that lay strewn across the floor. It also chased away a thin layer of cloud from the sky, making the moon seem even brighter. Like a searchlight, Devereaux thought, illuminating another truth he'd been trying to hide from. His reaction to the blackmail material that had been left at Alexandra's. He'd convinced himself that shutting down whoever had sent it should be his first priority. But why? Lieutenant Hale already knew the truth about his family, so his job wasn't threatened. The press might make a stink, but he didn't care about public opinion. No. Alexandra's attitude was the key. And she'd already looked at the pictures. He couldn't make her un-see them. She must have a million questions. Questions only he could answer. Questions he was trying to avoid, by trying to find the blackmailer first. Because once again, he was scared of her response.

The wind picked up further and started to move some of the larger chunks of debris from the damaged roof. That was the physical fallout from the first revelation about his father, Devereaux thought. He hadn't been able to control where those pieces fell, when the beam broke after he'd slung a noose around it in the midst of his previous case. He'd just had to clean them up, as well as he could. And now he saw it was the same with this new information. He swung his feet onto the floor. It was time to forget about the blackmailer. Stopping him wasn't important. Facing Alexandra was. And then fixing whatever damage that might cause.

Chapter Seventy-six

Wednesday. Late evening.

ALEXANDRA READ THE CONTENTS OF THE FILE CAREFULLY, THEN PUSHED it back across the kitchen table. "You stole this?"

"Borrowed it without permission." Devereaux slipped the file into his briefcase. "I returned the original. This is a copy."

"And you did it because of a dream?"

"In a way. I kept dreaming about my father's house being demolished after he was shot. I couldn't understand why that had to happen if he was a cop. A hero. I couldn't find anything online to explain it, so I had to get my hands on his file."

"How long have you known?" Alexandra stood and moved to the window, keeping her back to Devereaux.

"Three months, give or take." Devereaux shifted in his seat. "Remember Ethan Crane, the missing orphan? It came up in connection with that investigation. I thought there must be a mistake, at first. A cover-up of some kind, or a conspiracy. So I talked to the guy who'd wound up partnering the detective on my father's case. He explained everything. How they fixed things to make it look like I was the son of a cop, not a murderer. To take the stink off me. Give me a shot at a future. And it wasn't just me they helped. There were others. Innocent kids who wouldn't have stood a chance otherwise."

"You make it sound so innocuous."

"Heroic is what I was shooting for."

"Anyway, you should have told me. Given me all the facts before burrowing your way back into my life. And into Nicole's."

"Would you have made a different decision, then?"

"I don't know." Alexandra turned to face him. "Maybe."

"Then I'm glad I didn't tell you. Because, listen. I was shocked, too, when I first found out. But what I realized is, it doesn't matter. My father was a monster. I'm not. Look at it this way. Is Nicole destined to become a lawyer, just because you're one? Of course not. We're not defined by the genes we inherit. Our destinies aren't set in stone. We're all responsible for our own actions."

"Do you really believe that?"

"I do."

"Then I don't know if that makes it better or worse." Alexandra left the room, then returned carrying the second white envelope that had been delivered to her door. "Take this." She handed it to Devereaux. "And go. Read what's inside. I need more time to think. I still haven't decided what to do about it."

Chapter Seventy-seven

Wednesday. Late evening.

THE CITY LOOKED CLEAN FROM THE GIANT WINDOW IN DEVEREAUX'S living room at the City Federal. The expanse of sparkling lights made it seem almost shiny. And best of all, it was distant. Separate. Contained on the far side of the glass like an exhibit at a museum. Devereaux could shut it all out whenever he felt the need to isolate himself.

The envelope was different. It was the opposite, sitting on his coffee table like a bulging intruder, demanding attention. Just like the file about his father had done when Devereaux brought it back from the police archive three months earlier. And it was just as unwelcome. Devereaux picked it up and tipped out the contents, dreading the prospect of another stack of sickening images. But there were no photographs on the pages that spilled out. Just words and numbers. Columns and columns of numbers. And together, they formed a picture far more damning than anything Devereaux had seen in the previous package Alexandra had passed to him.

The figures formed a detailed financial record that someone had constructed for a corporation called Foughtthelaw Acquisitions, going back twenty-five years. It was an investment vehicle, specializing in long-term development projects in what were now some of the most gentrified districts of Birmingham. Nothing new had been added to its portfolio for over two decades, but the proceeds had continued to roll in and the value of the original properties had skyrocketed. One building, for example, had been purchased for $20,000. It was now estimated to be worth over $2.7 million.

It was the first piece of real estate Devereaux had ever owned. He'd paid for it with a bag of cash he'd taken from a crack dealer, right before helping the guy leave town for good. It was another form of neighborhood improvement, he'd figured at the time. He didn't regret it. He'd happily do the same thing again. Only he'd do a better job of hiding it. Foughtthelaw Acquisitions was the first smokescreen corporation he'd set up. It was from the days before the Academy, where he'd learned how to cover his tracks more effectively. Looking back, it was woefully inadequate. Alexandra had obviously linked it to him, due to its name and his love of The Clash. Joseph Oliver must have joined the dots, too, somehow. Though whoever he'd paid to pull the financial snapshot together was withholding two vital pieces of information. Where the capital had come from. And where the income was paid to. Not to mention all the tax code violations that were bound to be involved. The file was like a stick of dynamite without a cord or a detonator. Not a complete bomb. But more than enough to blow you to smithereens unless handled with extreme care.

This business was no longer an inconvenience, Devereaux realized. He was no longer looking at an awkward conversation with Alexandra, or an embarrassing article in the local paper. He was looking at serious jail time if the information reached the wrong hands.

He'd been wrong, back at the cabin. Stopping Oliver wasn't a luxury, after all.

It was a necessity.

Chapter Seventy-eight

Wednesday. Late evening.

How was he still not arrested?

Tyler Shaw flushed the toilet for the last time, dragged himself to the bedroom, and stood in front of his alcove. The officer had been right there. In that very spot. If he'd just reached out, pulled back the curtain, seen the icons . . .

If Mr. Quinlan hadn't stopped by the day before, and prompted him to deal with the smell . . .

If the moron athlete had turned right instead of left, when he managed to slip away before the potion took its full effect . . .

There were a lot of *ifs*. Lady Luck had tossed a lot of coins, these last few days. And every single one had come up in Shaw's favor. That couldn't be a coincidence. It had to show he was on the right path. And he didn't have much further to go. A little more tidying up. A short drive, there and back. A good night's sleep. A final run through the process. And then he'd be saying goodbye to the old, worthless Tyler. And hello to invincibility.

Chapter Seventy-nine

Wednesday. Late evening.

DEVEREAUX TURNED TO THE FINAL SHEET IN THE STACK OF PAPERS FROM the envelope. It wasn't printed, like the others. It was handwritten. A bold, blue dollar sign filled three quarters of the page. And a phone number was scrawled across the bottom.

Devereaux called the number and was immediately greeted by a generic cellular network voicemail announcement. He tried again, and got the same result. This time he left a message:

"Hello? My name's Cooper Devereaux. I just saw your advertisement. I'm interested in what you're selling, so call me back. As soon as you can. I'll leave you my cell number so you can reach me direct."

Devereaux was frustrated not to reach Joseph Oliver right away, but he figured the delay wouldn't be a major problem. Oliver wouldn't do anything stupid as long as he believed he was going to get what he wanted. And the extra time would give Devereaux the chance to prepare himself a little more thoroughly. He thought for a moment, then opened the directory on his phone and pulled up an out-of-hours number for a contact who worked at the Support Services Bureau over on Fourth Avenue.

"Devereaux?" Spencer Page answered on the second ring. "What can I do for you, buddy?"

Page was something of a pariah to most of the detectives in the department. He'd come through the Academy, spent five years in uniform, and only switched to a support role after a long stay in the hospital due to a fire escape collapsing under him while he was chasing down a suspect. Superstitious cops feared that his bad luck would rub off on them. Macho cops sneered that he was too chickenshit to drag his patched-up ass back out on the street. But Devereaux didn't react in either of those ways. He was never going to turn his back on someone else who'd reinvented themself. He thought Page had made a smart move. And he appreciated the real-world perspective that Page brought to the job. His time at the sharp end had taught Page that in some situations, corners need to be cut. Procedures flexed. Budgets ignored. Information kept on a need-to-know basis . . .

"I need the location of a cellphone." Devereaux reached for the piece of paper with the number scrawled across it. "I'm guessing it's in Miami, but I need to be sure. And this needs to stay between you and me, Spencer. Nothing official. No court orders. No records."

"Goes without saying. When do you need the info?"

"How soon can you get it?"

"Depends which network the phone's on. But within the hour, for sure. Leave it with me. I'll be as quick as I can."

Devereaux hung up, took a can of Battlefield from his refrigerator, and crossed back to his living room window. He scanned the surrounding streets and offices, desperate for something to distract him from the impatience that was boiling inside him like acid. He saw that lights were still burning in two of the windows in the Wells Fargo building, half a mile away. Devereaux took a long pull on his beer and wondered who was there. Maybe a couple of guys vying for promotion. Prepping for some big deal they were desperate to win. Pretending to work late, but really having an affair. Or maybe—

"Spencer?" Devereaux snatched up his phone the moment its screen began to glow. "Have you found it?"

"No." Page sounded disappointed. "Sorry, buddy. The phone's switched off. There's no way of knowing where it is. But I've flagged it. Discreetly. If it gets turned on, you'll be the first to know. Besides me, obviously."

"Thanks, Spencer." Devereaux swallowed back his frustration. "I appreciate the help. One last question, though. Can you tell where it was, the last time it was used?"

"I tried for that, too. No dice there, either. The phone's never made a call. Never received one, either. Only your two attempts tonight, which ended up in voice—"

"Spencer—sorry." Devereaux felt his phone vibrate. "Got to go. Another call's coming in."

Devereaux disconnected, then realized it was a text he received, rather than another call:

910. 2. 15?

He didn't recognize the number because it would belong to a burner phone, but he knew who the message was from. Tom Vernon. It was a code they'd used since their school days, only then they'd relied on paper rather than SMS: *910* was a lower number than 911, meaning the situation wasn't urgent; *2* was their backup meeting place, Sloss Furnaces. And 15? was a question—*meet in fifteen minutes? Hell, yes,* Devereaux thought. Whatever Vernon had for him—whether he figured it was urgent or not—finding out had to be a million times better than sitting around doing nothing, driving himself crazy.

Sloss Furnaces was a jagged, rust-red slice of Birmingham's industrial past, sandwiched between First Avenue North and the railroad, a mile east of the City Federal as the crow flies. Iron production had ceased there even before Devereaux's father had died, and for years afterward the fate of the site hung in the balance as the developers and the conservationists slugged it out for control. Officially abandoned and unsafe, the place became a magnet for local kids. Devereaux had spent countless hours climbing the web of crumbling pipework, and the dozen rocket-shaped silos were ideal places to hide from irate foster parents. Back then Devereaux used to imagine they were escape pods, about to blast off and carry him away to a better world. Or at bleaker moments—especially when he was alone there at night—he imagined them as futuristic mining machines bursting back out of the ground, their pitted and scorched surfaces clear evidence of angry demons pursuing them up from the inner reaches of Hell. Now, though, the place was a National Historic Landmark. It had been for more than thirty years. That meant it was properly maintained, and secured at night. There was no way in after hours. Not officially, at least.

Tom Vernon was waiting at the foot of the one remaining ladder in the brick annex to the main furnace building when Devereaux arrived. The days when they were happy to scurry up the worn iron rungs and disappear into the network of aerial girders at the first sight of an adult were long gone, but it was still their favorite meeting place on the site.

"You got news already?" Devereaux embraced his old friend.

"You know me. I don't let the grass grow." Vernon passed Devereaux a cellphone with a photograph open on its screen. "See what you think. That was taken at the address you gave me. Is it the guy you were looking for?"

The image was small and the man in the picture was old and stooped, but Devereaux had no doubt. It was Joseph Oliver. "It's him. When was this taken?"

"An hour after we spoke. I had a guy I do business with in Miami get right on it. I was out of pocket when his message came in, so I couldn't call you right away."

"No problem." Devereaux felt the calm clarity begin to flow. He wouldn't have to wait for Page to locate Oliver's phone, after all. Or for Oliver to call him back. He could just hop on the first plane to Miami in the morning. Visit Oliver in person. See what he had to say for himself. "Is he still there? Is your guy still on him?"

"This is why I wanted to see you, Cooper. There's something you should know. I'm not sure what your deal was with this guy, but I have more news. A second message came. Not long after the first. The fact is, he's gone, Cooper."

"As in, gone away? Gone to the airport?" Was that why his phone had been off? He'd been on a plane? Devereaux was trying to figure flight times, wondering if there'd still be the chance to intercept Oliver at Shuttlesworth if he was coming up to Birmingham, before he disappeared into the labyrinthine clutches of the city.

"No, Cooper. He's *gone*. As in, my guy saw him take a phone call. Drink a fifth of whiskey. Change into a suit and tie. And blow his own brains out with a nickel-plated .22."

Chapter Eighty

Thursday. Early morning.

WHERE WAS DANIEL?

Diane McKinzie sat up in bed, instantly wide-awake. Her head was pounding. Acid was burning her throat. Her heart was hammering its way out of her chest. What had Daniel done? She had to remember. Break it down, piece by piece. Smooth the edges. Soften the tone. Change the emphasis. Make it into something that other people could accept . . .

Then she allowed herself to remember. Daniel had gone too far this time. He'd strayed from the protective shadow she'd strained for so long to cast over him. He was standing in the spotlight now, on his own, his actions plain for all to see. All. Including herself.

Diane lay back down. Suddenly she didn't feel afraid. She didn't have to be scared that someone would discover her secret. That ship had sailed. Not only sailed, but gone down with all hands. Which meant she wasn't responsible anymore. Daniel's fate was no longer on her shoulders. She felt a little guilt, for all the people she'd misled. Disappointment, for not having been able to make everything perfect for her son. Disgust, for some of the lengths she'd gone to, like offering herself to that odious private school admission guy over dinner at Gianmarco's on Sunday. Anger, at the condescending way he'd turned her down. But mostly she felt relief.

Relief, because she didn't have to lie anymore.

To other people. Or to herself.

Chapter Eighty-one

Thursday. Morning.

DEVEREAUX WAS WOKEN BY HIS PHONE.

His eyes had been shut for barely four hours when a Ramones riff started to blare out from his nightstand. He'd been too keyed up to sleep after meeting Tom Vernon at Sloss Furnaces the night before, and trying to weigh the implications of Joseph Oliver's suicide had kept him awake even longer. Would Oliver's demise make him safer? Or more vulnerable? Dead men can't make blackmail demands. But how much incriminating material was out there? And where was it? Devereaux didn't like the thought of some stranger—or worse, some lawyer—coming across whatever other information Oliver had stashed away about his past activities. And he couldn't help but wonder about the timing. Why had Oliver decided to punch his own ticket that particular afternoon, after so many years living under the radar in the Florida sunshine? Tom Vernon's guy said Oliver had taken a phone call right before eating his gun. Was that a coincidence? Had he received some kind of bad news that had pushed him over the edge? Or had someone tipped him off? Devereaux made a mental note to reach back out to Spencer Page. Have him find where that final phone call came from . . .

I must change my ringtone again, Devereaux thought as he scrabbled for the Answer button. The irony of "I Wanna Be Sedated" was too much for him to bear at that time of the morning.

"Detective? It's Officer Jackson. Do you remember me? Your lieutenant sent me out to your cabin with a message, back in June. Anyway, I just started a tour in Dispatch, and I think I might have something for you."

"Jackson? OK. What have you got?"

"It might be nothing, but I figured I should run it by you. Here's the thing. We were told Tuesday that the Bureau was interested in anything that came up on a couple of guys. Diane McKinzie, a journalist. And Keith Barent Johnson, a pencil pusher at the Board of Ed. McKinzie ran a red light, or maybe her kid did, from what I hear, but we passed it on and it was slaps on the back all around. Then something much more crazy happened last night, and no one wanted to know."

"Because they already know, dummy. Daniel McKinzie was a collar for those school fires. He's in a rubber room right now, at UAB."

"No, *Detective*. I'm talking about the other guy. Johnson."

"Oh. OK. What did he do?"

"There was a report of a disturbance at his premises. A guy was running around outside, after midnight. Some kind of foreigner, apparently. He couldn't speak any English. But he was making a hell of a ruckus. And get this. The guy was buck naked."

"What was the outcome?"

"A unit responded. A couple of neighbors got involved. Another guy showed up, claiming to be romantically involved with the naked dude. No arrests were made, though. Anyway, I thought if this doesn't fall under *unusual activity*, I don't know what does."

"It does sound pretty weird. Thanks, Jackson. I'll look into it, if I get the time."

Devereaux sank back down, wondering why his bed always seemed so much more comfortable when it was time to get out of it, when a snippet of a conversation with Diane McKinzie floated back into his head. It was something she'd said to him on the phone, two days before. She'd been complaining about having to write some gossipy blog post about a guy disappearing from a club in town, including insinuations about his sexuality.

Devereaux called Dispatch back and asked for Officer Jackson.

"Check one thing for me. Have any single adult males been reported missing in the last week?"

"Hold on." Computer keys rattled, then Jackson came back on the line. "One has. Last seen Monday night. A professor. And there's a note about a woman calling about her son, a graduate student, who didn't come home last night. There's no paper on that one yet. It's too soon."

"Thanks, Jackson. I'm thinking I might go talk to that pencil pusher, after all."

Chapter Eighty-two

Thursday. Morning.

NOTHING WOKE ALEXANDRA THAT MORNING. BECAUSE SHE HADN'T been asleep. She hadn't even gone to bed. She'd hit the Zinfandel pretty hard after Devereaux left the previous evening, replaying their last conversation in her head and trying to make sense of what she'd seen in the two envelopes. The second one, in particular. She'd often wondered where Devereaux had gotten his money from. He'd always evaded her questions about his finances. But now she knew. About some of it, at least. She had no idea how many other pies he had his fingers in, though.

Alexandra had moved to the lounge, taking the wine with her, and out of habit started looking at the evidence against Devereaux from the other side, searching for holes. For reasonable doubt. She didn't expect to find any. Experience told her that people don't invest legitimate money in illegal schemes. There are plenty of safer ways to build your nest egg, if you have nothing to hide. Ways that earn you interest, not prison sentences. But she hadn't actually asked Devereaux where the seed money had come from. She'd only assumed it was ill-gotten. And even if it was, as far as she could tell from the figures, there'd been no further activity for twenty-plus years. Maybe Devereaux *had* done something wrong two decades ago. But should he be condemned for it forever? Because who hadn't made a mistake, sometime in their life?

At some point between that thought and the end of the second bottle, Alexandra had briefly dozed off, sprawled out on her couch. She'd immediately started to dream. She'd seen herself in court. She was arguing a case against Devereaux. Counsel for the defense was Devereaux's father, lying dead on the floor but somehow speaking through the bullet hole that had killed him. Nicole was the judge, flanked by a pair of Barbie dolls. The jury box was twice the usual size. And it was full of the victims she'd seen in the photographs in the first envelope, complete with their knife wounds and severed limbs and oceans of blood.

Chapter Eighty-three

Thursday. Morning.

KEITH JOHNSON PRACTICALLY RAN TO GREET THE DETECTIVES WHEN Brenda Lee called him to reception at the Board of Ed building, later that morning.

"Thank you." Johnson grabbed Devereaux's hand and pumped it vigorously. "Thank you so much. I read about what you did. I can't tell you what a relief it is, knowing that the schools are safe. Anything I can ever do for you, just say the word."

"How does five minutes of your time sound, right now?" Garretty gestured toward the stairs. "Your office?"

Johnson got the detectives situated, offered them water, then took his place behind his desk.

"Is this about the other day?" The smile had faded a little from Johnson's face. "When I was late? Because if I was clocked speeding, or ran a red light or something, it was only down to me not wanting to keep you guys waiting."

"No." Devereaux shot Johnson a friendly smile. "It's nothing like that. We just need a little information. There was a report of a disturbance where you live, last night. We're looking for you to put a little meat on the bones for us. Help us figure out if we need to take a closer look at anything."

"Last night?" Johnson took a swig of his water. "That didn't really have anything to do with me. I don't know much about it."

"The report said it took place on your driveway."

"Not *on* my driveway." Johnson fiddled with the lid from the bottle. "More like, on the street *near* my driveway."

"OK." All the warmth drained out of Devereaux's voice. "Then tell us what happened *near* your driveway."

"Well, you know, it was late, and I was already asleep, and I probably can't really add very much to what I guess the other officers will already have told you."

"Did I ever tell you about a friend of mine?" Garretty leaned forward. "He went to college in Texas somewhere, just like you did. Only this guy was a football player. A real big prospect. Scouts came out to all his games. But one day, he didn't show up for practice. He was a no-show the next day, as well. Now, this guy, let's just say he preferred the company of other guys. There was a place he liked to hang out, whenever he had the time. But when the coaches started asking questions, his friends, they didn't say anything. They were worried that the scouts might be prejudiced sons of bitches, so they kept their mouths shut, thinking they were helping their buddy. When the campus police found the guy's body, it was too late to save him. But they said, if only they'd gotten to him a few hours sooner . . ."

"All right." Johnson screwed the lid back on the bottle. "I get your point. But listen. I'm not trying to hide anything. It's just, last night—it was all a giant misunderstanding. A couple of guys. Too much to drink. A stupid disagreement. You get the picture. It was all over real quick. Even the other officers who showed up agreed they didn't need to write chapter and verse about it."

"Forget those officers." Devereaux took out his notebook. "The couple of guys who were fighting. Give them names."

"I only know one. Tyler Shaw. He's a neighbor. I only came out and tried to help because I recognized him. I guess the other guy was his boyfriend."

"Which one was running around naked, raising hell?"

"The boyfriend. He was drunk out of his mind. Staggering about. Slurring his words so you couldn't even tell what language he was speaking. Tyler was so embarrassed. Luckily the officers were able to help him bring the boyfriend home before things got completely out of hand."

"And this Tyler. What's his address?"

"Give me your book. I'll write it down for you."

"How long have you known him?"

"Ten years. Maybe eleven?"

"How many boyfriends has he had during that time?"

"I don't honestly know."

"How can you not know? It doesn't sound like he's too worried about discretion."

"Why should he be? But that's not the point. He was away for three or four years. He only moved back to Birmingham a couple of months ago."

"Where had he been?"

"I don't know. I guess he couldn't bear to be around the house after his mom died. But he seems to be over that now."

"He lived with his mother before he left town?"

"Right. It was through her that I got to know him. She was a nice lady. She asked me to help him when he was struggling to find work after the economy tanked, back in '08 or '09. The Board was still spending some money, refurbishing a few schools, so I put a word in for him with a couple of contractors. He's an electrician, you see. And that's why he looked me up when he got back to town. He needed a reference for a job."

"Did he do any work at Jones Valley school, back in the day?"

"I think he might have. It had already been converted from a high school to a middle school, but the old 1960s building was no longer fit for purpose. It was a complete rebuild, that one. I remember thinking it was convenient for him, being just over the street from where he lived."

"And the address you gave me. That was his mother's house?"

"Right."

"That's good. Now, listen. One last thing. This is important. If you talk to Tyler Shaw, do not tell him about this conversation. Not a word. Are we clear?"

Chapter Eighty-four

Thursday. Morning.

Diane McKinzie hadn't left her bedroom yet.

She hadn't even gotten out of bed. Her phone had rung unanswered half a dozen times on her nightstand, then buzzed to announce half a dozen voicemails. They were probably all from Kelly Peterson. They were probably increasingly angry. Diane may well have been jeopardizing her job by ignoring them. But at that moment, she didn't care. Because she was transfixed. She couldn't tear her attention away from the three solid steel bolts, evenly spaced on the inside of her door.

Diane was going to miss her son, she knew. But she wouldn't miss those bolts. She could remove them, now that he was gone. She could go to bed at night without having to lock herself in to feel safe. She could get to work on fixing the dents in the walls and the woodwork. Repair the broken picture frames. Replace the smashed light fixtures. Get new china. Channel her energy into her career. Take a course at the university. Travel. Read. Watch TV. Spend time without worrying about accounting for it.

She could start socializing again.

Maybe even start a relationship . . .

Chapter Eighty-five

Thursday. Morning.

"I REMEMBER THIS HOUSE."

Devereaux rolled to a stop at the side of Dowell Avenue and turned to Garretty. Jones Valley school—still fenced off and swathed in police tape—was on their right, and the address Keith Johnson had given them was facing it from across the street. "I walked by it every day for two years, before I switched high schools. I even remember seeing a boy playing in the yard, some afternoons. I wonder if that was Shaw? He was a skinny-looking kid. Wore weird clothes. And he was always on his own. Never seemed to be any friends around. Or brothers or sisters."

The detectives made their way up the path that divided the bunga-low's front yard, its stone slabs lifted in places by encroaching tree roots.

"I always liked this place. It was so neat and well kept. But look at it now!" Devereaux pointed to a circular flower bed, full of rocks and dried-up soil. "See that? It was always crammed full of plants. You could smell them from the street. The grass was . . . well, alive. The walls were sky blue, a bit like they are now, only freshly painted. Not faded and peeling. There were white shutters either side of both win-dows. I wonder where they went? And there was no need for security bars covering them, back then."

Devereaux held back, shaking his head at the state of the house while Garretty took the three steps up to the front door and rang the bell. There was no reply.

"What do you think?" Garretty turned to Devereaux. "Watch the place?"

"I don't know." Devereaux moved across and peered in through the front bedroom window. "Remember Irvin's profile? A guy who had access to the school. Was from the neighborhood. Lived with a relative, but doesn't anymore. Had gone out of circulation. Would be dangerous if he resurfaced. All on top of that weirdness with the naked boyfriend running around, and another guy reported missing? I say we should take a look inside."

"That's too sketchy. We'd never get a warrant."

"We don't need one. Listen. Can't you hear someone calling for help? Half muffled? With a slurry foreign accent?"

"No."

Devereaux strode back to the steps and slammed his foot into the front door, just below the handle. "Sure you do."

Chapter Eighty-six

Thursday. Morning.

ALEXANDRA HAD GIVEN HER DAUGHTER THE DAY OFF.

She'd made a brief attempt to pull together some exercises for Nicole to complete on her own, but her hangover had made even that much thinking impossible. She'd collapsed back onto the couch for another hour, feeling sorry for herself, then made for the kitchen to dose herself up on Advil and iced tea. She followed up the drugs with a hot shower, which took more of the edge off the discomfort. Then she went to look for distraction in the news sites on her iPad.

The first story to catch her attention was of course about how Devereaux had chased and caught Daniel McKinzie in the aftermath of the fire at Putman school. Alexandra was surprised Devereaux hadn't shot the kid, especially after she read about him getting doused in gasoline. And she was a little shocked to discover that Daniel was Frederick McKinzie's grandson. She remembered reading a couple of Frederick's groundbreaking articles when she was growing up, including Kathryn Thornton's spacewalk and the conviction of Governor Hunt, and had always cheered to hear of a guy from Birmingham cleaning up at the national journalism awards.

So in two generations it had gone from Frederick McKinzie, newspaper titan, to Daniel McKinzie, pyromaniac? How did that happen? Alexandra Googled the family. There was plenty of information about Diane McKinzie, Frederick's daughter, including links to all kinds of articles she'd written. But nothing about Daniel's father. He'd been out of the picture for years, it seemed. Diane had been bringing her child up on her own. Just as Alexandra had been, before Devereaux showed back up.

Would Diane have taken her husband back, if she'd had the chance? Or had she been the one behind them splitting up? Maybe she'd seen something in the guy she didn't like. Something she'd tried in vain to keep from being passed on to her child.

Alexandra thought of the picture she'd seen of Raymond Kerr and Devereaux. She wondered if Diane had any pictures of her son and his father like that. She switched apps on her iPad and brought up a shot of Devereaux and Nicole standing outside her house. She stared at it for thirty seconds. Then went and locked her front door.

Chapter Eighty-seven

Thursday. Morning.

IT TOOK TWO MORE SOLID KICKS BEFORE THE FRONT DOOR COMPLETELY gave way.

Devereaux went into the bungalow ahead of Garretty, and both men breathed through their mouths to save themselves from gagging on the harsh stench of antiseptic that hung in the air. The hallway was decorated with floral wallpaper, which was badly faded and starting to peel away in several places. There was an empty coatrack to the left, next to a framed photograph of a woman in her forties—presumably Tyler Shaw's mother, the previous owner of the house—and beneath that a scuffed pair of black leather work boots.

The dark wooden floor hadn't been polished in years, and it showed signs of water damage near one of the internal doorways. The detectives tried that one first, and found it led to the bathroom. It looked like it dated back to the 1950s, with cracked subway tile on the walls; tiny, hexagonal ones on the floor; and a heavy cast-iron bath with a newer showerhead above it. There was a small wooden table between the sink and the toilet, and a door to a closet in the far corner. The door was secured with a hefty padlock and a galvanized steel hasp, like the sort normally used on sheds or stables.

Devereaux picked up the table and used it to hammer the lock until the screws holding it in place gave way. Then he opened the door, and recoiled as the chemical stench grew even stronger. Inside the closet was a hot water cylinder, and crammed above that was an open-topped plastic barrel about four feet tall and two and a half feet in diameter. On the floor, wrapped in a grubby towel, there was a set of tools. A surgeon's saw. Two butcher's knives. And a pair of pliers.

"Cooper, look." Garretty was crouching down, his face close to the floor. "Blood." The remains of almost scrubbed away, black-brown flecks dotted the tiles. "There's more on the grout between the tiles above the bath." Garretty straightened up. "A bit on the shower curtain. Some on the toilet. But one area that looks clean." He pointed with his foot to a thirty-inch gap between the toilet and the bath.

"Shaw's definitely our guy." Devereaux frowned. "That'll be where he puts the barrel. The bones that Young found at the school, across the road? They'd been stripped with acid. This is how Shaw does it. He dumps the bodies in the bath. Cuts them up with those tools from the closet. Drops the pieces in the barrel and leaves them until the acid has dissolved all the flesh away. Then he pours the mush down the pan. It's like a production line."

"It doesn't look very solid." Garretty gingerly prodded the outside of the barrel. "Wouldn't the acid eat right through, if it's strong enough to dissolve human flesh? Wouldn't the bath be a better place for it? Why not just lie the body down and pour the acid in on top?"

"That depends on the acid." Devereaux pulled the top of the barrel toward him, sniffed, and immediately his eyes began to water. "There's at least one kind where the only thing it doesn't eat through is plastic. A crime scene guy told me about it once, swapping war stories over a couple of beers. Hydro something. Hydrofluoric, maybe? We'll get all this stuff to the lab, pronto. They'll tell us for sure. And think about it. A body will dissolve much quicker if you cut it up. More surface area."

"That's sick." Garretty backed away, his eyes also starting to sting. "And here's another problem. The bones at the school are old. This stuff looks like it's been used recently. People are missing now. If Shaw's done his thing with them, where are their skeletons?"

"I don't know." Devereaux shrugged. "They'll be around here somewhere, I guess."

"Gross." Garretty shivered, despite the warmth in the room. "Come on. This place creeps me out. Let's check the rest of the house. Look for signs of the boyfriend. Maybe Shaw hasn't turned him into gravy, just yet."

*

Devereaux and Garretty worked their way through the living room, dining room, kitchen, and back bedroom without finding anything else relevant.

"This is obviously where Shaw sleeps." Devereaux gestured toward the heap of unmade sheets on the mattress when they reached the front bedroom. "Wait. Hold on a second." Devereaux reached down and took hold of the cuff of a navy blue dress shirt that was almost hidden under the edge of the bed. He pulled it out, laid it on the mattress, and smoothed it down. Then he crossed to the ornate mahogany wardrobe next to the door. He took out another shirt—this one with bright cartoonish pictures of Saturn and Jupiter all over it. He brought it back to the bed. Laid it on top of the first one. And pointed to the three-inch margin of blue cotton that was visible, all the way around.

"Someone else was here," Devereaux said. "I hope those mutts in uniform didn't bring the poor guy back to be chopped up and flushed down the toilet."

"Here's something else." Garretty had opened a wooden jewelry box inlaid with delicate turquoise flowers, which he'd found on the nightstand. He slipped on a pair of latex gloves and lifted out a stack of laminated cards. "Drivers' licenses. They must be souvenirs of his victims." He shuffled through them. "Jesus, Cooper. There are twenty-two of them."

Garretty laid the licenses out on the bed next to the shirts and stood at Devereaux's side, looking at them. Reading each name. Studying each face.

"Well, the victims are all Caucasian," Garretty said after a couple of minutes. "It's hard to tell anything about age, because we don't know when he took them, relative to the expiration date on the licenses."

"There looks like three groups, to me." Devereaux started to form the licenses into separate lines. "We've got a bunch of older ones from Alabama. Eight of them. And one of those has been cut up and taped back together. Then eleven from out of state. They're from all over the place, coast to coast. Then three more from Alabama. All from Birmingham, in fact. And look. This one. I recognize the name. He's the missing professor. Diane McKinzie wrote a blog post about him when he disappeared. I remember her complaining about it. She thought blogging was beneath her. Anyway, that leaves two. My money says one'll be the naked guy from last night."

"Sven Erikkson." Garretty picked up one of the more recent licenses and pointed to the large blue shirt. "Sven was six feet six. Two hundred and sixty pounds. He'll be the guy."

"Sven was a monster." Devereaux took the shirt and held it out in front of him. "Hard to get the drop on a guy his size."

Garretty pointed to a pair of whiskey tumblers that had been left on the nightstand. One had been tipped over on its side. "Maybe Shaw slipped him something in his drink. That would explain the slurred speech when he tried to get away. Assuming it was him. I'll email a picture of his license to Keith Johnson, right now. See if he confirms the ID."

"Good plan." Devereaux swept up the rest of the licenses, then gestured toward the curtained-off alcove at the foot of the bed. "And then there's one more place we need to check before we get the hell out of this dump."

Chapter Eighty-eight

Thursday. Morning.

DIANE MCKINZIE STRAIGHTENED HER PAJAMAS AND SLID ONTO THE worn leather chair behind the giant mahogany desk in her father's study. She leaned back. Closed her eyes. And tried to persuade herself that she could still pick up a faint whiff of the countless Marlboros he'd greedily smoked for so many years. Next she looked up at the ceiling and smiled at the broad orange stain he'd always blamed on the cedar and sage candles her mother had insisted on burning to neutralize the odor. Then she dragged herself back to the present and lifted the lid off the dented cardboard file box she'd hauled out of the closet.

She'd had access to everything in her father's research archive ever since the day he died. There was some fascinating material in there. All kinds of details he'd uncovered in the course of his investigations but hadn't included in the published articles. *Stories are like recipes,* he used to tell her. *And facts are like spices. Add too many, and you'll spoil the dish.*

Diane didn't have enough experience of cooking to know if that was true, and she didn't really care. She just knew there were plenty of juicy secrets in those files. Maybe she should change direction. Start writing a book. An explosive exposé. There was plenty of mileage left in the Jefferson County sewer construction scandal, for example, according to what her father had found. Plus a few executives who hadn't been brought to book for their parts in the HealthSouth affair. And that was before she even started on the sports or political stuff. All in all, there was a ton of scope for her to get out of journalism before the listing, leaky ship sank the rest of the way.

Or, alternatively, she could put the information to another, more personal use. She'd only had the chance to dip into the files a couple of times recently, what with all the stress over Daniel sapping her energy. Now she could put that right. Take the box in front of her, for example. It held the papers relating to Detective Devereaux and Raymond Kerr. She could revisit the whole sordid story. Take it slowly this time. Dig deep. Who knew what other nuggets she might find in there? And what else she could do with them?

Chapter Eighty-nine

Thursday. Morning.

DEVEREAUX YANKED OPEN THE CURTAIN THAT COVERED THE ALCOVE AT the foot of Tyler Shaw's bed and found himself staring directly into the empty, lifeless eye sockets of a human skull.

The skull was one of seven. Each was positioned at the center of its own separate shelf, one above the other in a perfectly aligned vertical column. Each shelf was painted a different color of the rainbow. Red at the top, through to violet at the bottom. The sides and back of the alcove were matte black. Tiny crystals were sprinkled everywhere, and the ones on the side nearer the window were gently twinkling in the morning sun. Small tea-lights were set on both sides of each skull, resting on what Devereaux realized were upturned human kneecaps. The candles had all burned out, as had the sticks of incense that protruded from the vertebrae that were stacked up in threes at the outside edge of each shelf.

"Are these real?" Garretty stretched out a hand toward the highest skull, but stopped short of touching it. "They're so shiny. They look like they're made of plastic."

"He's coated them with something." Devereaux gazed at the porous, sponge-like bones that dangled down at the rear of the skull's nasal cavity. He peered through the narrow, angled apertures that would have carried the optical nerves to the brain. He recoiled from the gleaming triangular teeth that clung to the jawbones, their roots seeming long and exaggerated without any gums to bed themselves down in. He traced the meandering stitch-like joins between the curving plates of the skull itself. Then he turned away and fought to recover his train of thought. "Something to preserve them. Like varnish, maybe. Remember that one skull he dumped at the school? The lab said it had been damaged by heat. I bet that was his first one. I bet he tried to bake it, but that didn't work. So he changed tack."

"You might be right, Cooper. That might be *what* he did to them." Garretty's nose wrinkled in disgust. "But answer me this. *Why?* And what kind of guy are we dealing with here?"

Chapter Ninety

Thursday. Morning.

TYLER SHAW COULD FEEL THE POWER. ALREADY. IT WAS A DAY EARLY. HE was ahead of schedule. It was a miracle. Only it was real! He could *feel* it.

The previous night, it had hit him. Out of the blue. He was heading for the door, still planning on going home and grabbing a little rest before starting on his final day's work. But before he could step outside, he felt something change. Inside himself. At last. And it made him realize, he didn't need his job anymore. It didn't matter if he got fired. Let Mr. Quinlan do whatever he wanted. Very soon, employment would no longer be important. So in the short term, wouldn't it be better to stay at the source? Let the power continue to build until the next evening, when it would be time to put the final piece in place?

Shaw had prepared himself and settled down to sleep. But before he allowed himself to drift away he took some time to reflect on all the people who'd led him to the brink of this transformation. The people who'd given their lives for it. And he gave thanks for what they'd done. He swore to always remember them. To honor their sacrifice. To live his new life as a tribute to them, and never return to the pitiful way he'd been before.

Chapter Ninety-one

Thursday. Late morning.

Hawkins & Leach—where Tyler Shaw worked—was not far from Avondale Park, on the opposite side of downtown from his house. Taking Sixth Avenue South would have given Devereaux and Garretty a straight shot after they'd cleared Elmwood Cemetery, but Devereaux didn't like their chances with the traffic so he kept going straight on Green Springs and then merged north onto I-65. It meant going around three sides of a square, adding three miles to the journey, but it avoided the whole area around the university and the hospital and saved them a good five minutes, which is all that the detectives cared about.

Devereaux worked his way from the highway down Fifth Avenue as far as 38th Street South, then turned off into a long, roughly paved cul-de-sac. He rolled the Porsche past a succession of small businesses—a wholesale florist, a typewriter repair shop, a recording studio, a dog grooming parlor—until they reached Hawkins & Leach's wide, rectangular building at the far end of the strip. Devereux thought it looked like someone had actually taken two unrelated buildings and jammed them together. The left-hand half was built of brick, neatly pointed, with shrubs lined up in wooden barrels at the base of the walls. Inside was a reception area with a shiny, blond wood counter, two upholstered couches for visitors to use while they waited, a couple of offices for admin staff, and a large, bright presentation room for making pitches to potential new clients. The other half was like an old-school workshop. There was a stock section with floor-to-ceiling metal shelves full of all kinds of electrical components. An area for assembling the bespoke systems the company specialized in designing. A test rig, used by the maintenance team. And in the back corner, with a full-width Plexiglas window to ensure a clear view of everything that was happening, was Cam Quinlan's office.

Quinlan slammed his phone back into its cradle, veins bulging in both temples, and turned to face Devereaux and Garretty.

"The stupid . . ." Quinlan's hands balled into fists as he battled the urge to pound on the already-dented metal surface of his desk. "OK. All right. Here's the deal. Tyler Shaw—the obnoxious little shit, I knew there was something seriously wrong with him—didn't show up for work this morning. Again. But Melinda, my moron assistant, for some reason I'll never understand, has a soft spot for him. She knows he's on his final warning and didn't want him to get fired, so she didn't tell me he was AWOL right away. She figured she'd give it till lunchtime, and try to track him down herself."

"Did she have any luck?" Devereaux took out his notebook.

"No." Quinlan crossed his arms. "She has no idea where he is. Nor do I, I'm ashamed to say."

"Was he supposed to be here?" Devereaux pointed to the observation window. "I don't see many people around the place."

"The engineers are all out visiting clients." Quinlan scowled. "Shaw was supposed to be, as well. He's costing the company money."

"We'll need his client's address." Devereaux flipped open his book.

"There's no point." Quinlan shook his head. "Shaw didn't show up. Melinda said the client already called and complained. This kind of thing sucks. It really hurts our reputation."

"Is there anywhere else Shaw could be?" Garretty took a step closer to the desk. "Visiting a supplier? Picking up spare parts? At a doctor's office? We need you to think, Mr. Quinlan. Forget about your business for a minute. A man's life could be at stake."

"Sorry." Quinlan stared at the ground for a moment, then reached for the phone. "OK. Here's an idea. Shaw has a company truck. It has a GPS tracker in it. I can't promise you he'll be with it, but I can at least find out where it's at."

Chapter Ninety-two

Thursday. Early afternoon.

Tyler Shaw's truck was in a clearing in the forest about six miles southeast of Devereaux's cabin. When he was given the location, Cam Quinlan was afraid the security tracker had malfunctioned. He thought that the middle of nowhere was a strange place for a wanted man to go. Devereaux wasn't worried, though. Taking refuge in the woods made perfect sense to him.

Devereaux left the Porsche next to Shaw's truck, and he and Garretty continued on foot along the narrowing track as it skirted a dense stand of cottonwood trees. After they'd walked a quarter mile beyond that they caught sight of a wooden structure at the far side of another clearing, nestling at the edge of a deep expanse of tall pines and screened on three sides by clumps of thick gorse bushes. They crept closer and saw it was a cabin, much like Devereaux's only in far better shape. A galvanized steel chimney protruded through its solid new roof. The walls had recently been stained a deep brown color. And a constant, unwavering blue light was shining through the single window to the side of the door, suggesting a source of electricity had been installed.

Keeping low, moving slowly, and with their weapons drawn, the detectives eased forward until they reached the rough wooden wall of the cabin at the opposite end from the door. They then crabbed sideways until Devereaux was directly below the window. He pulled out his cell-phone, selected its front-facing camera, and raised it like a periscope until he could safely see into the room on its screen. Then he gave the OK signal to Garretty, pivoted around, stood up, and slammed his shoulder into the door.

Tyler Shaw opened his eyes as the door broke off its flimsy new hinges and Devereaux and Garretty came storming into the cabin. He was lying on his back, naked, on a blue satin sheet that was draped across the four-foot-high stone-topped platform he'd built in the center of the room. On a slab below it Devereaux could see a mass of human bones—femurs, tibias, clavicles, vertebrae, ribs, plus a bunch of smaller ones he couldn't name—all laid out in intricate shapes and patterns. Shaw had mounted blue lamps on stands in each corner of the room. He'd painted strange blue symbols on the walls and the ceiling. At each corner of the platform he'd attached a six-foot pole. And on the top of three of these poles, angled downward as if focused on Shaw himself, he'd mounted a gleaming, freshly-varnished human skull.

Chapter Ninety-three

Thursday. Early afternoon.

Alexandra took her favorite aluminum Rimowa suitcase from the closet and threw it onto the bed. She opened it. Unfastened the straps. Then stepped back. What should she pack? She looked around the room and thought about her clothes. Her jewelry. The family photographs on the dresser in their silver frames. The ornaments she'd inherited from her mother. The mementoes from the foreign trips she'd taken, after college. She had a lot of stuff. And she couldn't take all of it. So how did she narrow it down? Which things held the true value?

She was still wrestling with the problem five minutes later when Nicole scampered into the room, needing an extra pair of hands to help fix a broken Barbie. That was it, Alexandra realized. She had her answer. Being with her daughter was the only thing that mattered. But there was a problem with that. *Her* daughter was also Devereaux's daughter. Half of Nicole's DNA came from his side of the family.

Alexandra had been able to ignore that fact before. She'd named Nicole for her own mother, and Devereaux had been absent for the first seven years of the little girl's life. But now Alexandra had seen the photographs of Devereaux's relatives. And she'd seen the bond that had grown between him and Nicole. A bond she feared might be even stronger than the one she shared with the kid. So with that in mind, what would be the point of going anywhere? She couldn't leave Nicole. Which meant she couldn't leave the part of Devereaux that existed within Nicole.

Running away would be futile.

And besides, why should she be the one who had to leave? It was her house!

Chapter Ninety-four

Thursday. Early afternoon.

SHAW SAT UP WITH THE DISTANT, BEMUSED LOOK OF A MAN COMING OUT of a trance. Then his attention latched onto the two detectives who were suddenly in his space, crowding close to him. He registered the guns in their hands. Saw the disgust on their faces. Felt his brain explode into life. And then there was no more time to think. He just sprang down from the wooden platform. Shouldered Garretty aside while he was still reeling from the sight of all the bones and skulls, and dived through the cabin's wrecked doorway.

Garretty jumped out after him and fired off two quick rounds, but he couldn't get a clear shot as Shaw twisted and weaved through the thick belt of pine trees. Devereaux raced past Garretty, dodging between the tall trunks and ducking under the narrow, razor-sharp branches. Garretty followed, slipping on the layers of decaying leaves that covered the ground and stumbling over the jumble of hidden roots and semi-buried rocks. But hard as the detectives pushed themselves, Shaw—naked and barefoot—was steadily pulling away from them.

Devereaux and Garretty emerged almost simultaneously into a firebreak—a straight-sided, twenty-foot-wide channel cut into the forest—and could see that Shaw had plowed on ahead, far into the next section of trees, and was gaining further ground.

"I have an idea." Devereaux grabbed Garretty's shoulder. "You follow him. But stay to his left. Make as much noise as you can, so he can tell you're there. I know this area. There's a gorge, running crossways, straight ahead of us. It cuts all the way through the forest. It's deep. And too wide to cross. If you're to his left, he'll go to his right. I'll use the firebreaks. Get ahead of him that way. We'll trap him in between us."

Devereaux sprinted away, making much better progress over the smoother, open ground. He kept going until he reached a firebreak that ran at ninety degrees, then took the left-hand track and strained to move even faster. He kept up the pace until he drew level with the final patch of trees before the forest gave way to the uneven, rocky rim of the gorge. Then Devereaux crouched down and peered around a dense clump of gorse. He had a clear view along the undulating line of pines. There was no sign of Shaw. But Devereaux could hear someone crashing around to his left. Was it Garretty, having lost his prey? Or Shaw, doubling back toward his cabin? Or making a break for his truck? Devereaux cursed beneath his breath and twisted around to scan the area on the other side of the bushes.

Devereaux saw the flash of an outstretched hand through a gap between two trees. Then an arm. And a naked torso. It had to be Shaw. He must have heard Garretty but responded by veering off diagonally rather than going straight then right. He was on course to emerge from the forest twenty feet from where Devereaux was waiting. That was much closer than Devereaux had expected. And even better than he'd hoped for. It would give Shaw far less chance to turn back and dive for cover in the undergrowth if he sensed the ambush.

Devereaux held his breath and waited until Shaw was almost in the open before stepping out from his cover, gun raised.

"Stop right there. Police."

Shaw glanced at Devereaux without breaking his stride. Surprise flashed across his face, followed by a hint of amusement. Then he summoned another burst of acceleration and launched himself toward the far side of the gorge. He traveled fifteen feet through the air, legs still pumping, then gravity took its toll and he plummeted down, disappearing from Devereaux's view.

Devereaux ran forward and reached the rim just in time to see Shaw smash into the rocks at the base of the gorge, thirty feet below. Shaw's body crumpled on impact and he ended up sprawled out on his back, his right leg folded up beneath him. His left arm was twisted the wrong way at the elbow. His head was jammed against a lichen-covered boulder, and a stream of blood was beginning to stain the velvety surface a dirty brownish-red.

Devereaux started to scramble his way down the side of the gorge. It was steep and slippery, and he struggled to keep his footing on the wide patches of scree. He frequently had to slither between the rocks and tree stumps, slashing his hands as he grappled for support, but he finally made it to the bottom without suffering any serious harm.

Shaw was still breathing when Devereaux reached him, and a look of confusion and disappointment was clouding his eyes.

"I needed all four, I guess." Sticky red bubbles were forming in Shaw's mouth and nostrils as he spoke. "Three wasn't enough. I should have waited for all four . . ."

"Don't try to talk." Devereaux checked the pulse in Shaw's neck. It was fast and weak. "We'll get you to the hospital. Get you patched up."

"If I had all four, I'd have the power by now." Shaw's eyes opened wider. "I just needed an artist. I had a scientist, already. And a musician. And a jock. That pain-in-my-ass meathead . . ."

"I'll find my partner." Devereaux started to stand. "See if we can get a helicopter out here."

"Wait!" Shaw grabbed Devereaux's sleeve with his right hand. "Listen! It was the final step. Don't you see? The others—all of them—they weren't enough. Not one by one. I could have gone on forever, but I'd never have got it right. I needed four, together. The right mix. The right setup. That was the only way to end it."

"I need to get you some help." Devereaux brushed Shaw's hand away. "You're not in great shape."

"No." Shaw grabbed Devereaux's sleeve again and hung on tight. "Don't leave me here. Everyone always leaves me . . ."

"You need a doctor. And I'll get you one, if you just let me go."

"Then what?" Shaw's voice was fading. "If they do fix me up, what'll they do next? They won't understand. They'll send me to jail."

They'll give you the needle, Devereaux thought. "Maybe. That's not up to me."

"I can't go to jail. You know what happens to people like me in jail. Everything I've done. Everyone . . . It would all be for nothing.

Please . . ." Shaw grabbed weakly for Devereaux's gun. "Can't we just end this here?"

"Not like that, no." Devereaux pushed Shaw's arm down onto his chest. "But maybe we could let nature . . . I don't know. Tell me something first. All those people. Why did you hurt them like you did? Kill them? Chop them up? Take their body parts?"

"I didn't do it to hurt them." A tear appeared in the corner of Shaw's eye. "I never wanted that. I just wanted someone to stay with me. But no one ever would. I went all around the country, searching, but it didn't help."

"And butchering a bunch of people did?"

"You don't understand." Shaw tried to grab Devereaux's arm. "I had to do that to get the power so that next time, they'd stay. But I was doing it wrong. One at a time's no good. I found out, I needed a special chamber to harness the power. With four at once."

"By *chamber* you mean the way you set up that cabin?"

"Right. I found out I needed to build a chamber, but how? Where? Then I came back to Birmingham. Someone left me that cabin. An old lover of mine. I thought, what's the point of this? Who needs a log cabin in the twenty-first century? Then I knew. It was my way to stop the killing. It was—"

"Cooper?" Garretty appeared above them, peering over the rim. "Are you OK?"

"I'm fine." Devereaux stood up.

"What about Shaw?" Garretty took a step closer to the edge. "He looks pretty banged up. Is he a goner?"

"We don't know." Devereaux made eye contact with his partner. "We haven't found him yet. We need to keep searching. Say, for another half hour. Then I'll call it in. We can have Fire and Rescue come and deal with his body."

FIELD REPORT

When he perfected the gadget using nothing more than a handful of everyday household items, the genius demonstrated an astonishing degree of innovation and technological mastery. When he successfully deployed the gadget, time after time, right under the noses of the police and the FBI, he displayed extraordinary resilience and determination. And now? It's time for his improvisational skills to have their moment in the sun.

Just like other luminaries before him, the genius's conduct has come in for some unwarranted criticism. Like Oppenheimer, for example, his motives have not always been understood. Like Oppie, early in his career, he's been obliged to continue his work in new surroundings. And in those surroundings, the genius is not standing still. He's recruiting drones to assist with the next phase of his plan to rebuke the society that has so disgracefully disrespected him.

The authorities have inadvertently provided a nice large pool for the genius to fish in. Most of the other inmates seem capable. Many are rock stupid, of course. But all of them are desperate for a leader . . .

Chapter Ninety-five

Thursday. Afternoon.

DEVEREAUX TOLD GARRETTY THAT HE WANTED TO USE THE DRIVE BACK into the city from the forest near Shaw's cabin as a chance to crank up the stereo and finally road test the Porsche's recently repaired rear speaker. But that was just an excuse. The truth was, Devereaux didn't want to talk to anyone.

The sight of Shaw's body lying twisted and smashed on the rocks at the bottom of the gorge had brought echoes rushing back of the photos of his father's victims. The parallel between the images would have been unsettling enough at the best of times. But on that day it only served to remind Devereaux that somewhere out there, Joseph Oliver had left a stash of incriminating material. The kind of material that could wreck his life as surely as the fall had wrecked Shaw's body.

With the needle hovering around 90 the Porsche flashed past the off-ramp from I-65 to Wine Ridge. But they weren't going so fast that Devereaux didn't notice the billboard at the side of the other road. It showed a bolt of lightning breaking through a mass of black clouds and smiting a smug-looking forty-something in a sharp suit who was standing outside a bar with a glass of wine in his hand. Below the image was a single line of text. *Be sure your sins will find you out.*

Really? Devereaux thought. *Will they? We'll see about that.* Then he wound the volume down for just long enough to strike a deal with Garretty: two dinners at the Red Pearl in return for ducking out of the Shaw paperwork.

Garretty climbed out of the Porsche at the entrance to police head-quarters on First Avenue, then Devereaux worked his way around to Stephens, which he took north to I-20/59. He followed the highway past the outskirts of the airport, looped around the southern tip of Forest Hill Cemetery, and merged to stay on I-20. He slowed to go around the long sweeping bend, two and a half miles later, and glanced to his right in the hope of picking out the street where he'd had his near-miss with Daniel McKinzie. Then he picked up the pace again and kept going as far as Irondale. It was a totally inefficient route, he knew, but driving fast helped to clear his mind and he was feeling much more focused as he cut back to the southwest on I-459. Here he really let loose, overtaking everything in his path for ten straight miles until he reached I-280, which he used to approach Mountain Brook from the south.

Bill Adama opened his front door on the fourth ring of the bell. He was wearing green silk pajamas, which gave his over-tanned face an unhealthy orange pallor. He was unshaved. His hair was unwashed. And he was barefoot. When he saw Devereaux he nodded, then stepped back and gestured for him to come inside without saying a word.

The hallway floor was covered with foot-square gray tiles, highly polished, with a contrasting Greek key border. The walls were finished in eggshell white, with eight identically-sized framed prints of Euro-pean sports cars from the 1950s and '60s lined up on each side. There was no furniture to clutter the space, and no internal doorways—only an open archway leading to the living room at the back of the house—but two giant chandeliers hung on chains from the double-height ceil-ing. They were a curious mixture of traditional polished crystal in the center, surrounded by dull iron rods that were formed into protective outer spheres.

Adama closed the front door and launched himself at Devereaux, swinging an aluminum softball bat he kept near the entryway with all his strength. Devereaux jumped back, the tip of the bat whistling past his chin and smashing the picture of a Bugatti. Adama moved for-ward, swinging the bat again. Devereaux stepped out of his reach. He paused for a split second while the bat completed its arc, denting the wall between a Maserati and a Lamborghini, then he lunged forward. He grabbed the barrel of the bat with his left hand. Pulled it out of

Adama's grip. Flipped it around so he was holding it by the handle. Then jabbed it straight into Adama's solar plexus, leaving him on the floor in a sobbing, gasping heap.

Devereaux dragged Adama to the living room, bundled him onto one of a pair of cream leather couches that were lined up in front of a wide picture window with a view of the manicured back yard, and gave him a minute to recover himself.

"Do you want to tell me what that moment of madness was all about?" Devereaux lowered himself onto the opposite couch, still holding the metal bat.

"You killed him, you bastard." Adama spat out the words.

"You need to be a little more specific."

"Joseph Oliver. I told you where he was, and you killed him. Or had him killed. Just like you threatened to."

"That's not what happened, Bill. Joseph Oliver was at home in Miami, where you said he'd be. You get credit for not lying about that, by the way. I sent a guy to watch him. My guy saw Oliver take a phone call. And after that he blew his brains out."

Adama slumped forward and hid his face in his hands.

"I came to ask if you were the one who gave him the heads-up I was looking for him. I guess you've answered my question."

Adama let out a long, slow groan.

"What was the deal? You were supposed to deflect attention away from him, so he could lie low and enjoy life in the sun?"

Adama nodded. "We had it all mapped out. He moved away and changed his name. I stayed here as his last line of defense."

"Hence the aborted contract on him. You were walking a fine line there, my friend."

"No, I wasn't." Adama raised his head and stuck out his chin. "Those other losers would never have gone through with it. They're total wusses. I made them see that. Backed them off completely. And then I put it out there all about how I'd gone ahead on my own. Which added fuel to the smokescreen. Who's going to waste their time going after a dead man?"

"And if someone persisted anyway, you were supposed to tip Oliver off?"

"Right." Adama straightened up a little. "I was his early warning system. If someone got too close he was supposed to leave town. He was supposed to have a case packed at all times, good to go, twenty-four/seven. Why didn't he just do it, like we planned? I can't believe he lied to me."

"Lied to you, how?"

Adama sighed, pulled out his phone, fiddled with it for a second, then slid it across the floor to Devereaux.

It took a minute to read the whole message, then Devereaux closed the phone and tossed it back. "It's not really a lie. He doesn't say he never planned to leave. Just that he got too old. I guess he didn't have it in him to start over, somewhere new. You can understand that, right?"

"No." Adama was suddenly angry again. "I can't understand that. And I sure as hell can't accept it. We were supposed to be together in the end. The two of us. That's what he promised. That's why I did all this. And now? He strings me along my whole adult life, then says, *Sorry, our future's too much trouble to stick around for*? After all the times he swore to me he'd do it? God, I hate him now. I wish I'd never met him."

"OK." Devereaux leaned forward. "So Bill, explain one thing to me. Why *did* you do all this? Why did you shield the guy, after everything that happened? I don't get it."

"It's simple." Adama looked Devereaux in the eye. "I loved him."

"Loved him?" Devereaux held up his hands. "After he preyed on you? Victimized you? When you were so young? Still at school, even? And all those other kids, too?"

"Age doesn't come into it." Adama's voice had gained a harder edge. "And I wasn't a victim. The others might have seen it that way, but not me. They just didn't understand him like I did. And yes, he did some wrong things with some other people. But who hasn't? How about you, Devereaux? Are you going to sit there and tell me you're pure as snow? Because I remember you at school. I know the kind of stuff you were into."

"No." Devereaux shook his head. "You're right. Let's not go down that road. Let's get back on less weird ground. So. You and Oliver. This arrangement you had. Were there payments involved? Or was it all—what?—*altruistic* on your part?"

"Don't mock me. You don't understand, either. And yes. There were payments. But that's not why I did it. He had some money he'd inherited, and there was no one else for him to leave it to."

"Oliver was a lot older than you. Did you talk about what would happen if he died first?"

"He wrote a new will, years ago." Adama's throat tightened. "Everything comes to me. He offered to make it that way. I didn't ask."

"Everything? Are you sure?"

"Yes. I saw it in black and white."

"Good." Devereaux switched the bat to his other hand. "That simplifies things. Because here's the problem. He had an item that belongs to me. I want it back. That's why I wanted to get in touch with him. And now that he's not in a position to return it himself, you can do it for him when you take possession of his stuff."

"What is it?" Adama leaned forward. "How will I recognize it? Is it valuable, because—"

"Don't get excited. It has no monetary value. It's purely sentimental. Something that reminds me of my younger days, is all. And you won't have to recognize anything, because this is what we're going to do. My attorney will contact you, later today. You'll hire him. He'll handle the whole process of the inheritance. My thing, he'll put on one side. Everything else, he'll pass on to you. Untouched. And he won't even charge you his usual fee."

"No way." Adama got to his feet. "That's bullshit. My attorney will handle it. Give me a description of this thing you claim is yours. I'll have it appraised, and if you can prove—"

"Bill, sit down." Devereaux pointed the bat toward Adama's midriff. "Maybe your grief's affecting your memory. Maybe you've forgotten what happened the last time you failed to cooperate. And the stakes have just been raised. You've admitted to aiding a known child molester. Jail would be a particularly bad place for you to be right now."

"Fine." Adama slumped back down. "I'll go with your attorney. You can have your *thing* back, whatever it is."

"Good. And obviously our arrangement is confidential. No one gets to hear about it. Not even your wife."

"I don't have a wife."

Devereaux raised his eyebrows.

"OK. Technically I do. But we're not *married* married. I did it as a favor so she could get a green card, years ago, before gay people were allowed to get married here. I haven't been in the same room as the woman for a decade now. Longer, maybe."

Devereaux sat in his car on the block-paved driveway and sighed. He could see sleepless nights ahead of him, trying to make sense of all Adama's craziness. He shook the thoughts from his head and focused instead on evaluating the steps he'd taken toward recovering whatever incriminating material Joseph Oliver had left behind.

Progress was satisfactory, he concluded. Though he wouldn't be truly happy until all the pictures and financial records and any other details that had resurfaced were safely in his hands. He pictured opening the heavy cast-iron stove in his cabin, feeding every last shred inside, and lighting it on fire. Then he started the Porsche's engine, selected Reverse, and was about to release the brake when his phone rang. It was the number from the final sheet of paper in the second envelope that had been delivered to Alexandra's house. Joseph Oliver's number, which he'd called the previous night before he'd learned the man was dead.

"Who is this?" Devereaux kept his voice calm and level. "And how did you get hold of Joseph Oliver's phone?"

"Who's Joseph Oliver?" The man at the other end of the line sounded irritated. "And don't waste my time with stupid questions, Detective. Get a pen. Write this down. It's when and where we're going to meet. It's got to be this afternoon. That's non-negotiable. Meet me where and when I say, or any chance of reaching a deal will be dead in the water. And that's something you'll regret for the rest of your life. I guarantee."

Chapter Ninety-six

Thursday. Afternoon.

ALEXANDRA PUT THE SUITCASE BACK IN THE CLOSET. SHE'D MADE HER decision. She couldn't turn her back on Devereaux. Not again.

Some of the times they'd shared recently had been really good. The meals they'd cooked together. The wine they'd drunk. The late evenings they'd filled, after Nicole had gone to sleep. The trips they'd taken to Railroad Park, and the Birmingham Museum of Art. It was like they were coming together as a real family. When it was just the three of them, things were great. It was only factors from outside the home that were causing them problems.

There were two main areas that worried Alexandra. Devereaux's past. And his job. His past was out of her control. She couldn't change it, so she'd just have to learn to live with it. And his job? The way he let it encroach on family life? That did need to change. But she had to remember, Devereaux was new to all this. He'd been thrown in at the deep end as a parent, with conflicting priorities and calls on his time. She'd had seven years to learn. To adapt. He hadn't. He'd been absent. That wasn't his fault. But it had left a huge gap. And he clearly needed help to bridge it. Her help.

All she had to do was set some solid ground rules. Establish a common understanding about the important things in their lives. Which she was sure she could do. If she could only find a way to make him listen to her . . .

Chapter Ninety-seven

Thursday. Afternoon.

THE SKINNY, TWITCHY-LOOKING GUY CAME OUT OF HIS GRANDFATHER'S ramshackle house in the outskirts of Pleasant Grove, anxious not to be late for his rendezvous with the detective. Not much had gone right with the plan since day one, and there was no time left to recover from any more screwups. He checked his watch. Hurried across the ridged concrete driveway. Reached his dust-encrusted white Suburban. Climbed in behind the wheel. Slid the key into the ignition. And felt the cold kiss of steel against the back of his neck.

"Devereaux?" The guy put his hands on the wheel, where they'd be visible.

"Correct. Who are you?"

"My name's Kendrick. And I don't like having guns jammed into me."

"That's interesting. But unfortunately for you, the personal likes and dislikes of blackmailing assholes have never been a major concern of mine." Devereaux pressed a little harder with his untraceable .22. "Although I do have your number, so I'll be sure to let you know if that changes. Meantime, let's not drag this out. You have something I want. If you're smart, you'll hand it over, and you'll make sure I never see or hear from you again."

"I don't have it."

"Don't dick me around." Devereaux increased the pressure even further.

"I don't have it." Kendrick hardened his tone. "My job's to take you to the guy who does. That was always the plan. So your whole tracing my phone, or whatever you did, and breaking into my truck? That was a waste of time, *Detective*."

"Oh, I don't know." Devereaux drew back the gun and saw a small crescent-shaped smear of blood below Kendrick's ear. "I wouldn't say a total waste."

Chapter Ninety-eight

Thursday. Afternoon.

ALEXANDRA CLAPPED HER HANDS WITH RELIEF. SHE HAD THE ANSWER! They'd take a vacation. Somewhere quiet. Relaxing. Beautiful. Where Nicole could play, and she could get time alone with Devereaux. Plenty of it. Uninterrupted. They could talk. Straighten things out. Lay the foundations for a real future together.

The only possible wrinkle in the plan was getting him to agree to take time off work. But Alexandra had the solution for that, too. She'd get Nicole to ask him. He'd never say *no* to his precious little daughter.

Alexandra hurried down the landing. She knocked on Nicole's door. Opened it. Walked in without waiting for a reply. And saw her daughter sitting in the middle of her floor. She had a red marker pen in one hand and a Barbie in front of her. The doll was lying on its back on a piece of paper that had been colored in to look like it was covered with tiles. The doll's legs were bent back so far they'd almost snapped. Its right arm had been pulled off. And one half of a pair of scissors was sticking out of its stomach.

"I'm hungry, Mommy." Nicole didn't look up from the tableau she was creating. "When's Daddy coming home?"

"I don't know, Pumpkin." Alexandra was too shocked to lie. "Maybe never."

Chapter Ninety-nine

Thursday. Late afternoon.

KENDRICK TACKED THE SUBURBAN ONTO THE END OF A LINE OF SUVs
that had been dumped as usual in a no-parking zone near the ambu-
lance bay at UAB hospital. Then he jumped down and led the way past
the fountain, around the reflecting pool, and in through the entrance
to the main building.

The geriatric special care unit was down a level, in the basement.
Devereaux had been there before, earlier in the year. He recognized the
enclosed hum of the HVAC system and the bitter, oxygen-rich tang in
the air as they approached its bleached, acerbic corridor. And he was
again struck by the macabre image of the nearly dead being lined up
so neatly, already underground.

Kendrick stopped outside the last of the five rooms on the left-hand
side of the corridor and waited for its door to slide open. Then he
stood back and gestured for Devereaux to go in ahead of him. There
was an old man lying in the bed, wheezing loudly in his sleep. He was
completely bald, though the paper-thin skin stretched across his chin
and neck was flecked with white stubble. One shriveled hand lay on
top of the crisp baby-blue sheet, with a clip on its middle finger attached to a wire running to a socket on the wall. Kendrick approached
the bed and when the old man didn't stir he reached down and gave
the exposed hand a gentle squeeze.

"Granddad?" Kendrick leaned in close to the man's ear. "Wake up.
He's finally here."

The old man's eyes slowly opened, bloodshot and watery, and his face twisted into a cruel, disdainful scowl that transported Devereaux back in time more than two decades.

"Chris Lambert." Devereaux folded his arms across his chest. "You're still breathing. What a shame."

"Ever wish you had a time machine, Devereaux?" Lambert's voice barely rose above a hoarse whisper. "I do. Let me tell you. I wish I had one right now. I'd go back and stop you joining the Academy. Make sure you went to jail instead, where you belong. But failing that, I reckon there's another sweet spot I missed. From after that asshole Tomcik got too old for me to worry about him having your back. To before I got sick. That's when we should have done our business. It's too late for me to cash in now, I guess. But there's no reason for my grandkids to miss out, right?"

"The smell of your breath's making me sick." Devereaux fanned the air in front of his face. "So's your hypocrisy. Suppose I say screw your business. Invite you to bite me, instead. And leave you to take whatever secrets you think you know about me to your grave. Which I hope you'll be filling very soon."

"You could do that, I guess." Lambert paused to weakly clear his throat. "But it would be an awful shame. My grandkids would have to make do with seeing you rot in jail rather than enjoy spending your money. And you'd have to spend however long it takes these days for a dirty cop to get shanked in the shower knowing that you'll never learn the truth about your father."

"I already know the truth about my father, you senile asshole."

"You do?" A thin, mocking smile spread across Lambert's face. "So you know he was innocent? That he was framed and murdered by a pair of crooked cops? And you have proof of this? Because I do." Lambert tapped his forehead with his bony index finger. "It's all up here."

Acknowledgments

I would like to extend my deepest thanks to the following for their help, support, and encouragement while I wrote this book. Without them, it would not have been possible.

My editor, the inimitable Kate Miciak, and the whole team at Random House.

My agent, the outstanding Richard Pine.

My friends, who've stood by me through the years: Dan Boucher, Carlos Camacho, Joelle Charbonneau, John Dul, Jamie Freveletti, Keir Graff, Kristy Claiborne Graves, Tana Hall, Nick Hawkins, Dermot Hollingsworth, Amanda Hurford, Richard Hurford, Jon Jordan, Ruth Jordan, Martyn James Lewis, Rebecca Makkai, Dan Malmon, Kate Hackbarth Malmon, Carrie Medders, Philippa Morgan, Erica Ruth Neubauer, Gunther Neumann, Ayo Onatade, Denise Pascoe, Wray Pascoe, Dani Patarazzi, Javier Ramirez, David Reith, Sharon Reith, Beth Renaldi, Marc Rightley, Melissa Rightley, Renee Rosen, Kelli Stanley, and Brian Wilson.

Everyone at The Globe Pub, Chicago.

Jane and Jim Grant.

Ruth Grant.

Katharine Grant, my chemistry consultant.

Jess Grant, my anatomy consultant.

Alexander Tyska.

Gary and Stacie Gutting.

And last on the list, but first in my heart—Tasha. *There's still no shoe . . .*

About the Author

ANDREW GRANT WAS BORN IN BIRMINGHAM, ENGLAND. HE ATTENDED the University of Sheffield, where he studied English Literature and Drama. He has run a small, independent theater company and worked in the telecommunications industry for fifteen years. Andrew is married to novelist Tasha Alexander, and the couple divides their time between Chicago and the UK.

andrewgrantbooks.com
Facebook.com/AndrewGrantAuthor
@Andrew_Grant

About *the Type*

THIS BOOK WAS SET IN SABON, A TYPEFACE DESIGNED BY THE WELL-known German typographer Jan Tschichold (1902–74). Sabon's design is based upon the original letter forms of sixteenth-century French type designer Claude Garamond and was created specifically to be used for three sources: foundry type for hand composition, Linotype, and Monotype. Tschichold named his typeface for the famous Frankfurt typefounder Jacques Sabon (c. 1520–80).